Bo Henry
at
Three Forks

Daniel Bradford

Savant Books and Publications
Honolulu, HI, USA
2018

Published in the USA by Savant Books and Publications
2630 Kapiolani Blvd #1601
Honolulu, HI 96826
http://www.savantbooksandpublications.com

Printed in the USA

Edited by Eleonor Gardner
Cover Art by Saydee Lanes
Cover by Daniel S. Janik

13 digit ISBN: 978-0-9972472-7-5

First Edition: January 2018
Library of Congress Control Number: 2017961718

Dedication

I would like to dedicate this book to my mother, Hazel, my father Derle, and their eleven siblings who showed me the true meaning of family. Over the years their examples have guided me to make wise, moral, financial and social choices throughout my life. Their inspiration became the characters I have created.

Acknowledgements

I must thank several people for their contributions in the creation of this novel, none more important than Charyl "Sherry" Wojtaszek. It has been her dedication to my work that has kept me motivated and I cannot thank her enough for her technical contributions. None of my work would have seen the light of day without Sherry.

Doctor Randall James has my never-ending gratitude. It was his contribution that ended years of my floundering without a publisher when he brought Savant Books and Publications into my life.

In addition, I must thank Daniel Janik and the staff at Savant for their support and encouragement. I never knew how much preparation a publisher put into a single novel. Thanks to them for this opportunity.

Eleonor Gardner, the editor on this project, not only performed all the difficult tasks of editing, but she taught me nuances about writing that I could not have learned elsewhere.

Saydee Lanes has graced every book I have written with her beautiful art work. I am fortunate to have found such a talented artist to illustrate my covers.

Lastly, I would like to thank Genni DeMarco for reading my story and offering her critical insights.

- Daniel D. Bradford

Dan Bradford

Chapter 1
Rustlers at Three Forks

Bodine Alan Henry was a young U.S. Marshal on his first solo assignment. Bo was born and raised in Harper's Ferry, Iowa on the Mississippi River lowlands in the northeastern part of the state, just south of Minnesota. He was the youngest of ten boys and had two sisters. His father and mother had two hundred and sixty acres under plow and his father was also the town blacksmith. Behind the family smith shop was another ten acres of pasture for their livery stable. Bo's brother, Derle, ran the dry goods store and built furniture while his other brother, Forest, operated the family's tack and blacksmith shop. Early on, Bo never liked the farm or attending school, but his dad would not allow any of his kids to skip school or their chores on the farm. As soon as Bo was old enough, he traded his farm work to help his father in the blacksmith shop. Working in town was better than being on the farm, as far as Bo was concerned.

As soon as Bo was finished with primary school, he got a second job working for Harper Ferry's sheriff sweeping up the cells, feeding the prisoners and running errands for the sheriff. Bo often slept in the jail's back room where they housed prisoners. After a year, the sheriff made him a deputy. Not much ever happened in Harper's Ferry, Iowa so it wasn't much of a job; Bo didn't even own a gun his first year working there. Bo had been serving as the town deputy for just over two years when Judge

Roads arrived in town. One afternoon, after the judge had finished trying his cases, he came over to the sheriff's office and asked if there were any men in town—with any law experience—who would be interested in becoming a U.S. Marshal. Bo didn't think twice.

Bo jumped at the offer. "Yes, sir. I want to be a marshal."

The judge smiled at the sight of the ambitious young man dressed in pants that were too short and a shirt with patches on the elbows—a boy in the judge's eyes—who had just bravely answered his call. "I had men in mind that were a little older than you, son. Being a marshal is a hard job and we'd like to have men with some experience in life before they go out to die. Do you even know how to use that gun on your hip?"

"I've been trying to teach him, but I'm not much of a gun hand," the sheriff offered for Bo. "He learned quick what little I've been able to teach him. We just don't have much use for guns around here."

The judge looked Bo straight in the eye. "I have to be back here in a year. If you can impress me with your gun handling, we'll see about that job as a deputy marshal. Deal?" He extended his hand to the boy and Bo shook the judge's hand.

"I'll do my very best, sir," Bo replied, excited about the future opportunity, yet slightly disappointed. The judge left the office, got on his horse and looked back at the office as he left.

"One year and don't forget," he called back to Bo who was watching him leave. The judge turned his horse south and rode quickly out of town.

That was three years ago.

Today, Bo was astride his horse, Buck, moving west toward Dodge City. The day was warm and there wasn't a cloud in the sky. The dry season had started early and the prairie was already a golden hue. Bo felt a twinge of excitement as he patted the warrants in his vest pocket for Carl and James Burser—two very bad brothers. The warrants for the Bursers were accompanied by four blank warrants.

The Burser brothers had robbed a bank and killed a bank teller in the process. The law never caught the younger Carl, but James had been tried and convicted and was due to spend the rest of his life in the Jefferson City prison when Carl and four other men broke him out of custody. The group of men had set up an ambush half-way between Jefferson City and Kansas City where the trail dipped and veered around a clump of trees. They had waited—ready to ambush—for hours for the wagon to appear. During the attack, two deputy marshals were killed and one was seriously wounded. Now, Bo rode west to capture the killers and bring them back to Kansas City, Missouri for trial in Judge Roads' court.

Buck—Bo's faithful companion—was a large stallion that stood nearly sixteen hands tall. Buck was a soft tan color with a coal-colored black mane and tail and matching four black socks. If you studied the man and his horse as they rode across the countryside together, it was easy to tell that Buck was the one in charge. Buck carried his head high and there was pride in his step. He knew just how to coax an extra apple out of Bo or have Bo scratch him in just the right places. He had his human trained. Buck owned Bo, not the other way around and neither the horse nor the rider wanted it any differently.

Approaching a small rise in the trail, Bo could see the tops of two trees just on the other side. Off to the northwest he noticed a small stream running down under the trees. As Buck cleared the rise, Bo spotted four men under the trees about one hundred feet in front of him. Three of the men were circling a fourth man astride a swayback nag; the fourth man's hands were tied behind his back. Two of the men had their horses in the middle of the trail, angrily barking orders at the third man. "Come on, hang him, Clive, and let's get this over with." Clive was between the man with his hands bound and the treeline. He was trying to slip the loop of a rope around the fourth man's neck.

They paused when Bo called out to them. "What seems to be the problem here?" Bo said smartly. As he rode up closer to the men with Buck, he recognized three of men. Their faces were strangely familiar; he had warrants in his pocket for them. Marlin Bitter, a nasty enough man who liked giving orders, was sitting astride his horse in the middle of the trail to the south of the trees waving his rifle in the air. Along with the rifle, he carried an old, neglected pistol with the barrel sticking out the bottom of the holster. All that yelling and gun waving caused Jed Young's horse to nervously swing around and back into Marlin's horse. As Bo studied the scene before him, Judge Roads' words rang through his head: *Protect those we serve, protect other marshals and above all else, protect yourself.* These were the men who shot and killed Marshals Ben Parson and Lester Cousins and seriously wounded Big Bill while breaking Carl Burser out of custody. The man clutching the rope with his right hand and a shotgun with his left, was Clive Wilson.

"This is none of your business," Clive said as he narrowed his eyes up at the stranger on his stallion. Clive let go of the rope and dropped it over the head of the man it was intended for. "This here is our slave and he ran off with one of our horses. He's more problems than he's worth. We're in our right to hang him and be done with it."

Bo decided not to address Clive directly. Bo had his left leg slung around the saddle horn and brought his foot over Buck's neck, putting his weight down on his stirrups. At that moment, Buck came to an abrupt halt. With both feet firmly planted in his stirrups, Bo gave Buck a slight nudge with his right boot and Buck took three steps to the left. Every muscle in the big stallion became granite as he moved hesitantly toward the strange cluster of men.

The fourth man in the group was Jed Young, who'd been silent until now. "He stole our horse. We've got the right to hang him if he stole our horse," he reasoned, recognizing deputy Bo Henry now. Jed Young was a tall slender man on the bay. He fumbled with his shirt pocket. "I've got the papers for him and the horse right here," Jed said.

Bo looked over at the man who was about to be hanged. It was plain to see he was scared out of his wits. He was a large, dark-skinned man dressed in tattered clothing. His shirt pocket was torn and the suspender strap for his right shoulder was broken. He had a section of rope for a belt tied in a granny knot at his waist and his boots were well past worn. His frame trembled and sweat dripped from his brow making his dark skin shine as he sat planted on his horse, gagged. His head hung low, resigned to the rough conditions the other men had put him through. The man hadn't fully escaped his fate just yet, and he knew it.

"If he was dumb enough to steal that horse," Bo stated. "You should have let him go. You boys do know that there are no slaves anymore? The war is over and all the slaves were set free."

The dark-skinned man on the scruffy horse struggled to speak through his gag and got a shotgun poked into his belly by Clive. "Shut up, slave," Clive said harshly. "He doesn't want to hear what you have to say!"

Bo's eyes darted from one man to the next looking for any sign of an aggressive move. His eyes were fixed on their hands. He could tell Jed was the only one of them that was experienced with a hand gun by the way it was tied down and the way the holster had been cut away. He could only think: *This is going to get tricky.* Just then, Clive began to pull his revolver out of its holster, which wasn't a good sign for Bo. Bo reacted to the danger instinctively and before the man's gun could clear his horse's head, Bo fired his Colt. A shot cracked through the air, causing their horses to jolt. The bullet struck the man squarely in the chest sending him off to Bo's right. He landed with his feet in the stream and his head landed under the big, captured man's horse. Bo's carefully measured second shot shredded the rope draped over the limb of the tree causing all of the horses —except Buck—to spin and buck wildly. In the chaos, the dark-skinned man, with his hands still tied behind him, was dumped butt first into the stream with the rope dangling from his neck.

Jed Young halted looking for papers he did not have and quickly reached for the gun on his hip. The barrel never cleared the holster, however, and Bo's next shot rang out. The shot was low because the horse Jed was riding had reared up. The bullet struck Jed in the sternum and sent him toppling backward over his saddle and face down in the dirt.

A bullet from Marlin Bitters' gun sizzled past Bo's left ear, alerting Bo to him. Shifting his gaze toward Marlin quickly, Bo fired a shot hoping to stop the man before he could possibly kill him. Bo's last shot hit Marlin in the left thigh. The shock of the bullet and the bucking of Marlin's horse sent him flying into the air and back to the ground hard on his back.

Again, Bo's eyes darted from one man to the other as he tried to anticipate where the danger would come from next. His Colt scanned along with his eyes; there was no movement. He spun the Colt twice before shoving it back in his holster. Buck didn't relax or let his ears come forward until Bo's feet hit the ground. Bo dismounted his horse and made his way around the messy scene to pick up all of the loose weapons. He brought them back to where Buck stood patiently and dropped them under Buck's belly where he could lay surveillance on them as he moved. The big stallion's ears laid back and he became a stone statue. Bo walked up to the big man who had been "enslaved" by the others. The man was now sitting up to his waist in the stream.

"Are you all right?" Bo asked. The gagged man nodded and muttered a few words but Bo could not understand anything he was saying. The big man wasn't sure if this was better or if things had just gotten worse. Bo pulled his knife from its sheath and cut the bonds from the man's hands. "There, that should help"—he extended his hand out to the man—"I'm U.S. Marshal Bo Henry. I guess it was a good thing I came along when I did."

The big man let out a sigh of relief as he removed the gag hastily, glad to be free, and then took Bo's hand to shake it. He pulled himself out of the water. "My name is Washington Daniel Blue. I'm from Chicago and I am surely not a slave. I want to thank you for what you did, sir." Daniel was choked up with emotion as he thanked Bo who had just saved his life.

A sound broke the silence. Bitters, who had been shot in the leg, had regained his senses and groaned. Bo looked over at him.

"Help me get this one fixed up and then we'll gather their horses," Bo said to Blue. "Oh, by the way, don't get too close to the big buckskin, Washington. He's a little particular about who touches him. It'll take a few days before he gets used to you."

Blue stopped Bo before he could say more. "I would prefer if you called me 'Daniel' or 'Blue'. No one uses my first name."

"That's fair, Daniel." Bo smiled back. "You can call me Bo or Marshal Henry if you'd like. I answer to either."

Bo ripped the sleeves off of Clive's shirt to use as bandages and wasn't gentle as he and Daniel patched up the remaining wounded man. Bo and Daniel—with some help from Buck—gathered the stray horses and then tied them to the neighboring trees so they could keep an eye on them. Staring up toward the sun, Bo and Daniel tried to determine how much of the day they had left. Ultimately, they decided that it was too late to continue and they wouldn't find a better place to make camp that had both water and shelter.

Bo picked up a shotgun that had belonged to one of the men. "Why don't you build us a nice fire, Daniel? I'm going up stream to find us some supper." Bo checked both barrels for shells and then disappeared up the southwest side of the stream.

Daniel built a fire from pieces of wood he found along the stream shore and put on some coffee that Bo had in his stash of provisions. A half-hour had passed since Bo had gone when Daniel heard the bark of the first barrel and then the other. Soon, Bo sauntered back into camp with the shotgun over his right shoulder carrying two cock pheasants with his left hand. "I'm buying supper tonight," Bo said walking toward Daniel and the fire.

The two men busied themselves with the cleaning of the birds, holding the birds steady with one hand and pulling feathers firmly out with the other. They split the birds and using a long, thick branch they had formed into a pole with a knife, they stuck the birds firmly onto it to mount over the hot fire. When the birds were finally propped up over the fire, Daniel found a satchel that had fallen off a horse during the scuffle containing flour, salt and lard. He moistened the flour with stream water and placed the soft, doughy lumps on a hard pan. Bo smiled at the mouthwatering aroma as the fresh biscuits fluffed up in the heat.

"You're going to have to teach me how to make those. I've never been able to get them to smell like that," Bo said.

Daniel nodded. "It's the least I can do after you saved my life today."

Bo put down his coffee cup and leaned toward Daniel. "That gets me to a delicate topic. My pa told me to never get into another man's business if he doesn't ask. You haven't offered, but I'm going to have to ask—what are you doing out here like this?"

Daniel's head slumped forward. "It's been just under a year now. My wife, Trisha, and I were living in Chicago. I was at school one evening when six or seven men invaded our neighborhood and kidnapped a dozen other negroes along with my wife. Sometimes, former slavers will raid the northern cities and take us to the South to be sold as indentured servants. I started looking for my wife by traveling south. I found out three months ago, that she was being taken west to be sold as an indentured servant. I ran into these three this morning"—Daniel gave a quick look toward the men Bo had defeated—"I wouldn't go with them and we got into a fight. If the one with the shotgun hadn't clubbed me over the head, I'd have had them."

Bo nodded. "Of that I'm sure. I thought my pa and my brother, Milt, were the biggest men I'd ever seen, but, you put them to shame, Daniel. What grade were you in at school? My pa made me stay in until I finished the sixth grade...I was about sixteen."

Daniel was a little embarrassed over his advanced education. "I was in my third year of college. I was studying to be an engineer. I want to go west and build railroads, eventually."

Bo was impressed. "You're only the second man I've ever met who went to college; Judge Roads is the other. You are also the only black man I've ever met. I come from Harper's Ferry, Iowa and we don't have any colored people there"—he extended his hand toward Daniel—"I'm glad to meet you on both accounts, Daniel Blue."

They both smiled and shook hands. After they finished eating and had fed their prisoner, Daniel gathered the plates and cups. He sloshed them in the stream and shook them dry. When the plates and cups were dry enough, Bo put them back in the sack. Then, Bo made one more check of his prisoner for the night as Daniel stoked the fire.

Bo pulled the bridle from Buck's mouth and gave him a pat on the back. "Go get a drink, Buck."

Daniel was puzzled. "Don't you hobble him at night? Won't he wander off?"

"It's the other way around," Bo laughed. "He thinks *I* should be hobbled at night so that I won't wander off. Buck's not going anywhere he doesn't want to and right now he won't get too far from the apples I have in my saddle bag. Besides, he's the best watchman we could have. Our prisoner isn't going to make a move that Buck won't challenge. You can sleep sound with Buck standing watch."

Daniel stopped for a moment. "Do you know who these men are? You never said if you had warrants on them."

Bo smiled. "The tall thin corpse over there is Clive Wilson. The one lying next to him is Jed Young. The one with the bullet hole in his leg tied to the saddle is Marlin Bitters. Say hello, Marlin," Bo mused, looking at Marlin who was nursing his wounded leg. "This here is Daniel Blue. Clive, Jed, Marlin and I met when they passed through Judge Roads' court."

Marlin muttered a couple of curses at the two men and complained about how much his leg hurt him. Bo pitched a small rock at him. "If you can't say anything nice, Marlin, I'll put a bullet in your other leg."

Marlin knew enough to shut up and rolled over to face his back toward Bo and Daniel.

"Judge Roads figured these three were on their way to Texas and then Mexico," Bo said turning back to Daniel. "We never figured they'd head back in this direction. They helped Carl Burser break his older brother out of jail right after the trial; two marshals were killed and one wounded during all of that. Judge Roads sent me out here to bring the brothers and their accomplices back. We never thought that I'd meet up with these three."

"What did the Bursers do?" asked Daniel. Bo was busy spreading his blanket out on the ground.

"They robbed a bank and killed a teller in Three Forks. I was headed in that direction when I came across you. Now, I'll have to take this mess into Dodge City and then I'll head for Three Forks. If you can see your way to help me, I'll get you two dollars a day for every day you're my deputy. I'm sure you could use the money and I can use the help." Bo pulled out his blankets and knelt down.

"I can use the money," Daniel quickly agreed. "And, I was headed to Dodge, anyway. I'd hoped I could find out which way they took my wife."

Bo flopped down to his back and pulled the second blanket up to his chin. "That's good. You can consider yourself a deputy U.S. Marshal for the next two days. Say, 'I will'."

"That's all there is to it? I will." Daniel smiled.

Bo grunted. "The Judge had me say more but I can't remember all of it right now. Good night, Blue."

Bo was asleep in minutes. It took Daniel a little longer. His near brush with death had left his thoughts focused on his missing wife, Trisha. He worried about adversities she might be facing as he lay staring at the vast sky. Eventually, Daniel drifted into a restless sleep.

Dan Bradford

Chapter 2
Getting Acquainted

There was a light breeze blowing from the south through the golden prairie grass causing the grass to sway from side to side. The sun was just making itself seen in the east when Buck nudged Bo awake. Buck stood over where Bo was asleep and snorted in his ear.

"OK, Buck. I'm up," Bo said still half-asleep. "Daniel, are you awake?"

"I am now," Daniel replied and rolled over. "I'll get the fire started and put some coffee on."

Buck shoved his nose in Bo's back and gave him another push. "All right, Buck. I'll get it." Bo reached down and pulled an apple from his sack and gave it to the big stallion. "There, are you happy now?" Buck snorted and wandered off to the stream.

Breakfast was a few strips of bacon from Bo's food cache and the rest of the biscuits from the night before. After breakfast and packing up the rest of their makeshift camp, Bo and Daniel loaded the two bodies onto the horses and then the prisoner was hoisted into his saddle. Bo tied Marlin's left foot to the right stirrup and his right foot into the left stirrup passing the rope under the horse's belly.

"That should hold you," Bo said, examining his work.

Daniel watched. "Why the elaborate tie-down?"

Bo stood up to comment. "This way he can't spur the horse, slip out of the saddle or kick me. His legs are right where I want them when I walk up to him." Bo gave the leg with the bullet hole a pat. "Isn't that right, Marlin?" Marlin just groaned and cursed Bo.

Daniel swung onto the biggest horse in the group, a bay mare. Bo was quick to see it wasn't the one he'd been riding the day before. "Daniel, why did you ever get that plug you were riding yesterday?"

Daniel looked over at him. "It was all I could afford," he replied.

Bo laughed at Daniel's reply as he spun Buck around and headed off in the direction of Dodge City. "Let's get going. I want to be in Dodge for supper."

The sun was low in the western sky when the marshal and his new deputy cleared the edge of town. Their first stop in Dodge City was the local sheriff's office. When they pulled up in front of the jail, a crowd gathered and began to make some noise causing the sheriff to come out to the road when he heard the commotion.

"What's going on here?"—the sheriff looked up as Bo flashed his badge to him—"I'm Sheriff Anderson. You must be the marshal I got a message from Judge Roads about. Judge Roads said you could be in our area."

Bo leaned forward in his saddle to address the sheriff. "I'm U.S. Marshal Bo Henry, Sheriff. I've got one prisoner for you and a couple that didn't want to come along quietly."

The sheriff took one of two steps off the porch to see the men draped over the saddles on the additional horses that followed him into Dodge City. Sheriff Anderson took a quick step back as Daniel slid off his horse to the ground. The sight of a man that large was a little unnerving for him.

"And who is this?" Sheriff Anderson asked Bo. Bo smiled; Daniel had had the same effect on him the first time he'd seen him stand up, too.

"This is Deputy U.S. Marshal Daniel Blue. He's helping me with the prisoner."

The sheriff felt a little more at ease knowing that Daniel was a marshal. "I'm sorry, boy," Sheriff Anderson said, turning toward Daniel. "You have to be the biggest man I've ever seen."

Blue scowled at him. "I'd prefer that you address me as Daniel or Marshal, sir—I'll answer to either."

"Yes, of course," the sheriff replied, still feeling uneasy as he watched Daniel take the knife from Bo and quickly slice the straps holding Marlin's feet in the stirrups. As two of the onlookers slid Marlin out of the saddle and helped him into the jail and deposited him in a cell, the sheriff noticed the prisoner had been shot. "One of you men go down and get Doc Adams," Sheriff Anderson said to the second man. "This one is going to need some attention. The rest of you go get a cart and take these bodies over to the undertaker's,"—the sheriff looked back to Bo and a few people in the crowd moved out of sight quickly—"have the other marshals told you about our agreement?"

Bo slipped off of Buck's back and let the reins drape over the hitching rail. He stepped up onto the porch and turned to face the crowd to speak. "I wouldn't get too near the buckskin. He's very particular about who touches him"—Bo turned back to the sheriff—"yes, the other marshals told me that my deputy and I keep ninety percent of all bounty for prisoners we bring in draped and sixty percent of all bounty on those who have to spend time with you, like Marlin, here. That's to cover their expenses and burials. We get to sell the horses and tack at the livery and the guns to the smith."

The sheriff nodded. "That's the agreement, Marshal. I expect the prison wagon will be here for the prisoner in a few days?"

15

"That's fine with us," Bo smiled. "By the way, Marshal Stanley said to say 'hello' if I got over this far. He calls you Andy, is that right?" Bo and Daniel led the way into the jail. "I'll send a wire off to Judge Roads and have the wagon sent over as soon as they can find a driver."

The sheriff ushered Bo and Daniel inside the jail before addressing Bo's question. "My name is Ben but everyone around here just calls me Andy. Let's get some papers signed, so I can get you paid in the morning." He paused for a moment as Daniel Blue passed him in the doorway and had to look up to see Blue's face smiling down at him. "There's coffee on the stove...help yourselves."

Daniel poured two cups of coffee and handed one to Bo. "Thank you, Sheriff Anderson. We've been on the trail all day," Daniel said.

Daniel had a little difficulty easing himself into the chair at the far side of the room. He set his cup down on the floor next to his chair as he watched Bo and the sheriff take care of their business. As Bo signed papers, Sheriff Anderson pulled out wanted posters from his desk drawer.

"The last posters I have on these boys are right here. I'll have to send a wire to Judge Roads to make sure the numbers are still good. I've got four hundred on Clive and Jed and six hundred on Marlin. These posters are at least a month old and I know they've done more damage since then. Are they the ones who helped the Bursers get out of jail and kill the two marshals?"

Bo nodded yes. "They're the ones. Carl broke James out with their help after his trial. That's when they killed the two marshals and wounded Big Bill. They tried James for the bank robbery and the killing of the teller at Three Forks but never caught Carl. He still has to stand trial for all of that. Marshal Blue and I are going to the livery stable and then up to the gunsmith's," Bo said, finishing the papers for the sheriff. "After that, it's a meal and a soft bed. We'll see you in the morning, Sheriff."

Sheriff Anderson pointed in the direction of the livery stable. "Chuck runs the livery. He knows Marshal Stanley and they've done business before. He'll take good care of you and your animals. There are a couple of people who've been looking forward to your coming to town. They say they knew you back in Kansas City. Our gunsmith is Rick Gustafson. I guess he's the one who sold you those Colts. Molly is our new hotel owner. She said she knew your family before Kansas City. She said to tell you she's got your steak done medium with a stack of potatoes just the way you like them."

Bo smiled. "So, this is where Molly wound up. Let's go Daniel, we're going to get fed good tonight."

The two men walked out of the jail and swung up into their saddles. Bo looked out to the south and could see the livery stable over the crowd that was still standing in the street. The owner of the livery had come out to see what was going on down in front of the jail. Daniel gathered the reins of the extra horses and dragged them behind him down to the livery stable. Chuck was standing in the doorway of the livery when they rode up. He was a large man wearing a leather apron. His nearly bald head reflected the sun from the sweat running down his face. He stepped back into the shade as they rode up.

"Good afternoon, Marshal," Chuck said. "I saw you ride in. Let's take a look at what you've brought me."

Chuck strolled around the horses, eyeing them carefully, as he checked out the tack. Bo and Daniel stepped out of their stirrups and their boots hit the ground with thuds. Bo walked around to where Chuck was standing. "Well, what do you think?" Bo asked.

Chuck scrunched up his face. "The tack is in good shape and the first two horses are resalable but I've got no use for the plug." Daniel hung his head. "He's all I could afford," he mumbled.

"That's okay, Daniel," Bo smiled. "Give us the usual and you can have the plug. Marshal Blue didn't have much to say in the matter when they gave him the horse."

"You're a marshal?" Chuck asked, surprised. He then looked up at Daniel who extended his hand to him, carefully.

"I'm Deputy U.S. Marshal Daniel Blue. It's a pleasure to meet you," Daniel said. Chuck extended his hand to Blue.

"Well, I'll be! It's a pleasure to meet you too, Marshal." Chuck turned to face Bo. "Does Judge Roads know, I mean, that you hired yourself a deputy?"

Bo shook his head. "I guess the sheriff 's sending him a message now. He'll know by morning."

Chuck laughed. "You'll have to tell me what the judge said when you come back to get your horses." He chuckled more as he went off to his office to get the money he owed Bo.

Daniel and Bo pulled the saddles off their horses and hefted them up on the top rail of the stalls. Daniel led the bay back to her stall and removed the bridle. Bo gently slipped the bridle off Buck and gave him a slap on the rump and Buck trotted off to the first open stall, then disappeared inside. A moment later, Chuck returned with the money.

"Here you go, Marshal. I put an extra ten in for the plug. As long as it came from a marshal, I guess I can afford that much. I'll get him to pull a cart for his keep. I'll have the bay and the buckskin saddled and ready to go in the morning."

Bo shook his head disapprovingly. "I'll saddle Buck myself. He's very particular about who takes care of him. I wouldn't want the two of you to get off on the wrong foot, if you know what I mean. You can curry the bay—she needs it. I'll be down after breakfast to take care of Buck."

"Whatever you need, Marshal," Chuck smiled. "Just let me know.

They'll both get some extra oats tonight. I'll see you in the morning." Chuck turned and went back into his office and Bo and Daniel gathered their guns and the rest of their gear as they headed out the door and toward the gunsmith's. The smith shop was across from the jail on the east side of the street.

By this time, the shadows of the building to the west had made their way to the porch of the gunsmith shop. Daniel pushed the door open and a small bell rang as they entered. The familiar face of Rick Gustafson emerged from the back room and rushed up to Bo.

"Well, I'll be, Bodine Alan Henry," Rick said. "I haven't seen you since Kansas City! How are you? How's your ma and pa? How are your brothers and those two good looking sisters? Damn! It's good to see you, son." With all the excitement of seeing Bo, Rick hadn't noticed the six-foot-four inch, two hundred and ten-pound mountain that had walked in behind Bo. "Oh my! And, who are you?"

Daniel extended his hand toward Rick. "I'm Deputy U.S. Marshal Daniel Blue, sir."

Rick tilted his head off to one side as he looked back at Bo. "When did Judge Roads start sending out deputies with first year marshals or... does he not know about this, yet?"

Bo lowered his head. "The judge doesn't know, yet. The sheriff is sending him a telegram tonight. He'll know in the morning. It was complicated. The three we brought in were about to hang Blue when I got there. We had a disagreement about the situation and you saw the results when I came into town. I needed help getting the prisoner and his friends into town so I made Daniel my deputy to give me a hand."

Rick looked at Blue and then back at Bo. "He's not wearing a gun, Bo. How much help could he have been?"—Rick paused for a moment —"Daniel, do you know that Bo here is the best shot I have ever seen in all my years? If you're going to be a marshal, you couldn't have a better teacher."

Now, Daniel lowered his head. "I'm afraid that no matter what Bo teaches me, I will never be any good with guns. I couldn't hit the barn wall if I was standing in the barn." Blue held up one of his massive fists. It looked like the end of a large fence post. "I use these," he continued. Rick looked at Blue's fist thoughtfully.

"That will do the job if you can get close enough," Rick said. "The problem out here, son, is that the type of men Bo has to deal with won't let you get that close." Rick thought about it for a moment. "I'll tell you what. I'll give you top dollar for the pistols, their rigs and ammunition. I'll trade you even up for the two rifles for what I have in mind for Marshal Blue. Come back tomorrow and I'll have you all fixed up."

The men shook hands in agreement and then Bo looked back at the door. "I guess we're headed up to see Molly now."

Rick stopped them from leaving and looked them up and down with a little disdain. "On your way up there, you may want to stop by the dry goods next door for some fresh clothes *and then* go up to Molly's for a bath. The duds you're wearing have seen better days and you've been too long on the trail."

Bo smiled at Rick, pleased with his suggestion and turned toward Daniel. "That's probably a good idea. I'll bet you can't remember your last bath or when those pants were washed."

After leaving Rick to his work, Bo and Daniel made their way quickly into the dry goods store next door. The owner came out from behind his counter to help them. All of the smells in the store reminded Bo of home. He stopped for a moment, closed his eyes, and thought back to his brother's store. He opened his eyes with a smile of remembrance on his face. Bo and Daniel picked out a fresh set of clothes. Bo had it easy; there were several choices in his size. He picked up a new pair of denim pants and a dark, green shirt. Daniel had more of a problem because of his large size. He ended up with a rust red shirt and a pair of black and gray striped pants. And he found a pair of black high-top boots that actually fit, along with a new belt. His next selection was more difficult.

"I need a hat," Blue said, looking up at the selection of hats that were displayed in the store. "The one I had yesterday floated downstream." Blue tried on just about every hat in the store, grabbing them swiftly with two hands and placing them on top of his head. The dry goods store had a collection of fine hats. After a few unsuccessful selections of standard wide-brimmed western hats in various shades of brown, it looked as though he would have to wait until they reached another town. Each time he looked in the mirror, it seemed the hat was only teetering on top of his head. The whole process was very discouraging. Suddenly, Daniel leaned over and hefted a hat from the store window—the only hat that had escaped his notice. Before he tried it on, he admired the hat's black, smooth, hard, felt and flipped the hat over in his hands to study its round-dome shape. He tried it on and it fit perfectly on his head. "This one will do. It even fits."

Bo looked over at his friend and shook his head. "You don't want that hat. It will cause more fights than it's worth. We'll find you something else..."

"I like it," Bo said, shaking his head in disagreement. "I've seen many of these on men in Chicago. They're popular back there."

Bo repeated what he'd said. "I can't keep fighting for you, especially over some dumb hat," he pressed. Bo was discouraged with Daniel's selection of a bowler hat. It would be the only hat of its kind between there and San Francisco. It was going to draw a lot of attention.

Daniel smiled. "Those fights, I can handle myself. This bowler hat is the one I want."

"Okay. Just remember I told you so, when someone takes a swing at it."

Bo settled up with the clerk and they headed out toward Molly's hotel. Molly's place was at the far end of the street and on the other side of town. Each time they passed someone, they got laughs and second looks because of Daniel's hat. Everyone in the barber shop stood up and came to the window as they passed by; Bo could hear the laughs coming from inside. They turned and walked across the street. A cowboy stopped his horse and waved them across as they passed in front of him. Daniel didn't pay any of them attention as he made his way across the street.

A few minutes later, they ambled into the hotel lobby. The lobby was a large, open area. Two small bistro tables, each with two ornate, cushioned chairs, flanked the hotel lobby doors. Dominating the center of the small lobby was a worn green velvet circular settee. A counter stretched across the width of the lobby with a hall at the left and the stairs going up to the rooms on the right. The slightly balding clerk had a black mustache, black vest and his white shirt sleeves were pulled halfway up his forearms by black garters. He wasn't ready for what he saw in front of him; neither were the two guests seated in the front of the lobby reading their papers. Both men dropped their papers in their laps to watch the sight. Bo and Daniel approached the hotel's counter and dropped their gear on the floor. Bo spun the registration book around and pulled the pen out of its holder. "We're going to need a couple of rooms for the night."

The clerk panicked. "Molly! I need you out here right now," he said in a strained voice. His eyes were staring nearly straight up at Blue's bowler hat. A few seconds later, Molly came up to the desk from her office in the back and took one look at Bo standing there. Molly was a large woman in her fifties. She had at least fifty pounds on Bo and stood two inches taller in her heels. She wore a blue, flowery dress that ran up to her neck with a frilly, white collar and white frills at the cuffs. Twenty years ago, every man in Dodge would have been at her feet, but, the years and the wrinkles had caught up to her.

"Well I'll be damned! Bodine Henry!" Molly declared. "That was you they were talking about this afternoon?" She sauntered out from behind the desk and gave Bo a hug so hard it nearly took his breath away. Molly was closer to Bo's dad's age than his. She leaned closer to Bo's ear to half-whisper. "How's your pa? You know he was the best-looking deckhand on that damn river?"

"My ma and pa are just fine, thank you," Bo said a little embarrassed. "When did you come to Dodge?"

She put her arm around his shoulders and gave him another hug, then went back to the business side of the clerk's desk. "What can I do for you today? A bath, a room and some of that apple cobbler you like so much?"

Bo signed the ledger and directed her attention toward his new deputy. "Molly, this is Deputy Marshal Daniel Blue. We're going to need all of that for one night. We have to get back on the trail tomorrow."

Molly's eyes went up and down Blue's tall frame. "I can take care of you, Bo, but—Marshal Blue here is going to be more of a problem for me here in Dodge"—she hesitated for a moment before continuing—"I don't…I can't put him up in one of my regular rooms. My other guests will have a fit." She stood behind the counter with her palms on its surface, thinking about the situation for a moment.

Daniel stepped forward, attempting to right the situation. "That's all right, Marshal Henry. I'll go back to the stable and spend the night there."

Finally, Molly spoke up. "I'll be damned if you will. I've never turned away a U.S. Marshal and I'm not about to start now. Let's get the two of you a bath and some good food. I'll figure this out while we eat. We can eat in my office out back. I eat out there most nights anyway."

Molly put Bo in the big, copper tub and Daniel in the makeshift shower that her help had pieced together in the storage shed. Washed and refreshed, with their gear quickly stowed away in Bo's hotel room, they were now sitting in Molly's office in their new clothes with Kansas City steaks with all the trimmings in front of them. Molly had set up a makeshift table with two planks and a couple of barrels. She had a white table cloth spread out over it and the settings were of her finest china and flatware.

After they had their fill of steak, Bo had two helpings of hot apple cobbler. The sweet, warm smell of cinnamon and baked apple wafted by his nose with every spoonful. Molly poured a jigger of brandy for Bo to go with his meal. Blue declined Molly's offer of brandy and sat back with his hot cup of coffee. Throughout the evening, Molly asked questions, mostly about Bo's pa, and Bo asked her how she got to Dodge from Kansas City. They shared some laughs and warm memories between each other and then it was time for bed. It had been a long day for Daniel and Bo; they were ready for bed. The sun was long gone and the lamps were all lit in the hotel lobby. They could hear laughter and music coming from the bar next door.

Daniel stood up to leave. "I guess I had better get down to the livery or they won't let me in."

"I told you," Molly said, standing up. "I'm not going to let a U.S. Marshal sleep in that dirty livery, especially after I just had him washed. I got a nice cot for you in the storage room out back. It's not much, but we made it special long—just for you. I had my help put an extra blanket out for you. You'll be just fine until morning. I know you want to get moving, so I'll have your breakfast ready as soon as the two of you get up."

Molly put her hand in her pocket, revealing a small, brass colored key and leaned over to give Bo the key to his room. While she did so, Daniel expressed his gratitude for her hospitality. Bo took his key and echoed Daniel's thanks. With the effects of the full meal and the length of the day hanging over them, Bo and Daniel retired to their separate accommodations, each looking forward to a soft bed and a good night's sleep.

Dan Bradford

Chapter 3
Boone and Crocket

Bo was up early and down at the livery before Daniel was up and dressed. He saddled Buck and gave him his morning apple while Chuck saddled Blue's bay. After settling his tab with the livery stable, he walked both horses to the jail before he joined Daniel for breakfast. It was a cool, crisp, calm morning and the first rays of the sun warmed his face. Molly was at the front door when Bo walked in.

"Good morning, Bo. I see you've been down to take care of Buck already this morning," Molly said, from her usual post behind the hotel desk counter.

Bo smiled, seeing her standing there. "He takes care of me on the trail, so I take care of him when we're in the big city."

Molly led Bo down the hall and to the left of the front desk, back to the kitchen. The smell of fresh coffee, biscuits and bacon got Bo's attention. When they entered the kitchen, they discovered Daniel sitting there with his coffee and waiting for his breakfast. The portly cook was at the stove with a white apron around his waist and a towel over his left shoulder. Bo and Daniel exchanged greetings and the eggs began to cook on the large stove just behind Daniel. The cook looked over at Bo and asked how he'd like his eggs. Bo nodded before he pulled out his chair.

"You can cook my eggs hard and make the bacon crispy." It wasn't long before the meal was done and it was time to say good-bye again.

Parting, Molly gave Blue a warm handshake and to Bo, a crushing hug. "Both of you look out for each other," Molly said pulling out of the hug. "And come back in one piece."

With that out of the way, Bo and Daniel crossed the dusty street and made their way several doors down past the barber shop, the gun smith's and the dry goods store to the jail where Sheriff Anderson was waiting for them.

"Good morning, gents," Sheriff Anderson said to them. "I trust you had a good night's sleep. I got a message from Judge Roads early this morning. He sent me the latest reward amounts on the three you brought in yesterday. I've got his okay to take these numbers to the bank as soon as it opens. He wasn't really happy with you adding a deputy, but he said to keep him until you get back to Kansas City. He'll figure out how to deal with it, then. He also sent over two more warrants for you."

"That's good news"—Bo smiled and turned to face Daniel—"I guess the job's yours at least until we get back to Kansas City…if you want it."

"Right now, teaming up with you is the best way for me to find my wife. I'm in until you kick me out," Daniel exclaimed.

"What's this about your wife?" Sheriff Anderson asked, puzzled.

"A little over a year ago, seven men forced their way into his home in Chicago and took his wife, along with several others of his people," Bo explained. "He first believed they were being taken south to be sold as indentured servants. As it turned out, they were headed west. I don't suppose you've heard anything about that many blacks being taken out in that direction?"

The sheriff scratched his head, attempting to trace his memories for anything that could be helpful. "If anyone around here had seen a group like that, I would have heard about it. I'm sorry, Marshal. No troop has come through these parts like that. If I hear of anything, I'll get word to you through Judge Roads." Just then, the sheriff noticed the banker hurry past the jail window on his way to his office. The banker was a short plump man with a narrow, brimmed hat, wide mustache and a black, pinstriped suit. "There goes Tom. I'll follow him down to the bank and get your money. Where are you going to be?"

Bo smiled. "We're on our way over to Rick's gun shop to see what he's come up with for Daniel. He said he had some ideas that would make Daniel a better shot. We have no idea what he's got up his sleeve but it should be interesting."

The three men left the jail and parted ways. Bo and Daniel stepped off the walkway and headed up the street. The sheriff turned to his right and chased after the banker who was already near his destination. As the sheriff approached Tom, he called out. "Tom, wait up! I've got some business for you this morning!"

As Bo and Daniel walked toward the gun shop, the sheriff's voice faded into the distance. Rick had just opened his shop for the day when Bo and Daniel rang the little bell over the door as they entered. Rick appeared from the back room when he heard the bell.

"Good morning!" Rick said cheerfully, seeing who had just come through for a visit. "You're going to have to wait for the coffee; I just put it on. I trust that Molly got both of you a good night's sleep and a big breakfast?"

Bo pulled up a chair next to the stove that had just been fired up. "I can't speak for Daniel, but, I'm as full as I have ever been. Were you able to come up with something for my deputy?"

For a moment, Rick disappeared into the shelves in the back of his shop and after a few minutes, he reappeared from behind his counter with a belt and double holster rig. "I think I have just the rig for a man his size." Rick slipped the belt around Blue and tugged on the buckle, just clearing the second hole. "Turn around Deputy and let's see the back side."

Daniel shuffled his feet as he pivoted around. "Well, how does it look back there?" he asked.

Bo laughed, examining Blue. "Like the cinch on a bucking bull. But, I guess you won't be sitting on it when you ride."

"It looks just fine, Blue," Rick said, backing off. "Just stay put and I'll get the guns that go with it." Again, Rick wandered behind his counter.

Bo leaned in a little closer. "I've never seen a rig like this," he said. "What kind of guns go in holsters this large?"

Rick came back out from behind his counter, this time with his arms behind his back to keep his surprise hidden from Bo. He dropped the two guns into Daniel's holsters at the same time. "There! See how you like the feel of those."

Bo took one quick glance at the hardware. "Well, there's one thing for sure, you won't miss the barn wall with one of those."

Daniel reached down and pulled one of the two very short twelve gauge shotguns out of its shiny black holster and saw a lever just behind the two large flat hammers. He pushed the lever to one side and the barrels dropped down giving him a clear view of the floor as he peered down through them. Both guns had semi-pistol grips and the breech of each weapon was delicately engraved. He took the stock under the barrels with his left hand and snapped closed the first gun. It made a loud click as it locked in place. Even though Daniel had never handled a gun before, it seemed the right thing to do. He retrieved the second shotgun with his left hand and held them side by side. It was clear that he'd never seen anything like them before.

Bo leaned in to take a closer look. "That's about the most beautiful pair of pumpkin mashers I've ever seen. What's etched on the barrels, Daniel?"

Blue looked down at the two guns to read the inscriptions, turning the weapons from his wrists. Between the delicate scroll work were etched names. Daniel read the gun in his right hand first. "The right barrel has 'Boone' on it and the left barrel has 'Crockett'." Then he read the second gun. "This one has 'Houston' on the right and 'Austin' on the left. As I recall, they were all at the Alamo. Whoever had these made must have known those men."

Rick knew what was on the barrels. He looked at Daniel. "You got the first part right. Boone and Crockett were at the Alamo, Houston and Austin were not. They were the fathers of Texas."

Bo took one of the guns from Daniel and looked it over. "Houston was president of Texas, as I remember."

Rick went behind his counter and pulled up three boxes of shotgun shells in his hands. "Here, this will get you started"—he tossed a box of pistol cartridges to Bo—"this is for your birthday."

Bo caught the box in midair. "Thanks, Rick. My birthday was a few months ago, but thanks anyway." He paused for a moment. "How did you come by those shotguns? I know you didn't make them up last night."

Rick came out from behind the counter toward Bo and Daniel, then pulled up one of the two chairs next to the stove that was off to the right of the door. "I had an old-timer come in here with them about a year ago. He said he was on his way west from Texas and he needed a grubstake. I gave him a good price because I felt bad for him. I figured that sooner or later, I'd get my money back."

Daniel was still admiring both guns. "I must owe you a big piece of change for these."

Rick smiled. "I've already sold the two Sharps you traded me yesterday. I got my money back and a little more. The guns are yours even up"—Rick hesitated—"there is one thing about those guns. I tried to tighten up the triggers last night. Here, let me show you." He took one of the shotguns from Daniel and demonstrated as he spoke. "You have to cock the hammers full back"—he held the gun close to Blue's ear—"when you pull the trigger, you can feel a click after the first barrel discharges. That's the trigger locking up with the second hammer. When you squeeze it again, the second barrel will fire. The problem is, if you pull too hard or quick, you're going to get both barrels at the same time."

Bo slapped his knee and laughed. "You're not only going to hit the barn wall, you're going to blow a hole in it big enough for Buck and me to ride through." He laughed some more. "Well, we're going to have to take you out and let you get a feel for those cannons before you have to use them."

Rick handed the gun back to Daniel. "The only way around that is to only cock one hammer at a time. Just remember to use the right barrel first. The gun won't fire if you just cock the left one."

Blue wasn't very familiar with guns and now he had two that were already a problem. "I'll try to remember that," he said, looking at Bo. "Are you sure I need these? I'm not very good with guns and these make me uneasy."

Bo tried not to laugh. "You'll be just fine. We'll stop after we're out of town and let you get used to them. Don't worry about it."

The bell over the door rang and the sheriff walked in. He shut the door behind him, looked at the men standing in the shop, and focused on Bo who was standing close to Blue discussing something. Bo turned to look at the sheriff.

"I've got your money from the bank and those two warrants from Judge Roads," Sheriff Anderson said to Bo. "He said you should write your birthday on them for the issue date and 'Happy Birthday'." He passed the money and papers to Bo who took them in both hands. Bo then moved to the counter and counted out three piles of money. The small pile he handed to the sheriff. "This is for your help, Sheriff."

The sheriff took the money and put it in his shirt pocket. "Thank you, Marshal. I appreciate your consideration."

Bo continued with the rest of the money he'd received from the sale of the guns, horses and tack. Adding a few more bills to the third pile, he took the large pile of bills, folded them in half, and put them in his pocket. He picked up the rest of the money and turned around to face Blue. "This is yours, Deputy. It's payday."

Daniel had been sitting on the window ledge at the front of the store after admiring the new items he'd received from Rick. He got up, slid the two shotguns into his new holsters and walked to Bo. He took the money from Bo and counted what he'd been given. "That's more money than I've ever had in my entire life. There must be two hundred dollars here."

Bo smiled "There's two hundred and seventy-three dollars there. I took out what you owed me for the new clothes and that ugly hat. You had better take good care of that money. We may not see another payday for a month or two."

Daniel rolled up the bills and pushed them down deep into the inside pocket of his vest as Bo shook hands with Rick and the sheriff. Bo turned to face Daniel. "We've got to get going. It's a long ride to Three Forks and I want to make camp at that stream we were at when I met you."

The men nodded in agreement. The four men stepped outside to find a young boy –who was trying to smile—standing next to the horses.

"I had to tie all of your goods to the bay, sir," the boy said. "The buckskin wouldn't let me near him."

Bo smiled. "That's all right. You did just fine."

He gave the boy a quarter as he put his foot in the stirrup. One short bounce and Bo was on Buck's back. Daniel eased himself up into his saddle and reached down to shake hands with Rick again. "Thank you for all your help," he said. "I'll take good care of them."

Rick shook Blue's hand. "I want them to take good care of you."

Buck was eager to leave town and didn't wait for Bo to point him in that direction. He spun around and headed north at a trot. Daniel had to spur his bay to get her to follow. They were on their way. Molly waved at them from the walkway as they passed and Daniel tipped his hat as they began to gallop—Buck was in a hurry.

The two men had been in the saddle for an hour when Bo spotted a place near a stream for Daniel to try his new weapons. Bo whistled to get his deputy's attention and waved him toward a good spot for target practice. Daniel followed, and both dismounted. Bo gathered, then propped up several sticks in a row, ordering Blue back about twenty feet. Daniel pulled the shotgun from the right holster and braced himself for the impending jolt.

Bo encouraged Blue to take the shot. "Go ahead, Daniel. It's not going to hurt."

Daniel cocked both hammers and squeezed the trigger. There was a deafening explosion. The recoil from the first shot caused Daniel to tighten his grip on the gun and that sent the second hammer slamming forward. The second shot was more than Blue was prepared for and the barrels of the shotgun recoiled upward and hit him in the chest with a sickening thud.

Bo shook his head. "Well, at least we got that part over with."

Daniel took a second or two to get his wits back. "You mean you planned that?"

Bo looked sheepishly at Daniel. "I wanted you to see what it would be like if you cut loose with both barrels. Now we know. It would be my suggestion that you only cock the right hammer first and then the left."

They both looked back in the direction of their makeshift firing line made of the sticks Bo had bundled together. The first barrel had cut the middle stick off about a foot from the ground and the stick on either side hadn't fared any better. Bo nodded his head approvingly.

"That's about what I expected," Bo said. "You're going to cut a hole in the barn wall about ten feet wide at twenty paces out. If you fire one of those things any further back than that, you're going to catch a lot of innocent bystanders in its path. Just remember, right barrel and then the left."

"I'll remember. I have to cock the right barrel first or I'll get knocked on my backside."

As long as they were stopped near water, they decided to make lunch of bacon, beans and a couple of biscuits and let the horses graze. Bo gathered the sticks Daniel had just cut in half with his shotgun and built a small fire. Daniel got a pot of coffee going to wash down their meal. There was the stump and a fallen tree for them to sit on. The stream made a turn at this point and the water made a bubbling sound around the rocks. There was no wind and the sun warmed up the day. While they were relaxing next to the fire, Daniel decided to ask Bo a question. "Bo, when you saved me, you pulled your gun and I could tell it wasn't the first time you've had to use it. When was the first?"

A sad look came over Bo's face as he thought back to that night. "I'd been working for the sheriff for just a little over two years. We had a couple of our usuals—Emerson and Alvin—in jail for being drunk. A stranger came to town and started causing a lot of trouble. The sheriff arrested him and brought him down to the jail. I had to take old Alvin out of one cell and put him in with Emerson. Neither one of them was sober enough to be a problem. When I pulled old Alvin out of the cell, the stranger grabbed him and tossed him into the sheriff. They both went to the floor and the sheriff dropped his gun. The stranger picked it up..." Bo had to stop for a moment.

Daniel encouraged Bo to continue. "What happened then?"

Bo looked back over at Daniel. "I pulled my gun and pointed it at him," Bo continued. "The stranger turned and was going to shoot me. The sheriff was under old Alvin. There was a lot of shouting and kicking from the sheriff. The stranger shot me in the side and I fell back against the desk. I was on my knees watching the stranger swing the gun on the sheriff. It all happened so fast. It was just a blur. I cocked the hammer and pulled the trigger. The recoil from that old .45 drove the gun back into my face. I don't know what I would have done if I'd had to shoot again. The bullet hit the stranger and shoved him back against the bars of the second cell. He dropped dead on top of the sheriff and Alvin"—Bo pulled up his shirt and showed Daniel the scar on his left side just below his ribs—"this is the reminder I got. I went to the trick shot man who came to town that next summer and asked him to show me how to not get shot again. He taught me everything I needed to know in two days. After that, I practiced every single day." He tucked his shirt back in. "Let's get back on the trail."

Bo put out the fire by kicking dirt on it.They gathered their horses and packed the rest of their materials, then started off in the direction of Three Forks. This was going to be a long ride.

Chapter 4
Two Cows at Three Forks

The two men spent hours and then days in the saddle. One mile seemed like the next out on the prairie, wide open nothingness. There was only the occasional unwanted rain storm to break up the monotony of traveling along the trail. They passed the time exchanging stories about their families and adventures. Bo had a leg up on Daniel because of his nine brothers and two sisters. It seemed there wasn't a day that went by when one of the brothers wasn't in trouble with their pa over one thing or the other, and the sisters spent a great deal of time patching up bruises, scrapes and egos. Daniel, on the other hand, had only one older brother and it seemed they hardly ever got into trouble growing up. Blue's brother had died several years before in an accident on the docks in New York. The death prompted his family's move to Chicago. Daniel's pa had died two years ago at the age of sixty-six and his ma a year later. The only family Daniel had left was his wife and now she had been taken from him.

It was early afternoon when Bo and Daniel first glimpsed Three Forks with its snowcapped mountains far off in the distance. They picked up their pace as they neared the edge of town. From that far out, Three Forks could have been any one of a half-dozen small towns Bo had been in the past two years. It especially reminded him of Cimarron, Texas, a town he'd been in just over a year ago. There were five or six store fronts on either side of the street. Some had fronts that extended out over the wooden walkways that ran the full length of the town. All the doorways had signs announcing the business inside, but only the saloon had a painted exterior. It seemed there was a curl of smoke rising up from each business proclaiming they were ready to accept their next customer. It had been a long ride and both men were eager to get out of the saddle.

Entering town, it didn't take long to find the local jail. Bo and Daniel watered their horses and hitched them to the rail in front of the jail's entrance. As they stepped into the jailhouse, they were met by the local sheriff who stood up as they entered and then extended his hand.

"You must be Marshal Henry," said the man standing behind the desk near the entrance eyeing them. The sheriff was a short man whose belly hid his belt buckle. "I'm Sheriff Matt Douglas. I got a message from Judge Roads stating that you would be headed this way. He told me to expect you and your deputy any time after yesterday." He looked Daniel up and down. "Is this your deputy?" he said with some skepticism.

Bo extended his hand to Sheriff Douglas. "I'm U.S. Marshal Bo Henry. This is Deputy U.S. Marshal Daniel Blue. He's been with me for nearly a month now."

The sheriff wasn't sure how to handle all of what had just entered his jail, but he did his best. He pushed his hand toward Blue. "I'm glad to meet you, Marshal." The sheriff turned back to Bo. "The judge says you are after the Burser brothers. They were the outlaws who robbed our bank here a little over a year ago. I thought you caught them and sent them to prison. What happened?"

Bo and Daniel pulled up the two chairs that had been next to the stove, sat down and then Bo filled the sheriff in on what had taken place after the Burser brothers were caught and jailed in Kansas City. "We never caught Carl. His older brother, James, stood trial and was on his way to Jefferson City when Carl broke him out of custody. They killed two marshals and wounded another in the process. We thought they would be on their way here."

The sheriff just shook his head in disbelief. "We haven't seen them in these parts since the robbery. We chased them east until we were well-outside our jurisdiction. We lost their trail after the second day."

Daniel asked his own question. "Sheriff, we're looking for another group that may have passed here about that same time. There would have been about seven white men with more than a dozen blacks with them. Have you seen them? They kidnapped the blacks from Chicago and were last seen headed in this direction. My wife was in that group."

"I have warrants for these white men and anything you can tell us would be a big help," Bo added.

The sheriff didn't have to think on it much. "You know, there were a couple of people from town who saw a sizable group camped about three miles south of town for a time. They had come down from Denver and spent part of the winter here. It got too cold for them and they headed south after a few weeks. I never got a look at them myself. I do know they bought out most of the dry goods store before they left. You may want to go down there and talk to Bill. He's the only one who really talked to them."

Pleased with the lead, Daniel shook the sheriff's hand. "I appreciate your help, Sheriff."

Bo followed, shaking the sheriff's hand, too. "Thanks, Sheriff," Bo said, with a firm handshake. "We passed a stable on the way into town. Can we put our horses up there for a day or two? We're going to be here for a little while. I want to ask around and make sure the Bursers haven't been seen."

The sheriff stood, then pointed in the direction of the livery stable. "You can put your horses up there, but you're going to have a problem finding a room. Our hotel is full up for the hanging. You can still get a soft straw pile down at the stable if you hurry. I'm sorry, boys, we don't have hangings around here very often and this one has the whole county in an uproar."

Bo had to know more. "What the hell happened? I had no idea you had a judge out here. When was the trial?"

The sheriff sat back down in his large barrel chair. "We've had several new families move in to start farming. They got deeds to some of the federal land along the river bottom. Up until now, it hasn't been a problem. A few days ago, this family came through and along the way they managed to pick up one of Mr. Mertauck's prize bulls. This is where the stories I got from Mertauck and the farmers differ. Mertauck tells me that when his two hands tried to claim the bull, the farmer shot one and sent the other one off without his gun.

"Mr. Mertauck went back with about twenty of his hands, took the bull and beat the hell out of the farmer and his fifteen-year-old son, who had also been shot. Mertauck wanted it all legal so they held a trial yesterday. Mr. Mertauck recruited some shopkeepers and his trail hands to serve on the jury. He was also the judge. It took about ten minutes for the farmer to be found guilty. Mertauck pounded his gun butt on the table and said they would be hung for stealing the bull and shooting his trail hand. Mertauck and his men were going to hang them right then and there. I had to convince them to wait until the day after tomorrow. I said that it had to wait to make it legal."

Daniel was concerned about the type of justice Mr. Mertauck had dealt himself. "What did the farmers have to say at the trial?" he asked.

The sheriff shook his head. "Mr. Mertauck wouldn't let them speak.

He said all he needed was the testimony of his trail hands because the farmers were all liars, anyway."

Bo shook his head. "Did you talk to the farmer and his son at all? Where are they now?"

"Yes," Sheriff Douglas nodded. "I spoke to them when they were first brought in. I've got them locked up out back."

Bo pushed past the sheriff, peering in the direction the farmer and his son were being held. "I want to talk to them, right now. Then, I want you to send a message to Judge Roads. I want him to know what's going on out here. You're not going to hang these men until I have an answer back from Judge Roads saying that he's in favor of it. If he's not, then I'm taking custody of these prisoners as the Federal Marshal in this jurisdiction. Are we clear on that? I don't want there to be the slightest chance of hanging innocent men."

The sheriff nodded his compliance and stood back to let Bo and Daniel back into the cell area. There was a heavy wooden door with steel bars off to the left of the sheriff's desk that led to the cell area. Bo and Daniel made their way through the jail's entryway and past a small table and chair. When Bo and Daniel made their way to the back of the jail, the farmer and his wounded son were sitting on a bunk in the last of the three cells. From the wounds marking their faces, arms, hands and their torn clothes, it was obvious that both had been beaten and stomped on.

"Is this the way they were brought in here or did you have something to do with this?" Bo asked Sheriff Douglas who had followed them back. Bo was enraged over what he saw. The sheriff was forced to back off when Daniel put his huge hand on his chest, preventing him from unlocking and entering the cell with them.

"No, Marshal. This is the way Mertauck brought them in," Sheriff Douglas said, putting his hands up—one hand holding a ring of jailhouse keys—at Daniel to communicate that he meant no harm. "He said they put up a fight when the trail hands tried to take the bull from them." Listening to the conversation, the farmer clutched his son and tried to put himself between the cell door and the boy.

Bo yanked the keys from the sheriff's hand and tried two before he managed to open the cell. As soon as he did, Bo and Daniel stepped into it, joining the farmer and his son. The farmer shrank back as the cell's door opened and tried to position himself between his son and the men entering. Bo reached out his hand toward the nervous father. "I'm U.S. Marshal Bo Henry, and this is my deputy, Daniel Blue. I'm here to help if I can. You have to tell me what happened."

The man pushed back. "I want to know what happened to my wife and daughter."

Bo looked over his shoulder at the sheriff. "Where are his wife and daughter?"

The sheriff attempted to make his way into the cell again, and again was met by Daniel's hand on his chest. He looked up at the big face and the scowl looking down at him and answered the question. "Your wife and daughter are just fine. They're camped about a half-mile south of town…a couple of other farmers' families are taking care of them."

Daniel turned back to the farmer, who seated himself on the bunk. "Please tell us what happened to you out there. We want to help you, sir." His deep voice was soothing. The man seemed to relax just a little. The stiffness of his frame softened.

"My name is Mark Weston. This is my son, Peter. Two days ago, a large bull lumbered into our camp and ran off our two milking heifers. My son isn't much good with a rope and he was only able to get it around the bull—at least the bull wouldn't run the heifers off any further. We thought they would wander back. We staked the bull out and went off to look for our cows. That's when the two trail hands came up on us! They accused us of stealing the bull!

"One of them pulled a gun and pointed it at my son and shot him. I shot the trail hand and turned the gun on the other man. I made him leave his gun and I told him to come back with our cows. And if he did, he could have his damn bull back. My wife patched up our son and the man I'd shot. It's wasn't long before we had twenty or more men with guns in our camp. They took my wife and held her while they beat my wounded son and me. They dragged us off and threw us in here. The next day they had a trial. They wouldn't let us talk at all and now they plan to hang us"—he reached over and pulled his son closer to him—"my wife's name is Pauline and my daughter is Mary. You've got to get some word to them. They must be worried sick by now!"

Daniel tried to calm Mr. Weston, who had become increasingly upset at mentioning his wife and daughter. "I'll make sure your wife knows what's going on and that the U.S. Marshals Service is in charge now," Daniel said.

Bo looked at Daniel. "Let's not step in too deep without the judge on our side. We have to wait until we hear from him."

Daniel wasn't going to take no for an answer. "You know damn well the judge isn't going to let this remain like this and we're not going to let these people be hung. Send the message to the judge and mark it 'Urgent'."

Bo turned to the sheriff. "You heard the man. Get that message off to Judge Roads, right now!"

The sheriff jerked just a little when Daniel's hand eased him toward the door. "I'll get it off right away, Marshal," the sheriff said, racing out of the cell and out of the jail. He quickly crossed the street to the stage depot where the telegrapher was located to send the telegraph to Judge Roads.

Daniel leaned over Mr. Weston and his son. "Don't worry, sir. I'm not going to let this happen to you. You'll be safe here and we're not going to let anyone come in here to hurt you anymore. I'll have a talk with the sheriff as soon as he comes back. We'll send a message to your wife. Is there anything specific you want to say to her?" His deep voice was soft and gentle as if he was soothing a frightened horse. Both, Mr. Weston and his son seemed to relax.

Mark reached out his hand to Daniel. "Thank you, sir. I appreciate all you are doing for us. Please tell my wife we're fine and that we have your help now. That will make her feel much better."

Bo locked the cell, leaving the Westons to wait for the next events to transpire and went back out to the office to wait for the sheriff's return. Daniel nodded to the father and son and soon followed Bo out. Daniel looked at Bo's worried face inquisitively. Bo was more than a little disturbed by what Daniel had said to Mark Weston.

"Daniel, I know you are worried about Mr. Weston and his son," Bo said, with a serious tone. "But we can't step out of our jurisdiction on something like this. What will we do if Judge Roads tells us to back off? What will we tell the man's wife then? I will feel just as bad as you will, but they will feel even worse. We have to be careful about what we tell people. We have a grave responsibility to these people and to the law."

They pulled up chairs and both sat quietly, thinking about what Bo had just told Daniel regarding what Daniel had promised Mr. Weston. The thought that Judge Roads may not agree made Daniel worry and begin to ring his hands.

Bo took out his watch to check the time. Nearly an hour had passed since the sheriff had run out of the jail to send the telegram. Daniel and Bo were beginning to feel concerned over the sheriff's absence. The coffee was nearly gone when the sheriff rushed back in through the jail's door.

"I waited to hear from Judge Roads," Sheriff Douglas said to Bo and

Daniel, who were seated with cups of coffee on the desk in front of them. "I knew you'd want to get his message right away." He handed the paper to Bo. Bo took it, read it to himself and then handed it to Daniel, who accepted it anxiously.

"Well, I guess you're off the hook, Blue. The judge agrees with you."

Daniel jumped out of his chair and hurried back to the cell where Mr. Weston and his son were waiting.

"The judge sent us this message and I guess it's as much your business as it is ours," Daniel said, feeling pleased with the verdict. He held the piece of paper up and began to read. "'Due to the fact that the prisoners were tried without the benefit of legal counsel, and that the alleged offense took place across county lines, and the fact that there is no appointed legal judge in this district, I will hear the case in Kansas City at such time, as the alleged defendants can be transported to my court. In the meantime, Marshals Henry and Blue will investigate and determine if a crime has been committed. Signed, Judge Henry Roads, Senior Judge, Federal Court System, Kansas City, Missouri, These United States of America'."

Weston broke down and sobbed when he heard the news. "I can't thank you enough. You and Marshal Henry have been sent by heaven! I will pray for both of you. Thank you, so very much." He reached out through the bars and shook Daniel's hand. Daniel accepted the gesture kindly and then returned to the sheriff's office where Bo stood up when he walked in.

"Let's get the horses down to the stable," Bo said, adding, "and get ourselves settled in for the night. I could use a good home-cooked meal."

The sheriff accompanied them to the door. "There's only one place in town—Maggie's Food Emporium on the other end of town. They cook a good meal down there. Tell them that I sent you and they may be able to find you a big piece of apple pie."

The two marshals shook hands with Sheriff Douglas and climbed back in their saddles. A few minutes later, they secured a place to sleep in the loft at the livery stable and were on their way to Maggie's for a hot meal. They turned right out of the livery stable and headed north up the street. They could see the brightly painted sign hanging out over the entry proclaiming that it was Maggie's Food Emporium and went inside. They found a spacious interior with plenty of seating at small tables and along the counter down the right side. They took seats at one of the tables at the rear.

After their second cup of coffee and a large wedge of pie, they sat back to figure out what would happen tomorrow. It wouldn't take long for the news of Judge Roads' message to make its way around town. Bo and Daniel spoke quietly to each other, working out scenarios between sips of coffee. When they tired, they paid their tab, and prepared to retire for the night, but just as they were about to leave, the door of the emporium burst open.

The well-dressed figure in the doorway was Mr. Mertauck with two of his trail hands. Surprised onlookers whispered the figure's name to one another, confirming his identity to Bo and Daniel. One of the cowboys had his gun tied low on his hip and his fingers were dancing over the grip. Mertauck walked straight up to Bo and Daniel.

"I just heard that the two of you have stuck your noses into my business," Mertauck said smartly. "I want to know how the hell you got the idea that I'm going to turn over my town and those cattle rustlers to you?"

Bo didn't look up at Mertauck. "If you know about the message I received from Judge Roads, then you already know where I got the idea," Bo said, not breaking his gaze to look at Mertauck and his men. The other diners fell silent as tension rose around them. "Those prisoners are under the jurisdiction of the Federal Court System and the U.S. Marshals' Service. If you can't see your way clear to that, then I will send a message to the nearest U.S. Army post and I'll have a detachment of cavalry here in a couple of days. I'm sure they will bring enough guns to convince you of my authority."

Mertauck stammered for a moment, turned and stomped out of Maggie's. Daniel smiled. "Would you really send a message like that?" Daniel asked.

Bo laughed. "No, but he had to think that I would. He may believe he could run us out of town but there's no way he wants to tangle with a troop of soldiers." Bo stood up. The other diners applauded as he stood. "I guess we have a couple of friends in town." Bo raised his hand in appreciation as he put his hat on and moved to the door. "I think we should make Mr. Mertauck our first order of business in the morning. I want to have a look at his spread and see if we can't find those two missing heifers."

Early the next morning Buck and Bo rousted Blue out of his comfortable bed of hay at the livery stable, pushing him awake. Buck was just finishing his morning apple and Bo had him saddled.

"Get up, Daniel," Bo called out. "Let's go down and have breakfast. I want to roust Mertauck and let him guide us out to his spread. If he beats us out there, we may never find those milking cows."

Daniel got up to his feet slowly. A bit later, Daniel stopped for a moment as he was nearly finished saddling his bay. "If we find the heifers, how are we going to tell whose cows they are?"

Bo slid into his saddle. "Mr. Weston told me his cows have tags on their ears. He gave me the numbers of each tag. If Mertauck doesn't know what the tags are for and he hasn't removed them, then we have him dead to rights on two counts of heifer rustling."

Bo's response got a laugh out of Daniel. "The steer baron is going to be arrested for cow rustling. I can't wait to see the look on his face when you put that one in his lap." Daniel hopped into his saddle and began following Bo toward Maggie's. "I wonder if Mertauck will recommend hanging for milk cow rustling."

When they completed the short trot to Maggie's, they tied their horses up to a railing outside and walked in. There were a half-dozen customers seated at the counter and at two of the tables. The smell of fresh coffee and frying bacon was mouthwatering. The steak they had with the potatoes and eggs was done just right. Daniel pushed his chair back and rubbed his stomach. "That was one of the best meals I've had in a very long time."

Bo and Daniel were just leaving Maggie's as Mr. Mertauck was entering. Bo stopped him at the doorway. "Mr. Mertauck, as soon as you've finished your breakfast, I will expect you to accompany my deputy and me out to your spread. We're going to want to see this bull that you claim was stolen. I'll want to talk to the other hand who was there during the original meeting between him and Mr. Weston."

Mertauck was as uncooperative as possible. He tried to push his way past Bo. "I'll take you out to my place, but I don't travel with the likes of your servant."

Mertauck's attitude and tone of voice were just enough to set Bo off. He leaned in with his nose only an inch or two away from Mertauck's face.

"Listen to me, you pompous ass," Bo said. His voice was very low and only Mertauck could hear him. "That man's name is Deputy U.S. Marshal Daniel Blue. He's my deputy and you will treat him with the respect due any other U.S. Marshal. If you can't live with that, then I guess I'm off to the telegraph office to send my message to Judge Roads requesting troops. Your other alternative is to back up and clear your holster right here, right now."

Mertauck didn't like the sound of either of his choices. He turned to one of his men standing next to him. "Have our horses saddled," he barked. We'll be leaving for the ranch as soon as we're done with breakfast." He turned and pushed his way past Bo and into Maggie's.

Once the other men were out of sight, Daniel took Bo by the arm. "What did you say to him that made him turn white like that?"

Bo smiled. "I just told him that you took it very personally the last time someone called you my servant and you broke him in half before I could stop you."

"You didn't really say that, did you?" Daniel smiled.

Bo laughed. "No, I told him that if he didn't cooperate I would send for the Army troops. Let's go down to the jail and see how our prisoners are doing. I want to make sure our message was taken to Mark's wife."

Bo and Daniel mounted their horses and rode to check in at the jail to make sure all was well. When they arrived, Sheriff Douglas kindly gave them an update that pleased them and the Westons were fine in their bunks. With that out of the way, they mounted up and waited outside Maggie's for Mr. Mertauck to emerge. They didn't have to wait long.

After Mertauck mounted his horse, they took off with Mertauck leading. It was going to take most of the day to reach his ranch house. They had been in the saddle for seven hours when Bo leaned over. "When do we get to your spread?"

Mertauck smirked. "You've been on my land for the past four hours." He spurred his horse and pulled away from Bo. The rest of his men joined him and left Bo and Daniel in their dust.

Daniel turned to Bo. "I don't think he likes you much."

They rode for another hour before they reached the large timber arch that stretched over the trail that led to the structures in the distance. The top beam of the arch displayed Mertauck's name flanked by his brand—designed with a bold letter "M"—burned into it. When they got close enough, they could see that the ranch house was raised up on pylons with two floors above the footings. The house had a tall pitched roof for the deep winter snows. The large, white house was set up on a berm that made it look even bigger. The grass in front had been worn away due to all of the horse traffic. The roof hung out over the wide front porch. There was a balcony on top of the overhang supported by a row of heavy white posts. There was a set of doors that led out onto the balcony from the second level. Nearby was another large single-level building with three-man doors down the long side. This was the bunk house. In addition, there was a very large barn and four other smaller buildings littered around the property. One of the smaller buildings was a blacksmith shop; Bo took particular interest in that building. The front of the building was open and Bo could see the forge glowing even from that distance. It reminded him of his brother's shop back in Iowa.

Mertauck dismounted from his horse in front of his home, while one of the hands took the reins. Mertauck stepped up to the porch and turned to face Bo and the others. His six-foot frame towered over them. His dark, tan coat was framed by the white pillars on either side of him. There was no mistaking who was in charge. In the distance, he could see the forms of two men on horseback passing under the ranch's arch and approaching him.

Mertauck turned to face Bo directly. "My foreman will show you where you're going to sleep and eat. I trust you'll be gone tomorrow?" There was nothing but disgust in his voice. He turned his back and stomped into the house.

The foreman was standing on the other side of the horses they had ridden in on close to the hand who had taken Mertauck's horse. He was the one who had his gun tied down when Bo first saw him in town. He was wearing a black leather vest, a black and red plaid shirt and a wide-brimmed, black hat. He needed a shave and a bath.

"You and your servant can stay in the bunk house in a room out back we have for guests," the foreman called out to Bo. "We eat at six."

The man holding Mertauck's horse was staunchly built with a heavy leather apron on. His shirt sleeves were rolled up to expose his large arms. He leaned over toward Bo, still leading Mertauck's horse. "Follow me. I'll show you where you can stable your horses. I'll make sure they get watered and fed tonight. Then, I'll show you where your room is in the bunk house."

Bo and Daniel followed the man to the barn. "What do you do here?" Bo asked Mertauck's hand. They dismounted and followed him, horses in tow.

The man smiled and after ensuring that Mertauck's horse was secure, stood close to Bo to speak with him. "My name is Bill Tunley," the man said. "I'm the blacksmith. That is one fine looking buckskin you've got there. Where did you find him?"

"He found me at my father's blacksmith shop in Iowa," Bo said, giving Buck a sincere pat along his back. "He's a little particular about who touches him, so I do all of that."

Bill hesitated for a moment. "Your pa's a blacksmith in Iowa? My pa and I had a shop in Ohio until he died and I came out here. That makes us damn near neighbors."

Daniel smiled. "It seems you have neighbors just about everywhere you go, Bo."

Bill looked up at Daniel and noticed Daniel's badge partially sticking out from under his vest. "You're a marshal, too?"

Daniel extended his hand. "I'm Deputy U.S. Marshal Daniel Blue."

Tunley was visibly a little reluctant to take Blue's hand, but after a second he shook the big man's hand. "I ain't never seen a black marshal before and I'm sure I ain't never seen any guns like that."

Daniel pulled one of his shotguns out of its holster and handed it to Bill for him to see. "Bo and a gunsmith he knows rigged these up for me." Bill accepted the weapon from Daniel and turned the gun over in his hands. Bill admired the tooling.

"They're so good looking, it's nearly a shame to shoot them," he said passing the gun back to Blue.

Now that Bill was in a particularly friendly mood, Bo eased a question into the conversation. "Do you know about the shooting out on the prairie a few days ago?"

"Sure!" Bill nodded. "Some sodbuster took one of our bulls and shot Little Tim over it. I'm not sure it happened the way they said, though. Little Tim is a hothead and I can't see him getting the second shot off. He likes to think that he's some kind of gunhand. We got a couple like that on this spread. Keep a close eye on the foreman, Carver, especially. He spends a lot of time out there shooting up the trees. He's not all that good. I saw a trick shooter come through our town several years ago who was the best I've ever seen. He could shoot the dirt out of a washer without hitting the metal. Damnedest thing I've ever saw."

Bo smiled. "I've seen the same shooter. He'd spin a large wheel and he'd shoot the tabs off of it while it was whirling around."

"I guess we are from the same town in different states," Bill said, smiling.

"This place has lots of buildings. Are these all of them or do you have any on other parts of the ranch?" Bo asked.

"We've got line shacks about fifteen miles apart all along the western property line," Bill nodded. "The boss doesn't want our cattle crossing the river, especially in the spring. He sends some of the boys out there to keep the herd out of the river when it's high."

Bo was interested in the line shacks, so pressed further. "Is there a line shack near where the shooting took place?"

Bill pointed off to the southwest. "Sure. It's off in that direction about ten miles. That would make it about three miles from where the farmers took the bull."

Bo tilted his head. "Does this ranch stock any milk cows?"

Bill laughed at the question. "The boss don't want anything on this ranch that don't come from a still or out of a coffee pot."

By this time, the horses were stabled for the night and Bill led Daniel and Bo to the bunk house where they would be sleeping. The walk to the bunk house was at least one hundred yards northwest of the big house and down the other side of the berm. The bunk house was a long single-level building with a covered walkway that led to the chuck house, which also had a covered walkway. The chuck house was as long as the bunk house but narrower. The kitchen was at the far right end and had four smoke stacks rising up from its roof. The three men passed between four big oak trees on their way. By this time, the sun had dipped behind the mountains far off to the west and a nightly chill was beginning to set in.

"The boss keeps this room for the boys who come back from town all drunk up," Bill said as Bo and Daniel walked inside. "He don't want them getting sick in the regular bunk house. It's mostly clean and the sheets are fresh. You'll do just fine in here. None of the men have been to town in a week or so."

Bo shook Bill's hand. "I'd like to talk to the range hand who was at the shooting with Little Tim."

Bill nodded. "That would be Jason. He should be in from the range in a half-hour or so. I'll send him to you as soon as I see him." Bill set off in the direction of the blacksmith shop.

Bo and Daniel each settled into a bunk to pass the time. Jason turned up about an hour later and Bo and Daniel asked him their questions that were meant to review his side of the story. It was clear from the conversations Bo and Daniel had had with the trail hands on the way to the ranch that everyone on the ranch had been told what to say; upon interacting with them they all told the same tale.

At supper Bo and Daniel found themselves sitting alone at one end of the two long dining tables with flat benches down both sides. Each man picked up his plate and tin cup from the stack as he passed in front of the kitchen doorway. The cook would fill each man's plate. There was a long table against the east wall displaying fresh coffee, biscuits, rolls and flatware. Other than that, the room was empty. There were nearly twenty men waiting to be fed. After supper, Foreman Carver sauntered down to their end of the table. He was the only man in the room still wearing his gun.

"I guess you boys have seen everything out here. You can go back to town tomorrow and hang that cattle rustler."

"We're not done, yet," Bo said without looking up. "We're going to take a look around tomorrow morning when there's better light. We may have to spend another night here."

Bo's response didn't please the foreman. "I'll have one of the boys go with you to make sure you don't get lost," he spoke through his teeth as his finger tapped on his pistol grip. "We wouldn't want anything to happen to a U.S. Marshal on our ranch, now, would we?"

Carver stomped out of the dining hall and Bo and Daniel decided it was a proper time to get rest for the next morning's investigation, so they retired for the night.

In the morning, Bo and Daniel were met by an older cowboy on horseback wearing leather chaps, a well-weathered hat and a red and white plaid shirt. His boots had seen much better days and his rope was limp—the sign that it had seen a great deal of use. He had a rifle on his saddle but no handgun on his hip. This was a real cowboy. By the way he sat in the saddle as he approached, it was evident that he spent more time there than he did on the ground.

"Good morning, Marshal. My friends call me Smitty," the cowboy said to Bo and Daniel who were just finishing saddling their horses next to the blacksmith shop. "I'm supposed to keep an eye on you while you look the place over. Is there any direction where you'd like to start?"

Daniel pointed off to the southwest. "We'd like to start with the line shack out in that direction."

Bo stepped into his saddle. Daniel followed Bo's lead and swung up on the back of his bay. Daniel followed Bo and Smitty off in the direction of the southwest pasture. Smitty's wrinkled face smiled. "I guess that's as good a place as any to start, gents. It's about ten miles out. We had better get going unless you'd rather spend the night out there."

They started off at a slightly faster pace, but soon settled into a walk passing the time listening to Smitty tell them about how he had been working on the ranch nearly since it began. Smitty shared that he was there when Mr. Mertauck brought in the first of the breed stock and made a name for himself and the ranch as having the best beef in the West.

"I was originally the foreman on this spread until Carver showed up with his fast gun and took my job," Smitty went on. "I've never claimed to be a gun hand and Mr. Mertauck thought he needed a fast gun to keep the town's people in line. Now, I'm just a line foreman. I keep the cattle out of the river in the spring and I spend most of my time out here. Don't get me wrong, I don't mind it out here. It's quiet and I get to do most anything I want. It's peaceful."

"Where were you the day of the shooting?" Bo asked him.

Smitty pointed off to the north. "I was up on the other end of this line with a herd of horses we were bringing in for sale. I wish I'd been down here, though. Little Tim is a hothead and if I'd been there, I doubt there would have been any shooting. Those farmers wouldn't take that bull. They wouldn't know what to do with him. He's too damn fat to eat. Everyone in the county knows he belongs to Mertauck, so they couldn't sell him. I don't know what they were doing with him in the first place."

Bo and Daniel just exchanged looks and didn't comment.

Bo, Daniel and Smitty had been in the saddle for three hours when they came up over a slight rise and saw the line shack with a makeshift corral on the south side for the horses. Smitty was puzzled over what they had found. "This shack hasn't been used for months," Smitty said. "I know. I stocked it about four weeks ago, just in case. What the hell are those steers doing in the pen?"

Once they got close enough to the line shack, they could see the animals in the pen were not steers. Bo shook his head. "Those aren't steers."

"Those are damn milk cows," Smitty added. "What are they doing in my pen?"

Daniel voiced what they all were thinking. "I think we've just found the farmer's missing cows. The farmer and his son *were* telling the truth."

Smitty was still puzzled and it showed on his face. "Maybe you had better tell me what's going on here," he said intensely to Bo. "We don't have any milk cows on this ranch. The boss wouldn't let us even if we asked."

Bo shook his head. "The farmers claimed that your bull wandered into their camp and ran off their heifers. The farmer and his boy tied up the bull to keep him from running the cows all the way back to your spread. Then, they started off to find their milk cows. That's when your hands came up and accused the farmer of stealing the bull. According to them, your Little Tim shot first and the farmer got him with the shotgun after his boy was hit."

Smitty lowered his head. "That makes a lot more sense than the story Chuck came back with. Chuck was with Mertauck when they caught up to the farmer and his son. We should get back and tell Mr. Mertauck about this."

Bo needed more proof. "First, I want to go down there and have a look at these cows," Bo said. "If they do belong to Mr. Weston, they'll have tags in their ears and a number on each tag. This won't take long."

The three men spurred their horses and made their way down to the pen where Bo dropped off of Buck's back and quickly verified the numbers. "These are the missing milk cows, all right"—he looked up at Smitty who was still in his saddle—are you sure this is Mertauck's land?"

Smitty nodded. "His property line is at least a half-mile further west of here. It stretches all the way to the river. We built the line shack here to keep it dry in the spring."

Daniel smiled down from atop a horse. "That means your boss has two stolen cows penned up on his land. I'd say that is rustling."

"That's what Judge Roads will call it, too," Bo said, swinging back up on Buck. "Let's get back to the ranch house."

Smitty and Daniel followed suit and the men continued forward. They rode at a fast pace all the way back to the ranch house to confront Mertauck. When they had finally arrived, Bill met them as they came in with the horses.

"You boys have been riding hard," Bill said, eyeing the horses. "I'll walk them down to cool them off. I'll put Buck in the barn and let you take the saddle off later." The men dismounted and Bill took their reins and went off toward the stable with the three horses in tow. Mertauck came out when he saw them ride up and watched as Bill took the horses.

"What's going on, Smitty?" Mertauck called out. Smitty walked up to his boss.

"We found the farmer's cows all penned up at the quarter mile line shack, Mr. Mertauck. They're in our pen... ."

Mertauck was enraged at the news. "Who the hell put that farmer's livestock in *my* pen?"

Bo stepped forward. "That makes you a cattle rustler, Mr. Mertauck," Bo said. "I'm afraid I'm going to have to place you under arrest," Bo called out to Bill, who was still at shouting distance. "Bill, do you want to saddle up a horse for Mr. Mertauck in the morning? He's going to be coming with us."

Looking back toward Bo and the other men, Bill smiled. "Sure thing, Marshal."

Bo took Mertauck's arm and began to pull him in the direction of the barn, but Mertauck pulled his arm free. "This is ridiculous. You can't arrest me for rustling when it was just a couple of milk cows. Rustling doesn't include milk cows! It's not the same thing as cattle"—he took a full step back away from Bo—"I own most of this county. You can't arrest me! Besides, it was Carver who said the bull was stolen."

Carver strode out of the bunkhouse when he heard all of the shouting to see what the commotion was about. He froze in his tracks when he saw that Mertauck was now attempting to cast blame on him. Mertauck pointed at him and accused him of lying about the stolen bull. "That sodbuster and his son stole the bull," Carver protested. "We never saw any cows with him. It was all a big lie."

Daniel corrected him. "We found the two cows in the southwest line shack pen. They didn't jump those rails on their own."

Carver decided to change his story. "You're the one who said we have to keep those farmers in line," Carver said, staring hard right at Mertauck. "And we can't let them start cutting up all the good grazing land for their crops!" He was yelling as he finished and gesturing wildly with his arms.

Mertauck was even more enraged. "What the hell have you done? You sent Little Tim out there to shoot that boy. I never told you to do anything like that! I told you to keep them off our land, not to start shooting people. You're fired!"

Now it was Carver's turn to be enraged. His head snapped from side to side because he didn't know who to blame. His eyes settled in on Bo. "This is all your fault. If you'd kept your nose out of our business, those sod busting bastards would have been hung by now. This is all your fault!"

Carver's hand dove for his gun, but before his fingers could grip the butt, Bo fired three shots. The first two hit the holster and smashed the hammer off the revolver. The third shot hit Carver's right hand sending him spinning and screaming in pain. Carver ended up on his knees facing Mertauck. By the time the first shot was fired, Blue had pulled his shotguns out and was panning back and forth to make sure there were no other cowboys who wanted to test Bo's gun. None of them moved. They were all in awe of what they had just witnessed. Mertauck's words were nearly a whisper as he stood in amazement. "Damnation! That was fast."

Bo spun his Colt twice before planting it in his holster. His eyes darted from one face to another; there were no threats looking back at him. They all knew that making a false move right then would probably get them killed. Half of them were looking at Bo and the other half were fixated on the twin, short barreled shotguns in Daniel's hands.

Bill pushed the horses into the pen and came running when he heard the shots. "What the hell is going on here?" he asked in confusion. It didn't take him long to figure out that Carver had tempted his fate and lost. He bent down to look at Carver's right hand. "I can stop the bleeding, but, he's going to need a doctor to fix this mess"—he examined the hand again —"you're never going to use this hand to eat with, much less pull a gun with, my friend. Someone give me a hand to get him into the bunk house."

Bill pulled Carver up and two other ranchers who had gathered at the scene helped lead him off.

Bo turned back to Mertauck. "I guess that lets you off the hook on the shooting and rustling. I'm not sure that you're not guilty of something else. I'll send a message off to Judge Roads as soon as I get back to town. I wouldn't go too far if I were you."

By this time Mertauck decided to be more agreeable. "There must be something I can do to make this right," he said. "I never meant for anyone to get shot over this. Can't we work something out?"

Bo smiled. "Perhaps we could come up with a plan that would make the farmers happy and you a lot of money."

The reference to money opened up Mertauck's eyes. "It sounds as though you've already given this some thought, Marshal. Will you have supper with me tonight? I'd like to hear what's on your mind. Go get washed up and I'll have two extra places set at the table."

Daniel looked at Bo. "You go ahead, Bo. I'd like to have my supper with Bill and the boys in the bunk house if it's just the same to you."

"That's your choice, Blue," Bo nodded. "I'll see you later."

Bo and Daniel headed off in the direction of the bunk house to get cleaned up. Bo would be going to his meeting with Mertauck while Daniel was off to supper with the trail hands. The fire from the cook stove was already curling high in the sky and the smells coming from that direction were making mouths water.

An hour later, Bo had finished a large piece of apple cobbler and his second cup of coffee in the dining room. Mertauck pushed back from the table and had his cook bring in his brandy. He couldn't wait to discuss the possible venture any longer. He lit a cigar and offered one to Bo who just shook his head. "I never got a taste for those things, but, I will enjoy some of your brandy," Bo said.

The dining room of Mertauck's home was elegant for that part of the country. The table was a dark wood that Bo wasn't familiar with and all six chairs matched. The heavy burgundy drapes hung all the way to the floor. The rest of the cabinets matched the table and chairs. Bo thought that his brother Derle, the carpenter, would like to see this.

"What do you plan to propose that's going to make the farmers happy and me rich?" Mertauck asked.

Bo leaned back, away from the table. "How much do you get per head of cattle you send to market?"

Mr. Mertauck didn't hesitate. He knew the number. "Two and a half to three cents a pound."

Bo smiled. "That's half of what they're getting for your cattle in Kansas City or Chicago. Why are you giving all that money away?"

Mertauck tilted his head at the question. "I can't get any more than that for grazing cattle that have been herded across two states. They tramp off all the fat I put on them here. I'm lucky to get that much for them."

"I come from Iowa," Bo said, leaning forward. "We grow corn out there and we sell that corn to the stockyards in Kansas City and Chicago. They feed it to your stock, fatten them up and sell that same stock for twice what they pay you. In a year, the railroad will be out here and you could ship your stock to market and get the corn fattened price for them. The trouble is going to be finding the food for them that will put the weight on them here. These farmers you're so willing to run off the land will be happy to sell you all the corn your cows can eat. The good thing for you is that now they need money and they would probably sell you in advance the corn they are going to plant next spring for a very good price."

Bo could see the numbers ripping through Mertauck's head.

"You want me to pay for a crop of corn that hasn't been grown, to feed to a herd that isn't fully ready for market, to be shipped on a rail spur that hasn't been built, yet? Have I got that right?"

"That's right," Bo nodded.

Mertauck wasn't finished processing all of his numbers. After a moment or two, he leaned back and took a sip of his brandy. "I think I should go with you to town tomorrow morning. I've got some farmers to talk to."

While Bo was having supper with Mr. Mertauck, Daniel was eating with the trail hands in the bunk house dining room. When the meal was over, one of the men sitting next to him asked about the twin shotguns that were dangling from his hips.

"Can I see one of your shotguns?" one of the men asked. "I ain't never seen anything like that before."

Daniel took both guns out and laid them down on the table in front of him. The men on either side of Blue picked up one of the shotguns and turned it over in their hands. Smitty was sitting across from Daniel. "Let me see one"—Smitty took the gun—"someone has gone and named each of these barrels." He took the second gun and looked at it. "These barrels are named after a couple of men who fought at the Alamo. Did you have these barrels engraved?"

Blue shook his head as he took the guns back from Smitty. "No. They were already etched that way when I got them. I do appreciate their meaning. Those men died to be free."

That thought brought quiet over the dining room. Retrieving his guns, Daniel stood up and went off to the bunkhouse to get ready for the night. He lumbered into his cot and tried to doze off. A few minutes later Bo turned up and Daniel propped himself up on the cot on one elbow.

"Well, how did it go?" Daniel asked.

Standing, Bo looked down at Daniel. "Mr. Mertauck is coming to town with us in the morning to speak to the farmers about buying their crops."

Daniel didn't have much to say. "Well, I'll be damned."

The next morning Bo, Daniel, Carver, Little Tim, Smitty and Mr. Mertauck were accompanied by two other trail hands on their way to town. One of the trail hands was driving a wagon with Carver and Little Tim secured in the back. Carver's hand was bandaged and he was moaning during the entire trip.

Once the travelers were in town, Carver and Little Tim were taken to the jail and Mr. Mertauck made arrangements for everyone—except for Blue—at the local hotel. Mertauck handed out the keys in front of the hotel building. Finding one less key was handed out than he had expected, Bo looked at Mertauck. "What about my deputy?"

Mertauck shook his head. "They don't have any more rooms."

Bo started to object but Daniel stopped him. "It's all right, Bo. I'll be just fine where I was the other night. I slept well there. Let's get our horses bedded down for the night."

Daniel turned and started down to the stables and Bo and Buck followed him down the street to have Buck secured in the stables, too. After the horses were secure, and Daniel had found a warm place to sleep, Bo checked into his room. Early the next morning, Bo met Daniel out in front of Maggie's Food Emporium. Bo stopped to wipe a bit of hay off of Blue's back.

"How did you sleep?" Bo asked.

Daniel nodded. "I slept very well. It was comfortable. How about you?"

Bo shook his head. "I had to share a room with Smitty. He makes more noise than a herd of buffalo. I would have been better off if I'd come down and opened a bale of hay with you."

They entered Maggie's and took a booth in the back of the place where they could talk without being overheard. They ordered breakfast from Maggie and sat back with morning coffee that she had brought to their table. Bo took a sip and then leaned forward. The place was beginning to fill up and he didn't want their conversation to be heard.

"I sent a message off to Judge Roads this morning," Bo said. "We're going to have to wait until we hear from him before we start up to Denver. I think that would be our best bet for finding out if your wife was with those men when they came through here. Maybe they left your wife up there."

Moments later, Maggie swiftly dropped hot plates before them and the men eagerly ate. Bo and Daniel had just finished their breakfast when a telegraph agent rushed in. "I've got your answer from Judge Roads, Marshal. I figured you would want to see it right way."

The telegraph operator handed the paper to Bo who took it with one hand, unfolded and glanced at it, then handed it to Blue. "These always sound better when you read them out loud."

Daniel took the paper and read it. "To: U.S. Marshal Bo Henry. I will send the wagon for your prisoners. They will be tried in my court. Please send your full report with the prisoners. Proceed to Denver and serve warrants for the abductors of civilians from Chicago. Good luck. Henry Roads, Senior Federal Judge, Kansas City, Missouri." Daniel felt a new surge of hope as he set the paper down in front of Bo. "I hope you have your report written. We should get started as soon as possible."

Bo smiled. "I'll finish my report today. We still have some business to take care of in town today. I'm sure the sheriff won't mind if we use his office while we're in town. We'll get started for Denver first thing tomorrow morning."

After Bo and Daniel left Maggie's, Bo spent the rest of the day writing his report and making sure Mark Weston was reunited with his cows. He presented the sheriff with the warrants and his report for the two men in jail. Later, Bo and Daniel sat in on the meeting that Mr. Mertauck had arranged with some of the local farmers during which they negotiated an understanding of what would take place and who was going to do what. It was a very good day.

The next morning couldn't come soon enough for Daniel who was eager to continue the journey that would hopefully lead him to his wife. Mr. Mertauck had made a gift of a pack mule and supplies to Bo and Daniel for their journey and he and Smitty stood in front of the hotel as Bo and Daniel passed on horseback to leave for Denver. Bo stopped to thank them for the gifts. "Your generosity will be greatly appreciated. Thank you," Bo kindly said to them as he passed. Daniel tipped his hat as he passed.

Mr. Mertauck waved back at them. "It's the least I could do for you giving me the opportunity to make all of that money."

Bo and Daniel cleared the edge of town and Daniel looked back at the mule. "I went through the packs. Mr. Mertauck provided everything we'll ever need on that mule. We even have a tent. Can you imagine that? We have a tent!"

Bo smiled. "Now, all we need is a name for your horse. I'm tired of calling her 'horse'."

"I've got a name for her," Daniel smiled back. "You can call her

Alala."

Bo was puzzled at the name. "Where did you find that name? I'm sure it has a meaning."

"It's a feminine version of a Greek battle cry adapted from the sound made by attacking owls," Daniel explained.

Bo nodded his approval. "That's good. 'Alala' it will be."

Chapter 5
Love at Yellow Bud

In Denver, Bo and Daniel quickly learned the story of the seven men who had come to town with wagons full of Daniel's neighbors. Together, Bo and Daniel had asked several store owners who the wealthiest families in town were and had been directed, first, to the O'Reilly estate called "Yellow Bud." Yellow Bud, located on the far northwest part of the city, was a large three level, dark brown brick home inside of a towering hedge with a barn, guest cottage and four small homes for the families that worked there. From Yellow Bud's third level you could look out over the entire city of Denver below. When Bo and Daniel rode up through Yellow Bud's tall hedged opening, they were met by a stable boy who reached out to take their horses' reins. Bo heard dogs barking inside the house.

As Bo slid out of the saddle, he kept Buck's reins in hand. "I'll take care of my own horse. He's a little touchy," he said to the stable boy who had reached for them. Bo draped the reins over the hitching post and took the seven steps up to the property's front door with Daniel right behind him. The massive dark, oak doors were nine feet tall with scrolled carvings on them. The doors were framed in a grey stone arch that towered over them and the landing.

Bo lifted a hand up to grab onto a large brass knocker, but before Bo could move it, the door opened from the other side and a slender black lady of nearly thirty stood in front of him. The woman wore a light gray, neatly pressed dress uniform with a simple white apron. Her hair was wrapped tightly in a white scarf. She stood with hands folded in front of her and had a stern look on her face. "May I help you, sir?" she said, with a smooth southern drawl. From the uniqueness of the sound her words made as they escaped her mouth, Bo could tell she could be from the deep South.

Bo and Daniel removed their hats politely. "I'm U.S. Marshal Bo Henry," Bo said with his hat in his hands. "I'm here to see Mr. O'Reilly. Is he in?"

"Mr. O'Reilly is in," the maid said, grabbing hold of the door and closing it just a bit. She peered out at them with one had firmly set on the door. "I'll see if he has the time to meet with you. Please wait here," she said before she finished closing the door. The brass knocker bounced on the door as the door closed; both Bo and Daniel jumped at the sound. Just as it clicked shut and Bo and Daniel had assumed the maid had gone to retrieve Mr. O'Reilly from deep inside the house, it sprung ajar. The unexpectedness caused Bo's mouth to drop open. He lost his breath as he stood staring at the young lady who was now in front of him, poised under the doorframe looking back at him. He studied her carefully. His eyes went from the sandy red hair—all in curls that fell over her soft shoulders —to the bright green eyes and the turned-up button nose that was framed by two rosy cheeks. She was adorned in a white, calico dress with small, light green flowers printed across it. Around her tiny waist she wore a matching light green sash.

"Darlene, don't make the marshal wait out here for papa," she said, looking at Darlene then turning to face Bo. "I'm Rose O'Reilly. Please gentlemen, come in. My father will want to see you in his study."

Her tiny five-foot-two-inch frame barely reached Bo's chin as he slipped in past her to move through the doorway. Bo couldn't take his eyes off her light pink lips and smiled as he passed. She kept her eyes glued to his chin and gestured toward the sitting room.

"My father will be with you in just a moment," Rose continued. "Please, have a seat." She turned back to the maid who had met them at the door. "Darlene, please see if there is something these gentlemen would like to drink. I'll go tell my father they are here."

Darlene entered the sitting room and Rose made her way through the house to retrieve her father. "Is there something I can get for either of you?" Darlene asked. "There is fresh coffee in the kitchen or we have cold milk and water. Mr. O'Reilly keeps everything else locked up."

Daniel looked at her trying to remember if he'd seen her in the Chicago neighborhood. "I'd like a cup of coffee, please"—he looked back at Bo whose mouth was still open—"would you like some coffee, Marshal?" The question brought Bo back.

"Oh, yes, coffee would be fine. Thank you," Bo responded quickly.

Darlene returned with a tray of cups and coffee just before Mr. O'Reilly entered the room. Bo and Daniel stood up and set their coffee cups down.

"Thank you, Darlene," said Mr. O'Reilly. "You can bring me a cup as well."

Darlene retreated from the room after setting the tray down on a small table. "Yes, sir," she responded.

Mr. O'Reilly was an older man who wasn't completely out of shape. His short beard was starting to turn gray and his charcoal gray suit was perfectly tailored while his black boots shone like a mirror. He was six feet tall and Bo sensed he commanded respect without demanding it.

"My daughter tells me you are a U.S. Marshal and you have business with me. What can I do for you and your servant today?" Mr. O'Reilly said.

Bo extended his hand. "I'm U.S. Marshal Bo Henry. This is my deputy, U.S. Marshal Daniel Blue. We're here on official business. We believe you may have been in contact with several men who kidnapped about a dozen free citizens from Chicago and brought them out West to be sold as indentured servants. Have you had any contact with such a group?"

Rose had been standing, listening just outside the door of the sitting room and rushed in. "Oh, Daddy! They were telling the truth. What a terrible thing! Those poor people." She turned back to the doorway. "Darlene, please come in here."

Mr. O'Reilly was taken completely by surprise by his daughter's entrance into the room. He wasn't sure how to react. He stammered for words. "I had no idea these people were kidnapped...I would have never been a part to anything like that. I do not believe in—nor did I ever deal in —slavery. I was told these people were indebted servants and if I wanted them to work for me, all I had to do was pay off their indebtedness. I paid off their debts and took them on as employees. I pay all of my help and they accrue no new debt while they are with me. They are all free to leave at any time they wish."

Daniel spoke up. "One of the women they took is my wife. I've been trying to find her ever since"—he turned to Darlene—"do you remember my wife? Her name is Trisha Blue. She would be about your size. She is light-complected with long, shiny black hair She likes to wear it up with a scarf, especially while she is working."

Darlene broke down and started to cry, so Rose pulled Darlene to her. "I remember her, Mr. Blue," Darlene said through tears. "She's not here. Those men said they had a better place for her than here. We were giving them trouble and they said they couldn't get any money for us if they continued to beat us, so they sold us first."

Daniel stepped up closer to Darlene. "Do you know where they were taking her?"

Darlene stopped crying. "No, Mr. Blue. They never said where they were taking any of us. I was just so happy when they left us here! Mr. O'Reilly and Miss Rose have been so nice to us—I didn't want to leave."

Rose hugged Darlene. "We care about the people who work for us. There are no indentured servants at Yellow Bud." Her voice was stern and commanding and stood up straight as she said it.

Bo's posture softened after Rose spoke. "I didn't mean to infer that you had indentured servants, Miss O'Reilly. I'd like to speak to everyone else they left in your care."

Mr. O'Reilly was still a little taken aback. "One of our cooks and two of the grounds keepers came from them. I'll have them brought in right away." He turned to Darlene. "Darlene, can you please have Kathleen, Jacob and Charles come into the sitting room right away?"

"Yes, Mr. O'Reilly," Darlene replied. Darlene dipped a little curtsy and backed out of the room.

Soon Kathleen entered the room, her eyes fixated on Daniel; it was clear she recognized him. Daniel knew her, too. "Kathleen, I'm Daniel Blue. Do you remember me from Chicago?"

A tear trickled down her cheek. "Yes. You and Trisha lived at the other end of the street from us. I remember you were the one who was going to college." At that moment she started to sob and tremble and Mr. O'Reilly helped her into a nearby chair.

Two men stepped into the doorway holding their hats in their hands. One of them looked straight at Daniel and smiled. "Daniel! What are you doing here?"

Daniel charged forward toward him. "Jacob Kindler! I was hoping it was you when I heard Mr. O'Reilly had employed a Jacob here. Are you all right? Have you seen Trisha?" Daniel put his arms around Jacob who returned the hug and then pushed back.

"I'm fine," said Jacob. "I haven't seen Trisha since they left us here. I'm sorry, Daniel. I don't have any idea where they were taking the rest. They never told us where any of us would be left."

The other man stepped in. "I remember seeing you in Chicago. You're that Blue kid who was going to college. I'm Charles Alan. Kathleen and I lived on the other end of the street. What are you doing out here?"

Daniel smiled. "I'm now a deputy U.S. Marshal and I'm out here looking for all of you."

Charles sank to his knees. "God be praised!" He put his hands over his face.

Daniel took him by his shoulders and helped him back onto his feet. "Do you have any idea where they were taking the others?"

Charles shook his head. "They never talked about that in front of any of us. I have no idea where they were going after they left us here—are you really a U.S. Marshal?"

"Yes he is," Bo stepped in. "He's my deputy and we have warrants to put those men in jail for a long time for what they did to you all. We'll make arrangements for you to return to Chicago as soon as possible."

Jacob stepped forward. "Daniel, we don't want to leave here. Mr. O'Reilly takes good care of us. I have a good job and good pay now, and Darlene and I have a nice place to live. We get to go to town nearly whenever we want and no one has raised a voice or a fist to any of us since we've been here. This is the first time in my life that I've felt like a real human being. Why would we want to go back to Chicago and live in that slum?"

Both Daniel and Bo were surprised by the strong feelings Jacob had expressed. Mr. O'Reilly smiled. "It's just as I told you, Marshal. I take good care of everyone who works for me. If I'd had any idea there were more than just these four with them, I would have paid off all of their contracts and set them free. I hope this has been of some help to you, Marshal."

Bo shook Mr. O'Reilly's hand. "I want to thank you, sir. We were hoping to find Daniel's wife. If anyone can remember anything else, it would be a great help to us. We're going to be in the area for several days. Judge Roads has issued two warrants for us to serve in the area and we have to track down the men who took these people."

"Daddy," Rose spoke up. "If Marshal Henry is going to remain in the area, he should stay with us. You wouldn't want him in that dingy hotel would you?"

The suggestion took Mr. O'Reilly by surprise. "No! I would be honored if you and Marshal Blue would stay with us," he said. "We have a guest cottage behind the main house. You are both welcome to stay there as long as you'd like." He paused for a moment. "There is one thing I would like to talk to you about. It's of a more business nature"—he turned back to the four servants who were waiting to be dismissed—"all of you can go back to work now. If you remember anything else that would help Marshal Henry, please let him know. Kathleen, make sure there are two additional seats for our guests for supper this evening and have the house staff make the guest cottage ready for them."

Kathleen stepped backward out the door. "Yes, Mr. O'Reilly."

Mr. O'Reilly then turned to Rose. "Please tell your mother we have guests. I have a matter to discuss with Marshal Henry. I'll see you later." He gave her a kiss on the forehead and turned her around toward the door.

"Yes, Daddy, " Rose replied. closing the door as she left the room.

Then Mr. O'Reilly turned back to Bo. "Your arrival today is most fortuitous, Marshal."

Bo was puzzled at Mr. O'Reilly's word choice. He looked over at Daniel to see his reaction. Daniel just stood there with his normal calm expression. *I'm going to have to ask Blue what that word means,* Bo thought. He looked back at Mr. O'Reilly. "What is it that we can do for you, sir?"

Mr. O'Reilly gestured for them to sit down in the seats near them and took a chair opposite them. "Most of my holdings are in mining, timber and land," he went on. "I have a substantial payroll each month. My mining payroll has been robbed twice and my timber payroll has been robbed once. All of this has happened during the last two months. This is a loss that I cannot afford. There are four or five men responsible for these robberies. The local sheriff has done all he can, but, these attacks occur outside of his jurisdiction. After the first robbery, I assigned extra guards, but that did little to stop them. They've killed two of my men." He paused for a moment and looked out the window when he spoke of the dead men. It was clear he had been very concerned for them. "I heard you mention Judge Roads; his wife's family has business dealings with my wife's family. I've met him on several occasions. If it would help, I would be happy to send him a message, letting him know that I have personally asked for your assistance."

Bo nodded. "The judge should know we're going to extend our time here to assist you. He'll want to provide us with warrants to cover any arrests we make in this matter."

Mr. O'Reilly stood up. "I'll have my staff take your horses out to the stables and bed them down. They will show you where you'll be staying and where we'll be having supper tonight, as well."

As Mr. O'Reilly spoke, he moved toward the study room door then opened it. He was surprised to find Rose standing in the main hallway. She smiled when she saw Bo. Her eyes never left him.

"I'll show them where the stables are, Daddy," Rose said. "Mother said it will be nice to have company from out of town. She said supper will be served at six."

Daniel walked across the entry to Mr. O'Reilly's office. He stopped at the doorway to ponder a large oak chess board. Its carved white and black ivory pieces were spread across the pattern with a game in progress. He looked over at Mr. O'Reilly. "Who is black, sir?"

Mr. O'Reilly was surprised at the question. "My foreman is playing the black. Do you play?"

Daniel smiled as he looked up at him and walked over to the chess board to examine where the pieces lay. "I used to play with one of my college professors. We tried to get a game in from time to time. If you're white, you can have him in checkmate in two moves."

Mr. O'Reilly came over to the board and looked down, attempting to see the strategy he had missed. "I don't see it, Marshal."

Blue explained the moves of the rook and knight that were obvious to him. "In just two moves."

Mr. O'Reilly smiled. "I hope you are here long enough to play a game with me. I haven't had a challenge in a very long time. I'm afraid it's hard to find players out here. It wasn't a problem when I lived in Lawrence, Kansas. As I recall, Judge Roads is a fair player himself. Have you had a chance to play him?"

Daniel shook his head. "I haven't met the judge as of yet. I'm looking forward to meeting him though."

Rose placed her hand lightly on Bo's arm and started toward the front door. As she did, Daniel looked up and saw that Bo was being led out of the room and decided that he had better keep up. "Rose, don't you think you should let the staff take care of the marshals' animals?" Mr. O'Reilly asked, noticing his daughter with Bo.

Rose glanced back over her shoulder at her father. "No, Daddy. I'll show Marshal Henry where the stables are. It won't be any trouble at all." She waited for Bo to open the front door. Daniel rushed to keep up.

Mr. O'Reilly followed them out to the front of the house where their horses waited. He took one look at Buck and was impressed. "Where did you ever get such a beautiful buckskin? He is a magnificent animal."

Bo made his way down the stairs past him with Rose following on one arm and took Buck's reins from the hitching rail. "My family raised a few buckskins from time to time. Buck and I have been together ever since he was a colt. He's my best friend and he's a little particular about who takes care of him. I'll put him away for the night."

"Perhaps Daddy will let me take you for a ride before you leave the area," Rose said. She hadn't let go of his arm, yet. "I know a few beautiful mountain trails."

Mr. O'Reilly wasn't sure of how to handle his daughter at this point. He had never seen her behave like this before. "Rose, Marshal Henry has a great deal to do while he's here. I'm sure he will be far too busy to go on trail rides with you."

Rose was not deterred. "I'm sure he'll find some time." She turned her back and walked away with Bo toward the stables. All this time Marie O'Reilly had been watching her daughter from a balcony overhead. Marie smiled as she turned and went back inside. A few minutes later, she descended the stairs to meet her husband who was in the main hallway. He extended his hand to her as she reached the bottom stair.

"What has gotten into your daughter, Marie? I've never seen her conduct herself like this before."

Mrs. O'Reilly smiled. "Has it been that long, William? If you remember, that's the way I looked at you the first time we met."

"That was different," William stammered. "Your father introduced us." He stopped for a moment and smiled. "I do remember how you looked at me. As I recall my stomach turned over and I couldn't speak. I'd never seen anyone so beautiful"—he paused—"this is different. She's only nineteen and he must be all of..."—he hesitated once again—"twenty-one or twenty-two."

Marie nodded. "When I met you, I was eighteen and you were twenty-two. I think we've taught our daughter well enough. She will make all the right decisions, I'm not worried about that. The only thing that has me worried is if her father will be wise enough to trust her. Come with me, I want to take a walk through our rose garden. We won't have the flowers for much longer this season."

Marie ushered her husband out the back door of the hall that lead to the gardens. The garden was nearly as wide as the house and extended back two hundred feet from the doorway. The landscaping tapered off and down to the south side. There were large trees guarding all of the open areas. At this time of the year, the aspen were turning yellow and the oaks had begun to turn red. The grass under the trees was beginning to be covered by the first shedding of leaves

The yellow roses were Marie's favorite. She paused several times to smell the fragrance of several of the plants as she moved through the garden. William smiled to see the delight that his wife derived from the garden. His pleasure came from her smile. His thoughts went back to his daughter. *I hope she can find as much happiness with her young man.*

In the stable, Rose watched Bo and Daniel bed Buck and Alala down for the night. She took notice of how much attention Bo paid to Buck's needs and smiled at the thought of their friendship. Bo turned to Slim, a stable hand who reminded him of Smitty, and gave him instructions for taking care of Buck. Smitty and Slim were two real cowboys cut from the same slab of rawhide.

When the horses were stabled and fed, Bo and Daniel, with their hands full of saddlebags and guns, followed Rose down the path that led to the guest cottage. When they had arrived, Rose opened the door to the cottage. The guest cottage was a split log, single-level building with three chimneys rising up from its split shake roof. There was smoke rising up from all three. Inside, there was a well-furnished living area and two bedrooms set off to the back. There were two sofas and two chairs spread out in front of a large fire place against the farthest living room wall that had a large fire already burning in it. There was no kitchen area in the cottage, just seating for four at a round oak table.

"Daddy had the staff bring down plenty of hot water for your baths. If you want your clothes washed, just leave them outside the front door and they will be taken care of. Someone will be here just before six to bring you up to the main house for supper," Rose said, then left to allow them to get comfortable and get some rest. With Rose gone, the two men made good use of all the hot water and soap. The bath was a rare treat.

Just before six—the time by which Rose had said they should be ready—Bo and Daniel were dressed in the best clothes they had; their pants had no holes and their boots were brushed. Jacob came to the guest cottage to retrieve them for supper. They came into the main dining room, led by Jacob, with their hats in hand and their hair combed. In the dining room, they found Mr. and Mrs. O'Reilly with Rose. Bo felt very uncomfortable. "I'm sorry, Mr. O'Reilly," he said. "If we had known we were going to be in such a fine dining room when we left Three Forks, we would have brought better clothes."

Mr. O'Reilly smiled. "Bo, if your hands and boots are clean, you're welcome at my table. I haven't always been a rich man. When I first came out here, I owned only two pairs of pants, two shirts and one pair of boots."

"As I remember," Marie added. "Your 'everyday' pants had holes in the knees from panning for gold and your dress pants had a torn pocket."

William smiled as he remembered. "The only thing I owned, that wasn't that worn, was my picture of you." He reached over and took his wife's hand. Marie squeezed his hand and smiled at him.

The O'Reilly family questioned Bo at length about his own family and where he was from. He told them about all the land his family owned and the buckskin horses they raised. It was apparent that Bo's family were good, hardworking people of reasonable means. The O'Reillys then turned their attention to Daniel who told them about his wife and how hard she had worked so that he could go to college.

"I was in my third year studying to be an engineer," Daniel said. "I wanted to come west and build railroads." His face became sad. "Now, all of that's on hold until I can find Trisha."

"Daniel is going to beat me at chess after supper," William commented. "He played at college. I'm looking forward to playing with you, Daniel. It's been some time since I've had a good game. While Daniel is beating me at chess, I'd like to talk to you, Bo, about how you plan to find my missing payroll."

Bo was about to say something when he noticed Rose looking steadily at him from across the table. Rose smiled and Bo turned his head toward her, catching her look. "I'd like to show Marshal Henry Mama's gardens after supper, Daddy. I want him to see them before it gets dark," she said.

Bo wasn't sure how to handle all of this but responded quickly. "Oh, yes. I promised Miss O'Reilly I'd visit the gardens after supper, sir. Perhaps, I could join you after that. I'm sure your game with Daniel will take some time."

Mr. O'Reilly was a little put out over this. His wife put her hand on his arm. "I'm sure the marshal is more interested in the gardens than he is watching you sip brandy and tell your mining stories. He can come in later for a brandy, after Rose has had a chance to show him our beautiful gardens."

William grunted a little. "Not too late, young lady. These men must be up early and start out after the men who robbed us."

Soon, supper was served and it was the best meal that both Daniel and Bo had ever eaten, topped off with peach cobbler; it was possible that Bo had found a new favorite desert. He sat until Rose stood up. "Would you like to see the garden now, Marshal?" Rose finally asked.

Bo rose and placed his napkin next to his plate. "I'd like that very much," he said and walked around the table. He then tucked Rose's hand under his arm and they left the dining room and headed off to the gardens.

William stood up. "Can I offer you a glass of brandy, Daniel?"

Blue shook his head in response. "I'm afraid I don't use either alcohol or tobacco, sir. I've never had enough money to enjoy either. Now that I have some money, I don't feel the need."

William smiled. "You're probably a better man for it. I still enjoy some of each. I hope it won't bother you if I partake."

Daniel was taken aback. He'd never met a white man who gave a damn what he felt and now he was going to play chess with a man who genuinely cared. *This is going to be a very interesting evening*, he thought.

Rose waited for Bo to open the door leading to the gardens. The sun had already set behind the mountain tops but the roses were still visible in the dim, early evening light and their fragrance permeated the garden. Rose slipped her arm through Bo's as they began to explore the gardens, walking through it slowly. Bo's heart was beating so hard he was afraid she could hear it. He was speechless.

After a couple of minutes of silence Rose spoke up. "Well, Marshal Henry, what do you think?"

Bo wasn't sure what to say. "The roses are very pretty and they smell very nice."

Rose was a little put out by the shortness of his answer. "I know all of that," she went on. "What do you feel about our home and my family?"

Bo couldn't think; his mind was swimming with thoughts. He didn't know where to start. "I think, I think…" He couldn't get it out.

Rose could see he was having a problem with his words. "What do you think, Marshal?"

Bo stammered. He knew what he wanted to say, but he could not tell Rose all of what he thought, because they had just met.

"I…" he began slowly, "think your home is beautiful and your mother and father are wonderful. You are a very lucky lady."

Rose was pleased with his answer, but disappointed that he hadn't included his feelings for her. "I'm glad you like my parents, Marshal. It's clear they feel the same way about you." She gave his arm a slight hug, which he returned. The gesture brought a smile to her face.

Marie was standing on her balcony which overlooked the gardens. She'd heard every word and smiled as she looked down on them. A tear made its way down her cheek as she remembered nearly those same words exchanged by William and her over twenty years ago. She turned, went back into her bedroom and waited for Rose's footsteps in the hall. As Rose passed her bedroom door, Marie opened it. "Rose, do you have a minute?"

Rose nodded. "Yes, Mama."

Marie held her hand out to her daughter who entered her mother's room and gently closed the door behind her. "Do you care for Marshal Henry?" Marie inquired.

Rose was surprised by her mother's question. She stood stunned, looking at her mother. She knew she couldn't keep anything from her. "Yes, Mama. I…think I care for him very much. Is that awful of me? I've only known him for one day. Am I so terrible?"

Marie wrapped her arm around Rose's shoulder. "No, you're not awful and it's never terrible to care for someone who feels the same for you. Does he feel that way about you?"

Rose looked up at her mother. "Yes, I think so. He didn't say it, but, I can feel it. Yes, Mama I think he does. Is that possible?"

Marie hugged her daughter. "Yes, that's all you need. It's all your father and I had when we met. He didn't have a nickel and it was my father who had all the money. We loved each other so much that nothing was going to keep us apart. That's why your father worked so hard when he left; he wasn't going to come back to me without being a success. I would have married him even if he had never found gold. All we needed was our love and that's all you will ever need. Don't let Bo leave without letting him know how you feel. If he's like your father, and I think he is, it will give him the strength to make you happy—no matter what it takes."

Meanwhile, Bo made his way into the study after leaving the garden with Rose where he found Daniel and William involved in a game of chess. William politely offered him a glass of brandy as he stepped into the study and when Bo accepted, William got up and poured him a glass.

William was waiting for Daniel to make his next chess move. "Your deputy is giving me more competition than I had expected," he said. "He is more accomplished than he led me to believe."

Daniel just looked up and smiled. Bo took a sip of the dark, amber colored brandy and then studied the delicately cut, crystal glass snifter. It was the best tasting liquor he'd ever had pass his lips.

"I'm glad the two of you are having fun," Bo said.

William handed Bo a slip of paper. "I've made a list of people you should interview," William said. "I put their locations behind each name. I'll give you directions in the morning."

The game went on for another hour before Daniel politely put William into checkmate and excused himself for the evening. Bo retired for the night, as well.

Early the next morning, William caught up to Daniel as he was making his way into the stable.

"Good morning, Daniel," he asked. "Can you give us a moment? I would like to talk to Bo before the two of you leave."

Daniel nodded. "I'll straighten up our tack," he said, then slipped off to one side of the stable doors to wait for Bo to have his conversation with Mr. O'Reilly.

Mr. O'Reilly entered the stable where Bo was saddling Buck. "Good morning, Bo. If you've got a couple of minutes, I'd like to talk to you."

Bo turned around to face Mr. O'Reilly. "Sure, what's on your mind?"

Mr. O'Reilly looked at the floor of the stable and then directly at Bo. "My wife and I were up late talking about you and our daughter. We love her very much and we don't want to see her be hurt. We also trust her judgment. Clearly, she cares for you and we can see that you seem to feel the same about her. Before the two of you decide about any future you may have, we'd like both of you to think about what that really means. We'd also ask that you and Rose take an appropriate amount of time together before you start talking about the details that will come up. We want you to be prepared to make the sacrifices that come with those details. Being with the person you care for and making it work, is one compromise after another, and those compromises cannot be only one way. Rose is having this same conversation with Marie this morning. If both of you agree this is what you want, we will give you our blessing to court—as long as you both take time to be sure. Do you understand?"

Bo was a little taken aback by what he'd just heard. He thought for a moment and smiled. "Yes, sir. I do," he replied politely. He was surprised at how quickly this was moving along and a little pleased as well.

They shook hands, both turned to leave the stable and stopped dead in their tracks when they saw Rose standing in the doorway.

"I'm sorry, Daddy. I didn't mean to listen, but I'm glad that I did. I talked to mother and she told me you were coming here to talk to Marshal Henry." She walked over and put her hand on Bo's arm. "I would never do anything to hurt either of you, but I do care for Marshal Henry. I want you to know that he and I will have a long conversation and we will come and tell you and Mama what we've decided."

Bo put his hand on top of Rose's. "It would seem that Rose and I have a lot of talking to do, sir…now that I'm sure how she feels about me." He looked down at Rose. "Daniel and I have a job to do first, then, we'll have that conversation. Right now, Daniel and I have to get into town and talk to the people involved in your father's business."

Outside, Daniel heard his name mentioned. "Did someone call me?" Daniel called from the other side of the stable.

"Let's get these horses ready to go," Bo smiled and called out to Daniel. "It's going to be a long day."

Mr. O'Reilly started out of the stable. "Bring your horses up to the main house and we'll get you fed before you leave," he said.

A few minutes later, Bo and Daniel led their horses up from the stable to the main house where they tied them to the hitching rail and went into the house for breakfast. After a delicious breakfast, Mr. O'Reilly stepped out to the front of the house to send Bo and Daniel on their way.

"I think you should talk to my employees in town, first. They have 'Den' after their names on that list I gave you. Everyone else is out at the mines. That will be an overnight trip. I'll send word down there to make sure they know you're coming and that they have a place for you to stay."

Bo looked again at the paper Mr. O'Reilly had given him. "I see the names with 'Den', for Denver, but the rest of them have different letters. What do they mean?"

Mr. O'Reilly smiled. "Those abbreviations represent the names of my three mines. The first mine I dug was the Marie-Ann, named for my wife. The second was the Rose-Marie, named for my daughter. The mine we opened last year is the Yellow Bud. I named it after this house which has come to mean so much to us"—he paused for a moment—"you'll find that my holdings are far greater than the mines. I own the city's largest bank, one of the hotels and a few stores. I also own a large piece of the railroad that runs from Denver to Cheyenne and I have a large timber operation north of here"—he handed Bo a second piece of paper—"this is a letter of introduction to the president of my bank, Lester Sims. He will help you in every way. He's been a trusted friend for many years."

Upon arriving in Denver, Bo and Daniel took their horses to the stable for water and a stall. After, it didn't take them long to locate the bank that Mr. O'Reilly owned. Once there, Mr. Sims met them in the lobby and asked them back to his office.

"Mr. O'Reilly's letter explains that you are both U.S. Marshals and that you are here to investigate the payroll robberies we've had. Where would you like to start?"

Bo took out his list of names. "I'd like to start by talking to these men," he said, handing the list to Mr. Sims.

Mr. Sims took the list from Bo's hand to study it. "Let's see, this seems to be everyone. Why don't we start with the first person who knew there would be a payroll and how large it would be? Then, we can send in everyone who came in contact with the payroll, in the order they learned about it." He stood up, went to his office door and opened it. "Would you please have Mr. Blackman come into my office?" he called out to an accountant, who was seated in the office across from his.

He shut the door then returned to sit at his desk. In a moment the door opened again and a short, thin man entered. "Yes, Mr. Sims. What can I do for you?" The employee looked suspiciously at Bo and Daniel.

Mr. Sims rose from his chair. "Tate, these are U.S. Marshals Bo Henry and Daniel Blue," Mr. Sims said. "They are here to investigate the robberies we've had." He gestured toward both Daniel and Bo. "Gentlemen, this is my head teller, Mr. Tate Blackman. He will be able to answer any questions you may have regarding the process of a mine and timber payroll and how they are put together. Tate, these men are here at the request of Mr. O'Reilly. We're to give them our full cooperation"—he gestured toward the door—"there's an empty office next to mine. You may use it to conduct your interviews. Just tell my secretary who you would like to see next and she will instruct them on why you are here and that they are to be fully cooperative."

Mr. Blackman led them to the office next door and let himself in. There was a small window behind the desk, also four chairs around a small table to the left of the door. Bo and Daniel took two chairs that kept their backs to the wall and Mr. Blackman sat across from them. Bo leaned forward. "Mr. Blackman, can you please tell us how a payroll is created and then how it makes its way from the bank to the miners? Please don't leave out a single step."

Daniel stood up and made his way to the desk. Opening the desk drawer, he found a pen and a stack of paper with which he could take notes. After taking his seat again, he prepared to take notes on everything that was being explained. Bo, glancing over at Daniel who was intently listening and writing, smiled as he said, "I knew there was a reason I brought you along."

Daniel gave him a light punch in the shoulder. "Don't get any ideas about calling me your secretary."

Mr. Blackman went through the entire process of taking the payroll cash out of the safe and counting it. He explained that it was counted at least twice more before it was locked in the chest and placed in the back of the wagon. Everyone who touched the cash had to count it and sign for it and the previous counter had to sign for the release of the cash to the next person.

He continued, letting Bo and Daniel know that each payroll was different for each of the three mines. The money for each location was packed in chests and placed on a wagon to go out to the mine to be distributed. The driver and guard were selected by Mr. Blackman from a list prepared by Mr. O'Reilly. After, the wagon was packed and readied to go. For added security, the route wasn't revealed to the driver until he and his guard were ready to leave. There were four routes that would take them to the mines and the route was selected at random each time. The final step was to send out a trailing guard to make sure the wagon wasn't followed. Each robbery had taken place at the most advantageous location on each route for that day.

After they had finished getting briefed by Mr. Blackman, Bo and Daniel spent the rest of the day interviewing everyone who had come in contact with the money, from the time the payroll was generated, until it was to reach the mine.

On the ride back up to the Yellow Bud estate, they reviewed the notes that Daniel had taken. "This reminds me of college," Daniel commented. "We took notes on everything. Let's see what we have." He read off everything he had learned about the payroll process and Bo shook his head to signal his understanding.

"I don't see how they could have figured out where to hit the payroll shipment at the exact time and place that was chosen. They may have gotten lucky once, but, not all three times. There has to be someone on the inside who's giving them the information—I just don't see how. Everything is random and at the last minute. The one thing that's not random is the day of the month the miners get paid."

Daniel scrunched up his face. "There is only one explanation, Marshal. They've figured out a way for an insider to let his partners know where and when the shipment would be coming."

Bo's head was sagging down with dismay. "How are we going to tell Mr. O'Reilly he has a bad apple in his bunch?"

Daniel smiled "What do you mean we have to tell him? I'm not going to get in the middle of that. This is your lady friend's father. I'll take care of the horses, you go tell him."

It was supper time when they finally made it back to the Yellow Bud stables. Mr. O'Reilly saw them when they were riding past the house and stepped out as they passed to meet them.

"How did it go today?" Mr. O'Reilly asked. Bo handed Buck's reins to Daniel, who had dismounted his horse, and dropped wearily to the ground off of Buck.

"I think we've made some progress, but, I'd like to talk to your people at the mines before we put it all together. This may be more complicated than it looks," Bo replied.

Daniel shook his head. "You can say that again." He trotted the horses down to the stables. Shifting uneasily, Buck wasn't pleased to let Daniel take off his saddle, but didn't cause any problems. Once the bridle was off, Buck trotted into the first open stall. Then, Daniel took care of Alala and had her bed down for the night. The stable hand moved around him in the stable as well, to feed and water the horses.

Daniel hauled all of their gear up to the guest cottage to get cleaned up for supper. When he finally made his way into the cottage, he found all of his best clothes washed and neatly folded on his bed. He looked over and saw the same had been done for Bo. There was plenty of hot water for two baths with fresh towels. "This has to be the work of Miss Rose," he smiled and whispered to himself. "Bo, you've got yourself one fine lady."

Daniel had taken his bath and was nearly dressed when Bo finally strode in from speaking with Mr. O'Reilly. As he entered, Daniel turned to face him. "Well, did you tell him?"

Bo shook his head. "No, I couldn't tell him now. I'll tell him after we have some proof. It's too soon."

It was Daniel's turn to shake his head. "Coward. Take your bath and get dressed. And when you get up to the house, you can thank Miss Rose for all of this. I'm sure she arranged it."

Bo looked around the guest cottage, stunned to see the clean clothes on his bed and the water for his bath. "She did all of this?"

Daniel smiled. "I'd say no she didn't, but, I'll guess that she made sure it was done. You had better thank her when you get up there."

When they had finally got to the house after showering and dressing, Bo took Rose aside. "I want to thank you for having our clothes washed and preparing the hot water for our baths. That was very nice."

Rose smiled. "That was the least I could do for all the help you're giving Daddy. Let's go in and eat. You must be starving."

For a time, the conversation at supper centered on the investigation until Mrs. O'Reilly turned it to issues of a less business nature. After supper, Mr. O'Reilly headed off to his study with Daniel for an evening of chess. It was easy to see the two men had bonded. Rose was not about to let Bo get pulled into that routine of brandy and chess in the study, so took his arm and led him off to the garden.

"We have several matters to talk about, Marshal Henry, and I'm not about to let Daddy have you tonight," Rose said as she led him out.

Bo didn't object. "I've been thinking all day about what your father said about us earlier—he's right. We have to talk about all of this and what it will mean for both of us in the future. This has been going far too fast."

The night air was full with the fragrances of the garden flowers and the half-moon was just beginning to shine on Rose and Bo. Rose looked deeply into Bo's eyes and then leaned forward and touched her soft lips to his. Bo's heart raced and he could hardly breathe. He placed his hand on hers and held it tightly.

Rose pulled back from Bo slowly. "I've been waiting for you to tell me how you feel since our first walk in the garden. You have to know how I feel."

Bo was having trouble speaking. "I had everything clear in my mind with what I wanted to say, and now I can't think of a thing. Is this the way it's going to be for us from now on?"

Rose squeezed Bo's hands in hers and smiled. "I certainly hope so. We know how Mama and Daddy feel about our courting. What will your parents say?"

Bo thought about it for a moment. "My mom is going to cry. My dad is going to say it's about time. My sisters are going to cry with my mom. My brothers are only going to ask me how pretty you are."

Rose smiled. "Well, what are you going to tell them?"

Bo didn't have to think. "I'll tell them to remember the most beautiful sunset they've ever seen," he declared, "and remember how the pasture looks in the spring when all the wild flowers bloom. I want them to think about the look on their faces when they saw their first baby born or what it is like when they see a new colt take its first steps. I want them to recall what the river looks like when the willow branches ripple in the water on a hot summer's afternoon. Then, take all of that and roll it up into one picture, and then, they will be close."

Rose choked up and a tear slid down her cheek. "Do you really mean that?"

Bo squeezed her hands in his. "I know it's not enough, but that's as close as I can get." His smile faded as another thought came into his mind. "There's one friend of mine that we are going to have trouble with," he continued. "He may come to love you as much as I do or he's going to be a big problem."

"Who is it?" Rose wasn't concerned but asked anyway. "I'll show him I love you and he will be my friend, too."

Bo wasn't so sure. "It's Buck. He's been my best friend since he was a colt. He takes care of me when we're out on the prairie and I take care of him when we're in town. He's saved my life more than once. We've never been apart. This is going to change his whole world. I don't know what to do about him."

Rose understood the relationship between Bo and Buck. She'd seen how they looked after each other. If Buck rejected her, it could destroy her relationship with Bo or break his heart.

"I know what this means to you," Rose said. "Let's go have a talk with him, right now. I'm sure I can win him over."

Still, Bo wasn't so sure. "If we're going to be together, then we should try this, now."

Rose took Bo's hand and they made their way through the kitchen, where Bo slipped two bright red, crisp apples into his coat pocket as they passed through the pantry on their way to the stables to confront Buck. As he went in to greet Buck, Bo asked Rose to wait just outside the stable door first. "Here," Bo said, before disappearing into the stable. "Take these apples and wait for me here. I'll call you when I think it's okay for you to come in."

Rose slipped the two apples—one at a time—from Bo's hands and into her pocket and peeked around the corner of the stable doors as Bo went in.

As soon as Bo was inside, the light from a single lantern lit up his face and Buck stepped out of his stall to approach him. Stooping his neck low, Buck balanced to rest his forehead against Bo's chest and waited to be scratched behind the ears. Bo wrapped his left arm around the big horse's head and began to whisper in his ear.

"Buck, there is someone I want you to meet. She's very important to me and I want you and her to be friends." Bo's voice was low and soft as he was telling Buck about all the good times they'd had and how none of that was going to change. "I don't know if you can understand me, but, this is very important to me and I need your help."

From the stable doorway, Bo waved his hand as a signal for Rose to come in. She walked in very slowly. Buck nudged Bo slightly with his nose as Rose got closer to them and Bo stepped back just a little. Rose extended her hand toward Buck, holding one of the apples and stood very still as Buck sniffed the apple and then took it gently from her hand with his mouth. Rose reached up and scratched Buck on the nose right where he liked it. She brought the second apple up to his nose, and again, he took it from her most carefully. Wrapping her right arm around his neck, Rose gave Buck a hug and without thinking, took a brush from the top rail of the stall and started to brush his mane. Bo almost rushed forward anticipating an unfavorable reaction from Buck but the big horse didn't move. Bo nearly went to his knees when he realized that Buck was calm. Buck continued to munch on the second apple as Rose brushed his back. He gave her a flick of his tail when she got to his rump. Rose moved up and passed under his chin and then brushed down his left side. When she was done, she gave Buck another hug around the neck and stepped back.

Buck took a half-step forward to rest his nose against her chest. She scratched him again around the ears and then he backed up and retreated into his stall.

Rose turned to look at Bo. "Now, that wasn't so hard, was it?"

Bo was stunned. "He won't let Daniel brush him. He even has a fit whenever Daniel takes off his bridle."

He took her hand and they started back toward the house. Buck had the last word as he whinnied from his stall. To Bo, it sounded like a laugh.

The next morning, they ate breakfast after Bo saddled the horses. The pack mule was loaded and ready to go and Daniel led the team up the path to the main house. Rose met them on the top step. She bounced down the remaining steps and offered Buck an apple. He nuzzled up to her to get scratched. Seeing Buck's genuine comfort with Rose, Daniel shook his head in amazement. "Well, I'll be," Daniel said in awe.

Bo looked over at Daniel. "She's got him spoiled. In just one day she's got him spoiled."

A few minutes later, Mr. O'Reilly appeared with another letter for Bo. "Marshal Henry," said Mr. O'Reilly closing in on them. "Please give this to my foreman. I'll set you up with a place to bunk and anything else you may need. He's a part-owner of the Marie-Ann. He wants these men caught as much as I do. If you're going to visit all three mines, I wouldn't expect to see you back here for at least five days. I have people coming back every day. You can send me a message through them if you need to. Our next payroll isn't due for nearly two weeks. Let's hope you have this figured out by then. Have a safe trip and good luck."

Rose gave Bo a little tug on his shirt and when he bent down, she leaned to whisper in his ear. "You, hurry back to me, Bo Henry."

Bo was speechless and blushing as he swung up on Buck's back. Rose leaned forward and whispered, "Take good care of him," in Buck's ear. Buck snorted as Bo spun him around and then headed down the trail to the south toward the mines. Rose smiled as she heard Bo mutter to Buck, "One day and she's got you spoiled rotten." They had been on the trail for several hours when they encountered a stream. They dismounted, watered the horses and ate a hard tack lunch of fresh biscuits from the O'Reilly kitchen that Daniel had found in one of the bags and a strip of jerky each from their trail provisions. They wouldn't be there long enough for a fire. "It must have been Miss Rose who left us this little something extra for lunch," Daniel said, tossing Bo a biscuit. "You'd better treat her right."

Before they could get back in their saddles, they were approached by three riders and a wagon. After introductions, Bo learned they were miners from the Marie-Ann on their way to the bank in Denver with the weekly production reports, a list of supplies they needed, and the papers regarding the upcoming payroll. One man on the wagon was from the Denver office and the other three were from the three mines. After a few minutes, it was easy to determine they knew nothing about the robberies other than the gossip that was being spread. They shook hands amongst each other and everyone went on their way.

Bo and Daniel were told by the three riders before their parting that it would take them another three hours to reach the Marie-Ann. They would spend the next day there and then travel the two hours south to the Rose-Marie. Their last stop would be the Yellow Bud mine, which was higher up the mountain and located north of the first two. To gather the information they needed, they planned to spend at least a day at each site investigating the grounds and interviewing people of interest.

Each stop was the same; at first they were met with some skepticism, but, before long Daniel had them examining his guns and the conversations became friendlier. After that, it was easy to ask questions and determine if any of the miners knew anything about who could have been robbing them. Every one of the miners was more than angry over having lost the payroll. It was important for them to be paid on time for their hard work and the delays were more than an inconvenience. By the time Bo and Daniel left the first camp, they had become friends with the miners. The morning crew had already gone down inside the mine, but the late morning crew gave them a hardy sendoff with good wishes. It was mostly the same at the Rose-Marie. On their way to the Yellow Bud mine they were met by the same wagon party they had initially encountered on their way to the Marie-Anne. It was now making its way back from Denver to bring supplies to the mines. The driver stopped and pulled out a telegram from his pocket. "I was told to give this to you when I saw you, Marshal," he said, stretching his arm out toward Bo with the telegram in hand.

Bo took the message from him and opened it up. He read it and then turned to address Daniel with what it said. "It's from Judge Roads. He wants to know what we're up to. I guess it's a scolding. I have to send him a report as soon as I get back. It says here that he's heard that the Burser brothers may be in our area and we should keep an eye open for them."

Daniel smiled. "Well, you have been a little distracted as of late."

Bo wasn't pleased with Blue's remark. "That's enough out of you, Marshal Blue." He turned back to the wagon driver. "Thank you. Will you be heading up to the Yellow Bud mine?"

The man shook his head. "No, I've got to get all these supplies to the Marie-Ann. They split the load and send Yellow Bud's supplies up from there. If you climb up this trail for another hour you should be there. Have a good trip, Marshal."

The driver snapped the reigns for his team and started up the trail in the other direction and Bo and Daniel continued on their way. It was midafternoon when the Yellow Bud mine came into sight. The mine foreman met them as they rode in.

"Good afternoon, Marshals. I'm Ken Cummings, foreman for the Yellow Bud mine. I've been expecting you. I've got you set up with bunks and a place at the dinner table—that was the hard part. These boys know how to eat. Follow me. You can talk to the men when they break for supper."

Daniel was a little surprised. "Will all of your crew be at supper?"

Ken nodded. "Mr. O'Reilly doesn't want us running three shifts in the mines. We send men in on the early morning shift and then the afternoon shift. Everyone is out of the mine by sunset. He believes that we shouldn't have to work all night, too. He told me the gold isn't going anywhere and two shifts will make us all just as rich as three. If I send anyone into the mine at night, it's to inspect the mine for safety reasons."

Bo smiled. *That sounds like Rose's dad*, he thought. He turned back to Ken. "Have you or any of your men seen anything unusual lately?"

Ken stopped for a moment to consider the question. "We've had what I thought were some poachers the last few weeks. We've seen their campfires at night. When I've sent some of the men out the next day, they'd moved. They never set up camp in the same place. That's why I figured they were doing a little poaching. They pan out a small area and then move on. We've never been able to find them to run them off of Mr. O'Reilly's land."

Daniel needed more information. "You say they were in too close to the mine?"

Ken chuckled. "No, they weren't close at all. Mr. O'Reilly's land extends nearly all the way to Denver. He's bought up all of the claims between here and the city limits. He's even bought up all the dry claims like mine. He paid me twice what it was worth. He told me that if we ever strike gold on it he will still make me a full partner like he did at the Rose-Marie with Pete Peterson. Every miner who works for Mr. O'Reilly gets some of the profits from the mine. He tells everyone who works for him, that if you put your blood, sweat and tears into a mine, you should get more than just wages for it. When they robbed the payroll, every man here took it personally. If we catch them, we'll hang them on the spot."

Bo shook his head to show his understanding. "That's why I'm here. Judge Roads wants the robbers in his court. If there's going to be any hanging, he'll do it legal.

Ken nodded. "I'm glad you're both here. I don't have the manpower to be chasing after poachers or robbers. It's hard enough to keep a mine like this running without those kinds of problems. Let's get you boys settled in. You can talk to the morning shift before supper." He looked over at Daniel and continued. "They'll want to see those shotguns of yours. That's all they've been able to talk about. Are they really engraved with the names of the Texas heroes?"

Daniel pulled a gun from his left holster and handed it to Ken for him to see. "They sure are."

Ken took the gun and turned it over in his hands admiring it. "I'm not much for guns but, this has to be just about the prettiest shotgun I've ever seen. It's a shame to have to shoot something like this, isn't it? Where did you ever find these?"

As they bedded the horses down for the night, Daniel told Ken all about how he'd come to have the two shotguns. Later, Daniel and Bo took their gear and went to the bunk house, where Ken showed them where they were going to sleep. The deep shadows had already crept down the mountain side and started across the flat plains to the east. A few of the miners were starting to make their way out of the mine opening. Lanterns were lit and the aromas from cooking coming from the shack were making everyone move a little faster.

Bo and Daniel got cleaned up and made their way into the dining hall where there were twenty miners seated around a table when they got there. Room was made for them at one side so they could sit. They all took a moment of silence to say a prayer for the food on the table and then the food was brought in. *If anyone was slow at this table, he would starve,* Bo thought. It reminded him a lot of what it was like when he was growing up with all of his brothers. After the main meal, trays of peach cobbler were brought out. It didn't last any longer than the meat and potatoes had earlier.

Daniel smiled. "You boys eat well for a mining camp."

Ken was sitting across from Daniel and Bo. "Mr. O'Reilly makes sure that none of us goes hungry. He said the mine can afford it."

"Is this everyone?" Bo asked.

Ken nodded. "We have two shifts with seven miners and one line foreman per shift. Four of us work above ground. We're all here."

"Can we see the shotguns?" one of the men seated next to Daniel asked. "Some of the men down at the Marie-Ann said you had a pair of shotguns that we wouldn't believe."

Daniel knew they'd want to see them and he was the only one wearing any weapons in the dining hall. He sent one gun to his right and the other one to his left. Each miner carefully wiped his hands before he took his turn looking them over. Daniel was compelled to repeat his story of how he became the owner of such a pair of beautiful guns.

Bo wanted to know more about the camp fires that some of the miners had seen off in the distance that Ken had reported to them earlier. "Who here saw the campfires north of here?" he asked out loud.

Doug, one of the men who had seen the fires, offered to share his story.

"It started about a month ago," Doug went on. "I spotted the glimmer of a campfire about a mile from here on the next ridge to the north. I didn't think anything of it. It could have been some hunters. When the campfires reappeared the next couple of nights in different places, I pointed them out to Ken. If they were hunters, they would have set up one camp and hunted from there. We thought they could be a couple of pan miners trying to work some of the small streams up in that direction. I went up a couple of days later to see if I could find them."

Bo looked puzzled. "How do you know there was more than one man?"

Doug tilted his head to one side. "I didn't at first. When I found their first camp site, I saw tracks for at least four men and horses. If they were just panning for gold, there wouldn't be four of them, and four hunters would have kept to one camp site. They had to be more serious prospectors."

Now it was Daniel's turn to be curious. "How do you know they were prospectors?"

"If you're not hunting or panning," Doug explained. "Then there's not much else to do up there. There are no trails to move on—there's just the mountain. On the other side of it is another mountain. What else could they be doing?"

Bo nodded. "That's a very good question. We're going back to Denver in the morning. We'll cut up through that area if you can point it out to us. We'll have a look and see if we can scout their trail. You boys have been a big help with this information."

After retiring for the night, Bo and Daniel were up early the next morning with Ken. They had breakfast and saddled the horses for the long ride back to Denver. Ken pointed to a landmark they could use to find the first couple of camp sites the strangers had used. Bo reached down and shook Ken's hand.

"Thank everyone for their hospitality last night. After we take a look at the camp sites, we're going to check out the location where they robbed the first payroll."

Ken pointed down the mountain, toward the location of the second robbery site. "If you head down there first, you can see both sites on your way back to Denver," Ken said.

Daniel looked over at Bo. "That's interesting," he said. "Do you think our campers may be the robbers?"

Bo nodded. "I'm beginning to think so. Let's get going. I want to be back in Denver tonight." He spun Buck around and then headed off to the north at a gallop.

When they reached the first robbery site, they dismounted and tied up the pack mule. Bo sent Daniel to the south side of the trail and positioned himself where they knew three of the highwaymen had concealed themselves, about halfway up an incline.

Meanwhile, Bo climbed up and stood on a large boulder at the top of the hill and called down to Daniel. "This is where the first of them made his appearance," Bo said. He pulled his gun out of its holster and thoughtfully looked back down the trail. "The trail is too narrow for the wagon to have turned around. And the hill is too steep to make a run for it and clear the gunfire—they were stuck. With four guns pointed at them, they could do nothing except give up the payroll."

Daniel climbed back up the trail. "I don't know much about this kind of thing, but it looks like the perfect spot to hold them up."

Bo agreed. "They used a shotgun to blast the locks off the boxes and they stuffed the payroll in their saddlebags. Four men could handle all that money with ease. The guard and the driver were lucky they didn't get shot. Let's go up and find that camp site."

They mounted the horses again and headed up the mountain to the second robbery site; it looked identical to the first. Bo shook his head. "These boys scouted these sites a long time before they hit the wagons. They knew exactly where to make their stand."

Daniel agreed. "I bet we find camp sites near both of the other robberies. They left nothing to chance."

It took Bo and Daniel a half-hour to locate the site where Doug had seen the fires. Bo got off of Buck and strolled quietly around the second camp site.

"There's no sign that they camped here more than once," said Bo. "They couldn't have seen the wagon coming from here, the trees are too thick. They had to know when it was coming before they left this camp. It was the same at the first camp site."

Daniel nodded. "Then, you do think these were the same thieves who held up the payroll wagon?"

Bo looked at Blue. "I sure do. We've got to find out where they've been camping for the last couple of weeks. It's obvious they haven't been back here. I bet they were camped out north of Denver when they hit the logging payroll. We should have a look in that direction after we check out that robbery site."

Dan Bradford

Chapter 6
Bad Guys Beware

Yellow Bud was in shadows by the time Bo and Daniel had arrived. They rode straight to the stables with the horses and the mule. It wasn't long before Mr. William O'Reilly and Rose appeared in the doorway to greet them. William was interested in how their trip had gone. "Were you able to find out anything from the miners?" William asked.

Bo hoisted the saddle off of Buck's back and slipped the bridle out of his mouth and gave the big stallion a slap on the rump; Buck trotted off to his stall. Bo reached out and pulled Rose to him and gave her a hug, then turned to face William to answer his questions.

"We found out a great deal from your men," Bo said. "They pointed us to where the robbers had been camped just before they hit your wagon. I'll bet they did the same thing on the north end of town before they robbed your timber payroll. We're going up there after we've given the horses a rest. We need to take a look at the site where they actually robbed the wagon."

William was impatient for more information. "Have you been able to find out who it may be?" he asked with an anxious tone.

Daniel shook his head. "No. We have some suspicions, but nothing solid, yet. We'll know more after we've had a look at the other site."

Bo and Daniel finished taking care of their animals and their tack before they headed off to the guest cottage for the night. Rose accompanied them as her father made his way back to the main house. When they arrived, they found hot water and clean clothes folded on their bunks. Rose smiled when she saw how they appreciated the clothes and the hot bath. "I appreciate all that you're doing for my father" Rose said. "Get cleaned up. Supper will be in an hour or so." She turned and closed the door behind her.

An hour later, Bo and Daniel made their way up the path through the garden to the rear door of the main hall where they were met by the maid, taken to the dining room and seated for supper. It was another elegant meal topped off with apple cobbler this time. When the meal was over, William invited Daniel to his study for a game of chess.

"How do you feel about letting me win tonight, Daniel?" William asked.

Daniel shook his head. "I'm going to have to decline tonight, Mr. O'Reilly. It's been a long hard day and I'm looking forward to a sound night's sleep. Perhaps tomorrow."

Bo was very tired also. "I'm going to follow Daniel back to the cottage as well. Being in the saddle all day and this fine meal have taken their toll on me." He stood up. "Mr. O'Reilly, I would like to know when you are going to send out your next payroll…I expect you are going to be attacked again."

Mr. O'Reilly stood up after him. "They brought the papers up to me today; I went over them this afternoon. I'll be taking them to Denver tomorrow. We'll be taking the buggy. It's a day we'll spend in town shopping. Perhaps you and Daniel would like to go with us. Your horses can run in the pasture and rest up while we spend the day taking in what Denver has to offer."

Bo was pleased at the invitation. "We'd be happy to go with you," he accepted. "We have a few things to purchase for ourselves. Also, I'd like to have another look at how an actual payroll is put together; we may find out how they are getting ahead of you on the shipments."

Rose was not pleased with the shortened evening. "If you all would please excuse me, I'm going to my room. I'll see all of you in the morning," Rose said, then stood up and left the dining hall.

Mrs. O'Reilly excused herself, too. "It's been a long day for all of us. Please excuse me, gentlemen. I'll see all of you tomorrow at breakfast." She smiled as she followed her daughter out of the room and up the stairs.

After Mrs. O'Reilly and Rose were out of sight, Mr. O'Reilly led Bo and Daniel to the rear doors of the main hall. "I trust you gentlemen can find your way from here," he said, as one of the staff members opened the doors and let them out. Bo and Daniel thanked him for his hospitality then stepped outside to meet the fresh air and began walking back to the guest cottage.

On the way back to the cottage, Bo asked Daniel for some help. "You have a lot more education than I do. I need some help with my words and my numbers. I sound like some county hick around Rose and her father. All of you use words that I've never heard before, except maybe from Judge Roads. I want you to help me do better. I want to learn more about numbers, too. I've seen you doing calculations with numbers and I know they're important. If you can show me why they're important, then I can learn how to use them like you do."

Daniel grinned. "It's not just knowing words, it's knowing how and when to use them; that's called, 'grammar.' I can help you with that. We'll pick up a couple of books tomorrow while we're in town. The numbers are going to be a little more difficult. There are different types of mathematics. I think we should start with geometry. It's the mathematics that I used to make sure the designs I created in school wouldn't collapse once they were built. We should be able to get a book about that as well. We will have lots of time while we're riding from one town to another to study. We'll get you started as soon as we solve the payroll robberies."

Bo seemed happy to have Daniel help him. He smiled and nodded approvingly at the plan to get books to study. Soon they made it to the guest cottage, took their shoes off and settled in for the night.

The next morning, Bo went down to the stables to take care of Buck and found Rose there giving Buck his morning apple. Bo just shook his head. "You've got him spoiled already," he said. Then, Daniel and Bo took the horses and their mule out to the twenty acre pasture that extended north of the barn. At that time of the morning, the grass was covered with a light frost and the breath of the animals was obvious as they trotted out into the open air. With the animals taken care of for the day, they went up to the main house for breakfast.

When they were finished eating the breakfast the staff had prepared, Bo, Rose and Daniel stepped out of the main house door to find the carriage waiting for them at the front entrance. Mr. O'Reilly helped Marie into the carriage and Bo assisted Rose. William handed his wife a folder containing his banking papers and then climbed in next to her. He was closely followed by Bo, who seated himself next to Rose. Daniel jumped up next to the driver and they were quickly on their way into Denver.

A half-hour ride from the Yellow Bud estate, Marie and Rose were dropped off at the O'Reilly family dry goods store before the carriage made its way to the bank. There, Bo watched intently as the process of preparing a payroll wound its way through the bank from hand to hand. He made a special note of everyone who had contact with the numbers and documents, then, with the actual money. At one point he stopped Mr. O'Reilly to ask a question. "Is this everyone involved in the process?"

William nodded. "Yes, except for the wagon driver and the riding guards. They won't be selected until the wagon is loaded and ready to go. That's when they'll find out which trail to take."

Bo nodded to acknowledge his understanding. "You told me the selection of the trail is made by Mr. Blackman just before the wagon leaves. That doesn't leave much to chance. Can you select the route instead of Mr. Blackman this time?"

"Of course. That's highly unusual, but it is my bank. Do you want me to choose one for the timber payroll or the mining payroll?"

Bo was a little surprised. "Which chest is the next payroll to go out?"

William pointed to the two chests at the far end of the vault. "The timber payroll is the one with the big brass lock. It's next. It will go out in three days. The mining payroll isn't due at the mines for another week after that."

Bo thought for a moment. "How many routes do you use for the timber payroll?"

William paused to think. "There are two routes that we use. The north route is the one where they hijacked us. The south route takes three hours longer. My men don't like to use that one unless they have to."

Bo smiled. "Set this payroll up to use the north route. If the robbers think we're trying to dodge them, they will set up on the south route. If they're getting inside help, then there won't be any doubt they'll hit the wagon on the north route. Daniel and I will take a ride tomorrow and look the north route over. I want to see if there's more than one place to set up their ambush or if they'll have to try an ambush two times in a row, at the same place."

After finishing up at the bank, the three men left and strolled down the street to the dry goods shop where they met Marie and Rose to stroll the town and do some shopping. Bo and Daniel picked out some finer clothes and a few supplies at the dry goods store. It was going to be nice to have another change of clothes for dinner, Daniel and Bo thought. Daniel located two books; one was on grammar and the other on higher math for Bo to read while they were on the trail. Daniel tucked the books away with the rest of his other purchases because he wasn't sure Bo would want Rose to see them. After the shopping was complete, they boarded the carriage where Marie and Rose were already waiting and returned to Yellow Bud for a quiet evening of brandy and chess after dinner.

The next morning Bo and Daniel were up and on the trail before the rest of the household had eaten breakfast. It would take all day to check out the north route and get back by supper time. As they rode toward the site of the first robbery, Bo decided that he wanted to meet with Mr. O'Reilly once more before the payroll went out. He was formulating some ideas that they would have to discuss. "Daniel, I think the best way to catch these men is to let them think they've gotten away with the payroll and then, follow them back to their camp. We can get them and the stolen payroll all at the same time."

Daniel wasn't so sure about Bo's plan. "You're going to let them take another payroll and then hope we can track them down and capture them…and recover the other payrolls? That sounds a bit risky to me."

Bo smiled. "We're going to switch the chest tomorrow just after it's out of town with one that has much less money in it. There will be just enough cash left to keep them convinced, but not anywhere near the amount of the original payroll. You're going to have to trust me on the tracking part. We'll go over the plan with Mr. O'Reilly after dinner this evening."

They checked out the location of the first robbery and then rode nearly up to the logging site. Bo was satisfied. "There doesn't seem to be any better place for them to rob the wagon than the original site. I'm betting they're going to go back to what worked for them the first time. If

Mr. O'Reilly's men are dumb enough to use the same route, then the hijackers are dumb enough to use the same ambush site."

Daniel shook his head. "I've been around you too long. That actually makes sense."

It was nearly supper time when Bo and Daniel arrived back at the Yellow Bud stables. They led Buck and Alala in and took care of them to settle them in for the night. Then Bo and Daniel made their way to the guest cottage to freshen up. When they opened the door to the cottage, they discovered their new clothes pressed and waiting for them on their cots, along with plenty of hot water in pails and in the tub for baths.

Daniel shook his head. "You think Buck is being spoiled? Buck isn't the only one being spoiled. Miss Rose is going to make you impossible to live with on the trail."

Bo didn't want to respond. "I don't know what you mean," he choked out. "She's just being hospitable."

Daniel chuckled. "Hospitable is when they let us stay the night and feed us once in a while. Fresh pressed clothes and a hot bath every night is spoiling us. Take your bath and put on your new duds. Miss Rose is waiting to see you in them."

Pouring the hot pails of the hot water in the bath, they each took turns taking a quick bath with a shave. Then they jumped into the new clothes they had purchased in town the day prior and exited the guest cottage. They nearly ran up to the main house where they were shown to the dining room by the staff. Rose lit up the entire room with her smile when she saw Bo walk in wearing his new outfit. He even had the neckerchief she'd bought him tied around his neck. Bo moved toward her and sat next to her. She put her hand under the table and lightly squeezed his arm, then leaned closer to him. "Mr. Henry, you look so nice tonight," she whispered.

Bo turned very red and he pulled his hands out from under the table and put them out in front of him. "Thank you for the neckerchief, Miss Rose. It's very nice."

After looking at Rose and Bo at the table, Marie glanced over at William and smiled. Seeing Rose and Bo together bought back so many memories for her. William noticed her glance and cleared his throat. "Bo, what did you and Daniel find out on the trail today?"

Bo was glad for the interruption. "We saw the first ambush site today. We think they're going to try again in the same place. We've put together a plan that we want to go over with you after supper." That comment evoked a little kick from Rose under the table. "Well, I mean, after you and Daniel finish your chess game," Bo continued, taking the hint.

After supper, William stood up. "Well, Daniel, are you ready to give me another lesson in humility?" he said, turning slightly toward Daniel.

Daniel smiled. "Mr. O'Reilly, you are much more skilled than you let everyone think. I believe you're just setting me up."

Bo stood up and helped Rose up. Marie watched them. "Not too late, Rose," she said to her daughter. "You have to let the marshal have some time with your father. They are going to have a very busy day tomorrow."

Rose pouted just a little. "Yes, Mama."

She led Bo out the back door and into the garden. "Mr. Henry, were you going to go off to father's study, rather than spend time with me?"

Bo wasn't sure how to answer. "No, Miss Rose, but there are some decisions that I have to have your father make first thing in the morning and they are very important."

Rose wasn't about to let Bo get away with that. "I'm sure they are all very important, but I want to spend time with you, too."

Rose and Bo continued to stroll through the garden, admiring the flowers as they went. After over an hour of conversation, a whispering voice came down to them from the third floor balcony. "Rose, would you please come up and help me with the menu? I think that Marshal Henry is needed by your father in the study."

Rose displayed a little pout across her lips. "Yes, Mama."

Rose and Bo moved to the back door and exchanged warm glances. Rose put her hand on Bo's arm. "I'll see you in the morning," Rose said as Bo opened the door and they went inside. Rose climbed the stairs at the far side of the room and Bo turned to the right and stepped into the study.

William looked up as Bo entered and smiled. "It looks like my daughter finally let you go."

Bo was a little disappointed that their night together had ended. "Her mother asked her to help her with something."

Daniel made his move, placing a chess piece along the board. "Why don't you tell Mr. O'Reilly what we would like him to do tomorrow morning, Bo?"

Bo pulled a chair up next to the chess table. "We want you to exchange the payroll chest on the wagon with one that has much less money, just in case we can't capture the hijackers. Bring the payroll back here. Daniel and I will take it to the logging camp later. We're going up the trail to the location of the first robbery and will find ourselves some cover that will give us a chance to trail them back to their camp. Once we've located their camp, we'll take them into custody. If they haven't buried their previous takes, we should be able to recover all or most of your money."

Mr. O'Reilly wasn't so sure about the plan and his concern spread over his face. "There are four or five men out there. How are you going to take all of them into custody with just the two of you? Shouldn't I provide some help?"

Bo shook his head, declining the offer. "No, sir. We can't take a chance on having the robbers spot us while we're waiting for them. They may have a spotter on the other side of the trail." Bo was even more worried about having someone in town tipping off the person on the inside. "Daniel and I will be just fine."

Mr. O'Reilly walked to his large safe and lifted out a small chest similar to the ones used by the bank. He removed all of the money contained in it except for the few dollars Bo thought would be enough to keep the robbers interested.

"They have to think they've gotten what they came for," Bo said. He looked at all of the money that had been in the chest. "Sir, may I ask why you keep that much cash here in your home?"

Mr. O'Reilly closed the safe and put the chest next to the table. "This is the payroll for the house, garden and stable staff. They are paid on the same day that the timber camp gets paid."

Daniel shook his head disapprovingly. "With that much money on hand here, you will be high on their list of places to rob. We'd better get the gang now or your home will be their next target."

William wasn't sure about that. "The money's in the safe. They have no way of getting to it."

"You have the combination. What would you do if they put a gun to Rose's head? How fast would you open it, then?" Bo reminded him.

William turned pale at the thought. "I would give them anything they wanted," he admitted. His voice was shaking.

Daniel put his huge hand on William's shoulder. "We're not going to let that happen. This will be finished tomorrow."

At that moment Jacob tapped at the door frame. "Excuse me, Mr. O'Reilly. I have some information for the marshals."

William looked up. "Come in, Jacob. What is it?"

Daniel stepped forward and gestured to Jacob. "What do you have?"

Jacob felt uncomfortable and it showed in the way he fidgeted slightly, unrelaxed, and looked around. He'd never been in Mr. O'Reilly's study before.

"My wife and I were talking earlier," Jacob went on, "and she just remembered something that she had heard those men discussing one evening while they were bringing us here. She heard them speaking about San Francisco. I don't know if that will help. She couldn't hear much more than that. They were walking past our wagon and they moved too far away for her to hear any more. I hope that helps."

Daniel looked back at Bo. "Do you think they were taking my wife to San Francisco?"

William nodded knowingly. "That would be reasonable to think so. There are many wealthy families out there who would pay good money for indentured servants and they would not be as liberal as I am"—he turned back to Jacob—"Jacob, you and your wife take the day off tomorrow. Go into town and enjoy yourselves." He pulled ten dollars out of his pocket and handed them to Jacob. Jacob's eyes opened wide at the sight of the money.

"Thank you, Mr. O'Reilly. Thank you, very much," he said, taking the bills carefully from Mr. O'Reilly's hand. He backed out the door and disappeared into the hall.

Bo looked at Daniel. "That gives us another reason to take care of all of this tomorrow. We've got to get these prisoners back to Kansas and then head out to San Francisco."

William set his jaw. "When you're ready to head west, just let me know. I'll have my personal rail car made available for you. The train will take several days off your trip. You can meet it in Omaha where I'll have it waiting for you."

The thought of being brought much closer to his wife gave Daniel a boost. "Thank you, Mr. O'Reilly. Your offer is very generous." Daniel stepped away from the chess table. "Perhaps we could finish this match tomorrow after we've concluded our efforts."

William nodded in agreement. "Under the circumstances I think that it would be best if we all got a restful night's sleep. I'll have my wagon readied in the morning and I'll intercept the payroll just after it is out of sight of Denver. I'll bring the original chest back here. We can transport it up to the timber camp the following day."

Everyone shook hands as they left the study. Daniel and Bo set out for the cottage to prepare their gear for the morning and William went upstairs to his wife, who was waiting for him.

Marie, who was sitting at her dressing table when William walked in, smiled and turned to face him. There were a set of doors leading out to the balcony on the far side of their bedroom and Marie's dressing table was to the left of the doors with two lit lamps on it; they provided the only light in the room. "What's the reason for the sad look? Did Daniel beat you that badly?" she asked.

William sat on the edge of the bed. "Young Bo insists that he and Marshal Blue can take the five robbers without any help. I'm worried. That's five to two and those odds are not good at all."

Marie walked over to William and knelt down in front of him, taking his hands in hers. "He's a brave and smart young man. I'm sure he knows what he's doing. If he thought he needed your help, I'm sure he would have asked for it."

William shook his head. "Under normal circumstances, I'd say you were right, but how much of an effect is our daughter having on all of this? Is he taking undue chances just to impress her?"

Marie smiled. "Our daughter doesn't need risky heroism to impress her and he knows that. You should have heard the way they were speaking to each other tonight. They seem to already love each other deeply, and they are making plans that go far beyond this house. They are both behaving just the way we would expect. "

William was shocked at what Marie had just said and stared at his wife, astonished. "You listened to their conversation?"

Marie stood up and sat next to William at the edge of the bed. The light pink, over-stuffed down comforter puffed up behind her as she sat. "The doors to my balcony were open and I was sitting at my dressing table brushing my hair. It was too much trouble to get up and close the doors." She stood, pulling back the comforter to expose the matching pale pink sheets. "Come to bed and don't worry so much. It will be much clearer in the morning." Marie and William then got into bed and fell into a deep sleep until morning.

The next morning was especially early for everyone in the house. The sun was just peeking over the plains to the east and making its way onto the facade of the mansion. The kitchen stoves were stoked and the smell of coffee permeated the entire home. Bo and Daniel had saddled their horses and brought them to the front of the house where they secured them. Rose met them at the front door with two cups of coffee. She handed the first cup to Daniel.

"Good morning, Daniel. Did you get a good night's sleep?"

Daniel took the cup from her. "I surely did, Miss Rose." He took a long sip and stepped past her into the main hall.

Rose passed the second cup to Bo. "How did you sleep, Mr. Henry?" Her voice was a little lower and she gave him a sudden light kiss on the cheek when she was sure no one was looking. Bo blushed, took the coffee and started past her. He was embarrassed and responded quickly. "I slept just fine, thank you, Miss Rose. "

They passed into the dining room and sat down to breakfast. When the meal was finished, the entire group went out to the front of the house to find the wagon and Slim waiting for Mr. O'Reilly. Two new Winchesters were propped up in the front seat. Smitty had his handgun strapped low on his hip. "I didn't think it would hurt to have a little extra firepower today," he said, patting this handgun as he spoke.

Bo smiled. "Not today, Slim," Bo said, as he slid onto his saddle. "I doubt you'll see any sign of them that close to town. We'll be on the east side of the trail, at the first ambush point. If they're going to hit the wagon from the bank, that's where they'll do it. Good luck."

Together, Bo and Daniel spun their horses around and headed off to the north and Bo waved to Rose as he looked back over his shoulder. William and Slim pointed the wagon south toward Denver to intercept the payroll shipment. In a half-hour they would meet the wagon.

Meanwhile, Bo and Daniel made a wide sweep to the northeast before they cut back to the west and the tree line. It took them two hours to reach the point where they imagined the robbers would strike. They concealed the horses in the small grove of trees and found a place to watch the trail where they wouldn't be seen. At least another hour would pass before the bank wagon would reach the point where Bo and Daniel were now waiting. Bo pulled a brass telescope from his saddle bag and extended it to its full length. It clicked as each of the three sections came completely out. "I can't see anything, yet. I wouldn't expect to see them until just before the wagon gets here. They're probably sitting back in the trees waiting until the wagon gets closer before they move down," he said, surveying the area where the robbers would be.

By this time, the sun had reached a point high over their heads. Daniel quickly slid over and draped a piece of cloth over the lens of the glass. "That's to keep the sun from reflecting off the glass and giving us away."

Bo looked at the cloth. "I can hardly see through it," he said, then yanked the cloth off.

Daniel took the cloth out of Bo's hand and put the material back on. "With the sun that high in the sky, they'll see the reflection off of our glass before they see us! If they spot us, it's all over. They'll run for sure. Just keep looking in the direction of that large rock they used last time."

Bo kept his eyes focused in the direction of the rocks. He pulled the glass down and rubbed his eyes. "I can't see anything anymore. You take over for a while," Bo said, holding the telescope in one hand for Daniel to take it. Daniel took the glass and began to scan the area slowly side to side, where they expected to see movement. It was another half-hour before Daniel poked Bo.

"I've got them," Daniel said excitedly. "They just slid in behind that massive rock. They'll be hidden from the wagon until it's right on top of them." Bo took the glass to observe what Daniel had just claimed to see and pulled the cloth from it, but Daniel replaced it. "Leave it on," Daniel whispered.

Bo looked through the veiled glass at the massive rock where Daniel had said the thieves were. "I still can't see a damn thing," he said, continuing to look in that direction. "Wait a minute! There's one of their horses. I can just make out the rump of one of their horses. That's got to be them."

It wouldn't be long now before the bank wagon came up the trail. The four armed men were ready to leap out from their hiding places.

Bo shook his head. "I see only four of them. I thought there were five."

Daniel took the glass. "Maybe there was only four to begin with. That should make it a little easier."

Again, Bo shook his head. "There are five. The fifth one is somewhere up in the trees keeping an eye on the whole thing. I can feel him."

While they were waiting, Daniel began to wonder. "You told me about the first time you had to pull your gun. When was the second time?" he asked Bo.

Bo thought about whether he should tell Daniel about the incident and looked at the ground in reflection. "I'd been with the marshal's service about a year," Bo went on. "I was walking down the street late in the afternoon on my way to court. The blinds were pulled down at the bank. I thought that was strange so I crossed the street to take a look. As soon as I opened the door, bullets started flying at me. I had walked into a bank holdup. I pulled my gun and started shooting back. It was over in a heartbeat. I'd killed one of the robbers and wounded the other two. The local sheriff ran in a minute later and I went out back and got sick. I don't know if I got sick because I shot them or because I didn't get shot. I remembered how much it had hurt when I got shot the first time. I don't ever want to get shot again…"

Daniel interrupted Bo when he saw the bank wagon for the first time. "I can see the wagon. It's about five minutes away. Here, take a look," Daniel said, holding the glass out for Bo to take. Bo quickly took the glass from him, then lifted the cloth and watched as the bank wagon approached the rocks. Bo yanked the cloth from the glass and studied every move they made. The four men jumped out brandishing their weapons, stopping the wagon. In two minutes, it was over and the robbers were on their way back up the trail from which they had emerged. Bo visually marked the place where they disappeared into the trees.

"I didn't hear any gunfire so the guards must be all right," Bo said. "Let's get over there and find the robbers' trail."

Bo and Daniel scurried back to Buck and Alala and mounted up, then rode at a strong gallop to the wagon. Bo kept going as Daniel paused for a moment to question the guards. "Are you all right?" he called out to them.

The two men were shaken. "We're fine. Go get them, Marshal," they replied uneasily. Daniel spun Alala around. "Go on up to the timber camp and wait for us there. We'll see you tomorrow."

Alala charged off to catch up to Buck who was at the tree line now. Bo had dismounted for a moment to check the signs the robbers had left. His time as a blacksmith was valuable. He could read every hoof print as though he'd made the shoes himself.

"They're headed straight up the mountain," Bo said as Daniel approached him with Alala. "They're not expecting anyone to follow. Even you could read this trail."

Bo climbed back on Buck and they made their way up the mountain with Daniel and Alala trailing behind. There was no attempt by the robbers to hide where they were headed, it seemed. Bo's only concern was that he would come upon them too quickly. Daniel kept Alala right behind Buck as they moved forward.

"How far up do you think they've gone?" Daniel asked Bo.

Bo turned around in his saddle sharply. "Ssshhh—they could be right in front of us," he said in a low whisper, then leaned over to take a closer look at the trail the gang was leaving. "We've got to be getting close."

After another ten minutes, Bo slid quietly out of his saddle and took Buck's reigns. The mountain was getting steep. He pulled his rifle out and let the reins dangle in a bush. Buck tensed up as Bo slid under Buck's neck. "We'll go on foot from here," Bo said. Daniel slipped off Alala and followed Bo through the trees after securing her. Soon they heard voices coming from a small clearing. Bo signaled for Daniel to move out to the right. Daniel nodded and made his way off to the right making sure he was quiet about it and remained unseen. Bo hunkered down and made his way forward. In a few steps he could make out three of the five men and their horses. He crept a little closer before he made his announcement.

"This is U.S. Marshal Bo Henry! You're all under arrest! Throw down your guns and step out where I can see you," he said in a strong, loud voice. Two of the men had been crouched down trying to start a fire while two others watched. When they heard Bo's voice, the two attempting to light the fire sprang to their feet. All of them spun around to peer into the trees in Bo's direction. The men were not about to surrender to one marshal.

"You are damn brave, coming up here alone to take on five of us, Marshal," one of them said.

Two of the men slipped off to Bo's right. Daniel was in a position enabling him to clearly see four men. He could only make out the fifth man's hat moving back and forth among their horses. Deciding to create some confusion, Daniel decided to call out.

"He's not alone! I've got Boon and Crockett up here with me," he called out unseen, referring to his guns

That announcement took the men by surprise and they began scanning where the voice had come from; one of them pulled his gun and fired in Daniel's direction. Two of the men dove behind a large bush for cover. Their bullets zinged past Daniel's head. One of the bullets chipped off tree bark, which hit Daniel, cutting his cheek. He dove back behind the trees.

"Are you all right?" Bo called out

"We're just fine," Daniel yelled back as more bullets flew at him.

Now there was rifle fire being aimed at Bo; Bo didn't react the way Daniel had. He pulled his gun and began to return fire. The men behind the bush fired at Daniel again. Then, more shots exploded in Bo's direction. There was a sickening thud as one of the bullets hit Bo causing him to spin around and collapse to the ground. Daniel saw the whole scene from his position. He leapt out from behind the tree and cocked both hammers of his shotgun, firing at the bush the two men were hiding behind. The resulting explosion shook the entire forest. The bush vanished. The two men behind it were lifted up and tossed ten feet in the air. Bo managed to get to his feet and stumble into the clearing. He fired twice, hitting one of the remaining two men. The fourth man dropped his gun and went to his knees, hands raised. Daniel rushed in with his second shotgun at the ready. He caught a glimpse of the fifth man mounting his horse. Bo fired at the escaping man and heard him cry out in pain as he rode off. Daniel kept his gun pointed at the kneeling man as he grabbed Bo before he slumped to his knees. Daniel shoved his gun into the kneeling man's face. "Get over here and help," he demanded.

The man hesitated. "My brother's hurt, too. Help him," the man objected.

Daniel was in no mood for any of this. "Get up and over here and help this man or I'll kill both of you where you are!"

The man sensed the seriousness in Daniel's voice so did as he was told. Bo had been shot in the shoulder and was bleeding badly. The robber and Daniel used the shirt sleeves of the dead men to stop the bleeding and then worked on his brother. When they were sure that Bo and the man's bleeding brother were stable, Daniel stood with the right hammer cocked on his shotgun.

"Who are you?" he asked the robber.

The man looked up. "I'm Carl Burser and this is my brother, James. He's hurt real bad. We've got to get him to a doctor."

Daniel grabbed Carl by the shoulder. "Get our horses and bring them over here," Daniel demanded. Carl walked over to the horses and cautiously brought them back toward Daniel. When the horses were still, they lifted Bo and James onto their saddles. Then, they lifted the two dead men and draped their heavy bodies over their own horses. Daniel tied the reins of Carl's horse to Buck.

"Get up there." He gestured with the shotgun for Carl to get into the saddle. Once Carl was mounted, Daniel tied his feet to the stirrups the way he had seen Bo do it. Then, he climbed up on Alala. "We've got a long way to go and if my friend dies, so do you."

Daniel ordered Carl to lead them down off the mountain, to the trail as quickly as possible. Neither of the two wounded men was doing well by the time they reached the O'Reilly's home. When the Yellow Bud staff had seen the horses drawing near, there was a rush of activity to get Bo off his horse and into the house. Jacob jumped on a horse and galloped off to fetch the doctor. Rose was nearly in a panic as they took Bo up to a bedroom on the second floor. James Burser was taken off to the bunk house and Carl was chained up in the stable. Rose hovered over Bo the entire hour it took for the doctor to arrive from Denver with his bag of tools and medicine. When the doctor arrived, he quickly climbed the stairs behind Jacob and excused Rose out of the room to get to work on Bo. After some time, the doctor finally emerged from the room and all those waiting outside, paused anxiously to hear of Bo's fate.

"Miss Rose," the doctor began with a serious look on his face. "He's going to be fine after his shoulder heals. He's lucky. The bullet only chipped the bone. I'm afraid he won't have full use of that arm anymore, though. Keep him in bed for a week or so. Let's let the wound heal. Now, where is the other man I have to see?" Again, Jacob led the doctor, this time to the bunk house to tend to James Burser. The doctor was gone for nearly two hours before he returned to the main house where William met him at the door as he walked in.

"How is your other patient?" William asked.

The doctor frowned. "He's not doing as well. The bullet hit him in the lung. I had to do a lot of cutting to get the bullet out and stop all of the bleeding. He's going to live, but, I'm not sure for how long. Wounds like that can take a man years after they heal. He's in for a hard life."

William followed the doctor out of the main house foyer and onto the front porch to see him out. "Thank you Samuel. I appreciate you coming all this way."

The doctor assured him that it was no trouble at all and went to his horse that one of the staff had secured outside for him during the chaos. Mr. O'Reilly shook the doctors hand after he got up onto his horse.

Suddenly, Jacob appeared before Mr. O'Reilly, running up to the house toward him, holding what appeared to be sacks in one hand. "Mr. O'Reilly, you've got to take a look at this," Jacob said with a sense of urgency. "We just went through the saddlebags of the horses Marshal's Henry and Blue brought in! They're full of money"—he handed the bags over to Mr. O'Reilly—"Marshal Blue should talk to the one we've got down in the stables. He's not making any sense. He keeps babbling about being cheated." William took the bags from Jacob and carried them into the house with Jacob following.

William turned to Kathleen. "Please have Marshal Blue join us in the study and bring us a pot of coffee."

"Yes, sir," she said, turning quickly to go and find Blue. Mr. O'Reilly went to his study to wait.

Soon, Daniel rushed into the room. "What is it? Kathleen said it was very important."

William had dumped all of the money from the saddlebags out on top of his desk. "This isn't anywhere near the amount of money they took from us in those robberies. What the hell did they do with the rest? This can't be even ten percent of it."

Jacob was standing in the door way. "That's all there was Mr. O'Reilly."

Daniel looked down at the heap of money, then stopped to think. "They must have split up what they had. They wouldn't have buried it because they were preparing to leave the territory when we caught up to them. One man got away but he wouldn't have had that much on him."

"The man down in the stable keeps saying he was cheated," Jacob spoke up. "What's that all about?"

Daniel turned toward the door where Jacob stood. "We believed there was someone on the inside giving out information. Let's go see if we can find out who that someone is, and the name of the gang member who escaped."

Daniel led William and Jacob out of the house and down to the stable where Carl was chained up. Carl watched as he men approached him.

William grabbed Carl firmly him by the shirt. "What did you do with the rest of the money? Who was the fifth man with you?"

Carl pulled back. "How did you know where we were? It was that lousy snitch, wasn't it?"

Daniel jumped in before William had a chance to respond. "We never found out who he is. He betrayed you by sending us a note informing us of your location and when you were going to ambush the next payroll. Who is he? He deserves to get what you're going to get."

At this point, Carl didn't hesitate to name the fifth accomplice. "It was Blackman," he went on. "He swapped out the chests before they were loaded on the wagons. He told us what was in the chests was our expense money and he would split up the rest of the take with us tomorrow. I figured he was planning to keep all of it for himself! I knew it! That no good son of a bitch! James and I were going to Canada to live like kings on our share."

William took a half-step back. He couldn't believe what he'd just heard. "Tate Blackman's been with me for years. How could he do this to me...to us?"

Daniel reached out and grabbed Carl's shirt and vest and picked him up completely off the ground with one hand. Carl was now nose to nose with Daniel. "Who was the fifth man?" It was more of a growl than a request.

Carl gulped. "It was Roman Christian...his name is Roman Christian. We met him in Kansas City a while back."

Daniel dropped Carl with a thud, then turned back to William. "We've got to get into town tonight and arrest Blackman before he figures out that we have his gang," Daniel said, then turned to Jacob. "Did you say anything to anyone about what has happened here?"

Jacob shook his head. "No, I went straight to the doctor's. I told him that someone had been hurt bad out at the house. He never had a chance to talk to anyone either. We came straight here."

Daniel turned back to William. "I think the three of us can handle Mr. Blackman. Let's get this finished."

Deciding to confront Mr. Blackman, Daniel, Mr. O'Reilly, and Jacob, quickly ventured out on horseback. In a half-hour they reached Blackman's home. When they rode up, it was dark outside but candles were lit from inside the modest house. They dismounted their horses and William knocked on the door. Blackman opened it.

"Mr. O'Reilly, what are you doing here? Is there a problem at the bank?" he asked, surprised to see his boss standing there.

William stepped into the front hall of the house. "There's been another robbery," he said with bitterness in his voice. "We caught the men and I know everything. How could you do this? Tate, I've treated you like a brother all of these years! If you needed more money, all you had to do was ask."

Daniel stepped around William. "Mr. Tate Blackman, you are under arrest for four counts of bank robbery." He spun Blackman around, pulled out shackles from his side pocket and snapped them over Blackman's wrists. Blackman was not a large man and he knew he had no chance if he tried to pull away from Daniel's grip.

"I've worked for you for years and I have watched you become more wealthy every day while I lived like this," Blackman said, angrily. "I was tired! I wanted what you have. I wanted more!"

Blackman sank to his knees and Daniel hauled him up. It was over. Daniel and William found the remainder of the stolen money in Blackman's home. A half-hour later they had Blackman locked up in jail in Denver and the men were able to end a rather successful day. They returned safely to Yellow Bud and checked in on Bo before retiring to meet the next day. The next morning, Daniel was back in Denver with Carl Burser. Once Daniel had him secured behind bars, he headed to the telegraph office to report to Judge Roads. Once there, he sent a message off to Judge Roads explaining what had occurred and waited for an answer. The judge responded that he wanted a full report of Bo's condition, details on the arrests that Daniel had made and that he would be sending the prison wagon as soon as he could get a message to the driver. It seemed that the wagon couldn't get to Denver to move Carl Burser for a week or more. Moving his brother, James, was going to take even longer than that. His gunshot injuries were going to take weeks to heal before he could leave Yellow Bud. Daniel spent his time taking care of his prisoner in Denver and the one he had at Yellow Bud. *I'm going to cut a deep rut in the road between Denver and Yellow Bud if I keep this up,* he thought. The wagon arrived eight days later. The prisoners, Carl Burser and Tate

Blackman were loaded onto the wagon and continued on their way to Kansas City where a trial awaited them. The driver delivered a message to Daniel before going on his way. "The judge told me to tell you that you and Bo are to take the train to Omaha and the steamer to Kansas City to testify at the trial for these prisoners. He seems to think it will be easier on Bo that way," the driver relayed.

Daniel and the driver shook hands and Daniel stepped back from the wagon. The driver smiled. "I think I'm going to keep your secret from the judge. I want to be there the first time he sets eyes on you," the driver said, as he ushered the wagon forward. "You've got to be the biggest man I've ever seen. Have a safe trip, Marshal."

Daniel watched as the wagon rolled out of Denver and stood watching it until it was out of sight. Daniel thought to himself. *Yes. That first meeting is one I'm looking forward to as well.*

Dan Bradford

Chapter 7
The Long Ride Home

For the first few days after Bo and Daniel's confrontation with Mr. Blackman, Bo lay, unmoving in a guest room at Yellow Bud. Days had passed but Bo hadn't opened his eyes and Rose never left his side, refusing to let anyone else take care of him. After a couple more days, he finally opened his eyes—just briefly. When he managed to open them fully, he opened them to Rose's beautiful face looking down at him. It had been a week since the doctor had operated on Bo's shoulder and he spoke for the first time. Rose's worried frown gave way to a glowing smile when she heard his voice.

"Have I died?" Bo asked, gazing at her.

She reached out and took his hand. "What would make you say something like that? You are not dead and I am so glad." She squeezed his hand.

Bo smiled. "I kept seeing an angel looking down at me. She was the most beautiful angel in the whole world. She kept trying to get me to drink some water. It had to be an angel."

Rose blushed. "It was me, silly. I've been so worried about you. You've been unconscious for days. I had to persuade you to drink water. Now that you are awake, I'll have some chicken broth brought up for you.

We also have a warm loaf of bread just out of the oven. I'll bring you a slice of that with fresh honey on it."

Bo nodded at her carefully so as not to move his shoulder too much. "That sounds very good," he said. "All of a sudden, I'm hungry. Could I have the bread and broth with a cup of tea?"

Rose was pleased to hear Bo asking for something to eat. The doctor had told them that he must eat to get his strength back. "I'll go down and have a tray sent up," she said, moving away from Bo. Giving his hand one last squeeze, she left the room. From the other side of the door, Bo could hear her speaking with someone in the hall. "He's awake, you can go in."

Daniel eased the door open and stepped in. He was wearing his best outfit and carried a package tucked under his arm. Bo attempted to sit up, but the pain in his shoulder was too much and it drove him back to the mattress. He tried to muffle the groan as he lay back down. "Take it easy, Bo," Daniel gently admonished him. "You've got a lot of work to do before you use that arm."

Daniel placed the package down on a chair that was set next to the bed. Bo rolled his head over to look at the package. "What's in the package?" he asked.

Knowing that Bo wouldn't be able to open the package himself, he picked the package up again. Daniel opened it and pulling the contents out of the heavy brown paper, held up a new set of clothes for Bo to see. "Everything you were wearing when I brought you back was ruined. Most of it had to be cut off, so Miss Rose and I went to town while you were resting and picked up a few new things for you."

Bo gave him a grateful look and reached out to Daniel's hand with his good arm. He had to know. "What happened to our prisoners?"

Daniel set the clothes at the foot of the bed and took the seat next to the bed. "Carl Burser and Tate Blackman were shipped off to Kansas City yesterday. We're going to move James Burser from here to the jail by the end of the week, maybe longer. The doc can keep a better eye on him there. He's not in good shape. The other two were dead at the clearing."

Bo was a little fuzzy on the details. "I don't remember shooting them. What happened? How did we end up with Mr. Blackman as a prisoner?"

Daniel lowered his eyes. "One of them shot you and I…shot both of them."

Bo looked down at the shotguns on Daniel's hips. "Did you unload both barrels at once?"

Daniel nodded. "I forgot. I cocked both hammers at the same time. It was a mess. I got sick after it happened. Carl Burser and I loaded everyone on the horses and brought you all back here. You nearly didn't make it. You were out for a week. The doc's still not sure if James Burser is going to make it. We got Carl to admit that Blackman was part of the plan so we went into town that night and arrested him."

A few minutes later Rose arrived with a tray of broth, honey bread and tea. Daniel said his good-bye and slipped out the door so that Bo could rest. Placing the tray down on a small table she had set up at the foot of the bed, Rose proceeded to feed Bo. She held the bowl of broth up for him and spooned—carefully—steamy and flavorful mouthfuls to him to sip. Rose lovingly dabbed the corners of his mouth before offering him the tea and honey bread. When he was finished, he slid down a little further in the covers and closed his eyes. "I think I'd like to take a nap."

Rose collected the spoon, bowl, and tea cup and returned them back to the tray then, leaned over him and wiped his forehead with a cool damp cloth. Bo was in and out of consciousness during the next three days. He slept for long periods of time with Rose sitting and watching him. When he was awake, he'd take a little broth and then drift off to sleep again.

The doctor visited at the end of the week. By that time, Bo had been recovering over two weeks. "Well, Bo. How are you doing today?" the doctor asked, observing him and checking his pulse.

Bo struggled to turn his head around to face the doctor. "I feel better today, better than I have since I was brought here."

The doctor extended his hand out to Bo for him to grab. "Do you feel like standing up?" the doctor asked. "I think you should begin taking short walks. At first, just around the bed, and in a couple of days I'd like to see you go downstairs. Your legs are weak from your being laid up for so long. I'm going to have Daniel get you up a couple times a day. I don't think you'd fall with his big hands helping you. We've got to get the rest of your body back into shape before we can start on your shoulder." He turned toward the door. "Daniel, would you come in here now?"

Daniel slipped into the room. "Let's get Bo up off the bed and take a look out the window. That would be a good start." Daniel slipped an arm around Bo's waist and Bo put his right hand on Daniel's shoulder as best as he could.

"Let's give this a try," Daniel whispered in Bo's ear. Daniel lifted Bo up off the bed and stood him up. Bo's legs were shaky but he made it to the window and back without any problems.

Once Bo returned back on the bed he looked up at the doctor. "That was farther than I thought."

The doctor smiled. "That's why we have to take it easy. You haven't used your legs in over two weeks. Take it easy and you'll do just fine."

Over the following days, they did take it easy and Bo made great progress. Ten days later Daniel came into Bo's room before lunch.

"I have someone downstairs who has been looking forward to seeing you," Daniel said to Bo. "Do you think you can make it down the stairs?" Bo nodded. "You're going to have to help me get dressed. I can't go downstairs like this. Who's down stairs?" Daniel didn't answer, he just smiled.

Daniel helped Bo into his new set of clothes. Among them was a new smoking jacket from Mr. O'Reilly. Bo took one look at it. "What is this? I've never seen a man wear anything so fancy."

Daniel helped him ease his right arm into the jacket and the other side over Bo's left shoulder and sling. "William thought you needed something to keep your good arm covered," Daniel said, looking over Bo to make sure his clothing was put on properly.

Bo grasped Daniel's arm to stand up and then made his way down the stairs to meet his mystery visitor. Daniel followed closely behind him. When they reached the bottom, Marie met them.

"Marshal Henry, it's so good to see you up and around. Just don't do too much too quickly," Marie said and then reached over quickly and helped Daniel get Bo out the front door and to the porch.

Bo looked down the porch stairs at an amazing sight; there was Buck in his halter with Rose holding the rope. Daniel couldn't get Bo down the stairs fast enough for either Bo or Buck. It was clear the two friends had missed each other. Rose slipped Bo an apple as he walked up to Buck. The big stallion took the apple gently from Bo's hand and then pressed his forehead against Bo's chest. Bo scratched him for some time. As Bo pulled back, he looked over his shoulder at Rose. "How did you ever get him to let you bring him up here?"

Rose moved closer to them. "Buck and I have become good friends. We've been going for walks the past couple of days. I won't even try to saddle him, but, he doesn't seem to mind the halter."

The afternoon meetings and apple became a regular part of their day for the next week. Each day Bo pushed himself a little further. Eventually, he removed the arm sling and began stretching his arm. By the end of the third week Bo decided it was time to get back in the saddle and Daniel helped Bo saddle Buck. By the end of the following week Bo was feeling more like himself again.

"I think I should get back to some practice. It's been weeks since I've used my guns," he said.

Rose wasn't so sure. "It's only been four weeks and I don't think you should be doing that now."

But Bo insisted on getting back into shape. First, he went out behind the stables and practiced his draw without shooting. Daniel stood behind him and watched. The speed wasn't there the way it had been, but, all the moves were right. Bo convinced Rose and William to let him go out further and practice. The following day Rose made a lunch and added a few beverages to the basket. William, Rose and Daniel went along to see what Bo could do now that he seemed to be back on his feet.

The four of them rode about a mile north of the house to a location that seemed perfect for Bo's practice. When they had settled on the place, they dismounted and tied up the horses then started in to a little clearing that was just ahead from where they tied the horses. Daniel picked up pine cones along the way as they passed through the trees. Mr. O'Reilly carried the lunch basket under one arm and Rose followed behind Bo. Once they reached the clearing, Bo stopped to talk to William and Rose as Daniel placed the pine cones at various locations in the clearing. The clearing was about two hundred feet long and one hundred feet wide. It was easy to see it had been a popular place for elk and deer to bed down. The ankle deep grass was matted flat. The heavy pine forest encircled them. Daniel walked back to Bo and stood facing him. William and Rose stood back. Daniel's eyes glimmered with excitement and he braced himself for the noise. "Go!" he yelled.

Bo spun around to face the pine cones and drew his Colt. He fired three shots, hitting three of the pine cones and sending them flying backward. He hesitated for a moment and then fired a fourth shot, hitting the last pine cone. As the fourth shot was fired, Daniel threw two more pine cones in the air over Bo's head. Bo dipped slightly to his right and fired two more shots, hitting both targets before they reached the ground. Bo exchanged the empty Colt with the loaded one, pulling the loaded Colt from its left holster. Though he had managed to hit his targets, Bo's left arm was still giving him problems. He could feel where the doctor had cut into his arm as he shot at his targets. The result of the damage made his movements rough and slightly uncomfortable

Daniel laughed. "You're getting slow. You allowed the last two cones to nearly hit the ground and you never saw the last stationary pine cone."

Bo took exception to Daniel's comments. "You hid that last pine cone next to the tree trunk and you threw those much closer to the ground than you usually do."

Before Bo had a chance to complain any further, Daniel threw three more pine cones over Bo's head causing Bo to spin around and draw his second Colt. Bo fired three shots in rapid succession and hit all three targets. Before he had a chance to recover, Daniel threw three more, this time in a slightly different direction. There were three more shots and three more hits.

Bo turned around to look at Daniel. "You're getting cagy."

Daniel smiled. "Now that's more like it. In a day or two I'll have you back to where you were before you forgot to duck."

William hadn't said a word until now. He watched a few feet, safely behind Bo, as Bo tracked and shot at his targets. "That was slow? That was the fastest thing I've ever seen! How did you ever learn to do that?"

Daniel looked over at Bo who was putting his Colts back into their holsters. "That's his work speed. He does all of his trick shooting with this Winchester," Daniel said, picking up the rifle and then handing it to Bo.

Bo took the rifle with one hand, then turned it on its side to check the weapon and prepare to shoot. "Just two this time, Daniel."

Daniel tossed two more pine cones up in the air, high over Bo. Bo shot twice and hit the first one just as he'd done before; the second one was a clear miss. He lowered the rifle and handed it to Daniel. His movements were jagged and he winced in pain.

"I'm not ready. The recoil is too much for my shoulder," Bo said. The pain in his shoulder was obvious to everyone. Rose rushed to his side and helped him sit on a downed tree. William brought over the basket with the lunch and beverages, recognizing that it was a great time to break for lunch. They unloaded the basket's contents, sat eating and talked for an hour before they started back toward the horses. They secured their belongings and mounted their horses to travel back to Yellow Bud.

When they reached the house after securing the horses in the stable, they found a message waiting for Bo from Judge Roads just inside the door on a silver tray resting on a table. Bo took the message to read it and then proceeded to tell them what was written. "The prisoner wagon will be here the day after tomorrow for James Burser," he said. "We must have our prisoner ready to go. We'll all be leaving in three days."

This was not what Rose wanted to hear. The last several weeks had been wonderful for both her and Bo. They had shared so many discussions about their future together, but his leaving so soon was not something that Rose had in her plans.

"Father, tell him he can't go," Rose pleaded with her father. "It's too soon. He's not ready to travel half way across country." She looked at Bo and then back at her father, but William didn't know what to say and paused for a moment.

"Rose, Bo has his duties as a marshal," he stammered. "He knows what he has to do. We can't interfere with that. If he says he has to go, then that's what he has to do. We don't want to make it any harder on him. I'm sure he'd rather stay here than make that trip."

Rose began to cry as she stomped off up the stairs and up to her room. "It's not fair," she cried.

Bo looked at Daniel. "Take Alala and ride into town in the morning. Make sure James Burser is ready to travel. Go over to the dry goods store and make arrangements for our supplies. We'll pick them up when we get our prisoner." Bo's head was hanging down with sadness. He turned and went up the stairs to his room to lay down. He knew that the next two days were going to be very difficult on everyone.

Daniel watched Bo go up the stairs, then turned to William. "It's as hard on Bo as it is on Rose. I know he doesn't want to leave."

William just lowered his eyes and then, walked toward his study. But before he entered the study, he turned his head to look back over his shoulder at Daniel. "Daniel, would you like a quick game before supper?" he asked.

Daniel gladly joined him.

The next morning, Daniel met the prisoner wagon and the driver in Denver as Bo had instructed him. Marshal Don Young had driven the wagon from Santa Fe with two other prisoners. His tour with the Marshals Service was as long as that of Judge Roads. Before becoming a marshal, he had been a hunter in Alaska and even tried his hand as a mountain man in Montana, as well as hunting buffalo on the plains. Judge Roads had given him some purpose in his life and he'd been a marshal ever since. He had a wonderful sense of humor and stories that were never ending. *This is going to be an interesting trip,* Daniel thought after meeting him and making his way back toward Yellow Bud to relink with Bo.

The next three days were so quiet at Yellow Bud that even the staff sensed the sadness creep over everyone. Bo and Rose spent as much time together as they could. Bo also spent part of everyday behind the stables where he exercised both of his arms, hoping to regain mobility of them. The trip to Kansas City was not going to be easy and Bo knew this. Over the three days, Rose was in the stable every morning with Buck's apple; even Buck could sense the changes going on around him.

The morning for Bo and Daniel to continue on their journey had finally come. As hard as it was to hold back, there were tears in everyone's eyes. Bo gave Rose a kiss as he stood out front of the main house, close to Buck. The words he wanted to say to her stuck in his throat. He put his hands on her arms. Rose could see he was having a difficult time getting the words out.

"I know it's hard, but I want to hear it," she whispered to Bo, squeezing his arm.

Bo fought his hesitation. "I think you are the most beautiful thing I have ever seen," he blurted out. "My heart is pounding and I can't catch my breath every time I hear you speak. I've never felt like this before."

Rose looked down, trying to focus on the toe of one of her white shoes as it peeked out from under the hem of her pink dress. It was embroidered with red roses and green leaves. "Would it make you feel any better if I told you I feel the same way?" she asked.

Bo felt his heart skip a beat. "Rose, I've only known you for a short time and I already can't imagine what it will be like now that I have to leave." Taking her hand in his, he pressed her hand to his lips, then Rose slipped her arms around Bo's waist and put her cheek against his chest.

"I know it's only been a short time, but I feel like I've known you my whole life. I don't want you to leave—ever!" Rose lamented.

Bo moved his hands to Rose's shoulders and pushed her away gently. "We've got to get back to Kansas City with the prisoner."

Rose lifted his hand to her lips one more time to kiss it sweetly and slid her arm around his waist as they turned toward the horses. "I know," she said.

He gently shifted her backward so he could get into the saddle. He placed his hand on the top of her head as she gave his leg a hug. Before she moved back to allow Buck and Bo to pass, she slipped one last apple out of her white apron and fed it to Buck. Bo pulled back on Buck's reins before he turned toward the trail for Denver.

"I'll be back soon," he said, then waved as he turned Buck and rode off. Daniel, who had been hanging back on Alala so that Rose and Bo could say their good-byes, shook William's hand. "Keep practicing your chess moves," he said to William as he watched Bo ride into the distance. He knew that it was now his turn to go. "We'll be back before you know it." He nudged Alala and caught up to Bo. Soon, they were out of sight.

Rose ran past her father, sobbing and went up to her room with her mother not far behind. They knew it was going to be a long day at Yellow Bud.

Meanwhile, the ride to Denver was quiet; neither man could say much to ease the pain that was caused by their departure. When Bo and Daniel finally reached the jail, they found that Marshal Young had already loaded the prisoners and was sitting on the wagon seat waiting for them. Bo smiled when he realized who it was. "Don, what the hell are you doing here?" Bo asked, nearing Marshal Young. "I thought the judge had you on desk duty until you retired."

Don smiled. "I told him you were going to need special care on the way back, so he let me do the driving. I didn't think it was going to take you all morning to get here or I'da come up to the house to get you. Besides, I wanted to meet this new deputy you hired. The judge hasn't talked about anything else since he found out"—he looked over at Daniel —"you don't do anything small do you, Bo?"

Bo looked first at Don and then back at Daniel. "I suppose the two of you have already had a laugh or two at my expense, haven't you?"

Daniel smiled. "Just a couple."

Don snapped the reigns to get the horses moving. "Let's get going," he said as the horses began trotting forward. The wagon gave a lurch and they were on their way. "The judge hasn't hung anyone in a while. I know he's anxious to see these three back in Kansas City."

Daniel and Bo flanked the wagon while the pack mule was strung out behind. The three prisoners bounced around inside the wagon as they traveled to Kansas City. James Burser moaned every time the wagon hit a bump in the trail. After the first day of travel, Marshal Young rode Alala and Buck followed alongside him while Daniel drove the team with Bo sitting next to him. Bo took out the books that Daniel had bought. They read the books together to help Bo learn what was inside. As Bo read from each book, he would sometimes pause to ask Daniel for an explanation. Refining Bo's ability to read became the norm rather than the exception for the rest of the trip back to Kansas City.

After more than two weeks of traveling trails between Denver and Kansas City, the prison wagon finally pulled up in front of the Kansas City courthouse and jail. The courthouse was an impressive three story building constructed of dark brown brick. The courtroom was a tall single story section that extended out to the north. There were eight steps from the hitching post to the top of the curved stairs. Bo had counted them many times on his way into that building. The jail was a single-level building built just to the south of the courthouse and connected by a tunnel. All the windows on both buildings were crowned with archways and a large matching archway extended over the massive oak doors in the middle of the landing at the top of the curved stairs. Judge Roads was out front to meet them. When they had slowed to a halt, jail guards opened the wagon doors from behind and took the two prisoners into the jail and James Burser was taken to see the doctor. Bo, Daniel, and Marshal Young secured their horses and mule as Judge Roads approached them.

Judge Roads looked over at Don. "Don, go up to the marshals' office and draw your pay. I put a little something extra in it for you for taking this trip."

Don smiled. "Thanks, Judge. I appreciate it," he said, then disappeared into the building.

Judge Roads turned back to Bo and Daniel. "Bo, I've had no less than two messages come in every day for the past three days for you from someone named Rose. I suggest that you get over to the telegraph office and send Rose a message that you arrived here in one piece. Go! Get out of here, and when you get back I want you in my office. We have to discuss what a U.S. Marshal can and can't do in the field."

"Yes, Judge," Bo smiled, then made his way toward the telegraph office, which was nearby.

When Bo was out of sight, Judge Roads turned to face Daniel. "You must be U.S. Deputy Marshal Daniel Blue," he asked, extending his hand toward Daniel. "I'm glad to finally meet you." He took Daniel by the arm and started leading him up the courthouse stairs into the court building. "I must admit, that when I first heard about Bo hiring you, I wasn't very impressed with what my young marshal had done. After I read your report about the arrest in Denver and how the whole thing happened with the Burser brothers, I'm damn glad he had you there. The job is yours as long as you want it, Marshal."

The lobby of the courthouse was a wide, open expanse, ringed with government offices. The tall dark oak doors to the courtroom were off to the right. There was a small desk to the left where the guard, Big Bill, was sitting. He kept an eye on everyone who came and went from the courthouse. The hall directly ahead led back to the office used by the marshals for their paperwork and to the judge's chambers used by the judges when the court was in session.

The stairs on the right hand wall had seventeen steps. These were another set that Bo had counted many times. They led up to the second floor where Judge Roads, his prosecuting attorney and staff kept their offices. The stairs continued up another seventeen steps up to Judge Driscoll's office and spaces for his attorney and staff to work in. Bo had been up there only once or twice since he had become a marshal. He never seemed to be able to get past Judge Roads' office.

Judge Roads and Daniel walked through the lobby and up the wide oak stairway to the landing on the second floor until they reached Judge Roads' office. They entered and sat down. Judge Roads took his seat behind his desk and Daniel sat down opposite him on the other side of his desk.

Daniel leaned forward. "Sir, I don't know if Bo has had a chance to tell you about my wife and her abduction with the others from my neighborhood in Chicago…"

Judge Roads nodded. "I've heard about the whole thing, son, that's why I'm giving you these seven blank warrants. I want you and Bo to leave as soon as you've finished with the Burser trial. This is your top priority." Judge Roads placed the warrants on the desk and tapped his index finger on them. "I've sent word ahead to all of the local jurisdictions to keep an eye out for these men. We'll find them and try them in my court. They won't get away with this."

They were discussing the situation for a few more minutes when Bo knocked on the door.

"Come in, Bo, and have a seat," the judge called out and Bo entered the room. "I've been talking to Daniel about the situation with his wife.

I've moved the Burser trial up on my calendar so that the two of you can leave as soon as it is complete. I don't need you here for the Blackman trial; I've already summoned all the other witnesses who are going to testify. I just have to find an attorney to represent them. Everyone knows they killed two of the marshals who were transporting them. None of the lawyers in Kansas City want anything to do with them. There is one thing that we have to take care of tomorrow afternoon, however. We need a formal swearing-in ceremony for our new marshal. I'll send the word out to court staff, the marshals' office and the sheriff's office and have them at the court house at three. I trust the two of you have better looking clothes? We can't have our newest marshal dressed in rags for his swearing-in ceremony. Be back here at three tomorrow and be dressed for the occasion. Now get out of here and have some fun tonight. That's an order, Daniel. You can tell me about those shotguns tomorrow."

Bo and Daniel both stood up and responded with, "Yes, Judge," in unison. They then turned, stepped toward the door and closed the door behind them.

Bo looked at Daniel. "Welcome to the U.S. Marshals' Service," he said. They shook hands, left the building, and took the horses and the mule down to the stables for feed and water. After, they headed to the bunk house for a bath and some rest. As they walked around the town, they noticed more than a few eyebrows raised with Daniel's arrival. They all knew Bo and not a word was said. For the most part, Daniel was accepted as one of the marshals which became evident when Bo and Daniel had dinner with the other marshals later that night.

The next day was filled with reviewing reports at the courthouse building. Daniel and Bo reviewed the reports that accompanied the prisoners when they had been brought in and those that had been prepared for the upcoming trial. Before they knew it, three o'clock had crept up on them. They moved across the hall to the courtroom which was filled with Judge Driskill, his staff, lawyers and the marshals who were in town. The court room was a tall, single story area with wide, heavy oak doors. As Bo and Daniel approached the doors to the courtroom, the bailiff smiled and reached for the door. "Good afternoon, Marshals. Everyone else is here. Let's get you in here and get things started.

Bo extended his hand to the bailiff. "Hello, Tim." They shook hands as Bo and Daniel went through the open doors. There were five rows made up of five chairs on each side of the aisle. In front of the chairs was a heavy, dark oak railing with a single gate that squeaked on its hinges as Tim made his way toward the front of the room. He scowled and looked down at it as he passed and thought, *I've got to get that fixed.*

In front of the railing were two large, dark oak tables with four matching chairs at each. The judge's bench was in the middle of the room at the front. There was one step on either side of the bench. To the right of the bench were two chairs. One was for testimony and the second was a padded chair for Tim.

The jury box was to the right of Tim's chair and it extended from the railing to the front of the room. Tim took his place to the right of Judge Roads, picked up his staff and bounced it off the floor as he announced loudly, "All rise for his honor, Judge Henry Roads!" Everyone in the room stood. Judge Roads looked over at Tim and scowled. "I'll get the gate fixed this afternoon, your honor," Tim whispered back.

Judge Roads tapped his gavel. "You may all be seated," he said. Judge Roads waved to Daniel as he and Bo came in. "Come up here, young man. You too, Marshal Henry. This was all your idea. I want you to stand next to Daniel while we swear him in."

The ordeal caused Bo to recall his own swearing in. Sadly, there had been no one to stand with him on that special day. "Yes, Judge," Bo said, then approached him with Daniel. The gate in the railing at the front of the court squeaked as Bo went through and took his place. He stood alongside Daniel facing the raised bench in the courtroom. Before the audience, Judge Roads recited the official oath for Daniel. At the end, he added a few extra sentences making Bo responsible for training Daniel in all of the duties required of a U.S. Marshal. When he had finished speaking, he peered over his bench, first at Daniel, who responded, "I do", to the oath, then he looked at Bo. "I will," Bo responded.

The judge smiled. "Then I pronounce you, Washington Daniel Blue, the newest deputy U.S. marshal of the Marshals Service. Congratulations, Deputy Marshal Blue," Judge Roads said, handing Daniel's badge to Bo. Bo took the badge and pinned it onto Daniel's chest.

Marshal Young jumped up in the audience. "Yahoo!" he shouted. Everyone in the room stood, shouted their approval and applauded. Judge Roads pounded his gavel and the crowd sat down.

"This is still a court of law," Judge Roads said sternly, looking out at the audience. "I want anyone involved in the Burser trial in this court room at nine a.m. tomorrow"—he paused for a moment—"the first round is on me at Casey's. Court is adjourned." His gavel struck the bench once more and he stepped down to shake Daniel's hand.

Those in the court made their way out of the building and down the street to Casey's where the marshals gathered for drinks and a good meal whenever they were in town. The saloon had also hosted the celebration for more than one new marshal in the past. When Bo and Daniel had arrived and found a stool to sit on, each member of their group came over to Daniel and welcomed him to the Service. Many had heard about the twin shotguns that Daniel carried from talk around town. Daniel pulled them out and broke them open when they asked. One by one, the marshals examined the guns with admiration. There were also more than a few jokes all in good fun about Daniel's bowler hat. Daniel really felt like part of the team—something he hadn't felt before.

After a couple of beers for Bo and coffee for Daniel, the group made their way to a table for supper. At the end of their meal, they were served a plate of apple cobbler. Bo took a bite and somehow it didn't taste the same after having the peach cobbler at Yellow Bud. Daniel noticed the sadness creep over his friend and he knew why. Bo and Daniel finished their meal, bid everyone goodbye, and retired to the bunk house for the night.

The next morning before nine, Bo and Daniel were seated in Judge Roads' court, waiting for the Burser trial to begin. The trial for the Burser brothers lasted three days and Bo and Daniel testified on the second day. Each day when court was recessed, Bo would hurry over to the telegraph office to pick up a message from Rose and answer her.

On the third and final trial day, the jury took only an hour to deliberate before they returned back into the courtroom with their verdict. The foreman took the slip from a jury member and passed it to Judge Roads. After the judge reviewed it, he nodded at the foreman who then approached the bench to read the verdict aloud. The foreman stood up straight and began. "We the jury, find James and Carl Burser guilty of all charges."

Those in the courtroom became unsettled and Judge Roads pounded his gavel to settle the noise erupting from the people in his court. The Burser brothers stood quietly. They knew what was going to happen next.

The judge leaned forward over his bench. "I cannot describe how much contempt I have for the two of you," he said, looking at the brothers directly. "You have taken the lives of two U.S. marshals, two of the best men I have ever known, and nearly killed a third. You have caused more pain for these families than I care to discuss. The law says I can hang the two of you at my discretion. I don't feel that hanging is enough punishment for what you have done, so it is the order of this court that you be remanded to the prison at Jefferson City for hard labor...for the rest of your natural lives without the possibility of parole. Take the prisoners away." He pounded his gavel twice and stood up. "This court is adjourned."

The guards dragged the Burser brothers out of the courtroom and over to the jail. The brothers would begin their trip to Jefferson City in the morning. Everyone else in the courtroom sat stunned by the judge's pronouncement.

Later that day, Judge Roads instructed a clerk to find Bo and Daniel to bring them into his office. Within an hour, the clerk returned with Bo and Daniel and sent them into Judge Roads' office.

"I'm sure the two of you want to get started as soon as possible," Judge Roads said as the men entered and took seats. "I've sent word ahead to Omaha so you can board the transcontinental railroad there. It will take weeks off your journey. When you're ready to come back, send me a message and I'll get you booked for the return trip. You can leave tomorrow if you want."

The idea stirred Daniel who was eager to get on course with finding his wife. "What do you think, Bo? Can we be ready by tomorrow?"

Bo shrugged his shoulders. "I don't see why not. It's going to take us the better part of a week to get to Omaha." Bo looked at Judge Roads. "How long will it take us to get to California?"

The judge thought about that for a moment, turning the calculations over in his mind. "I'm not sure. It depends on how many stops they make and how long they take at each layover. I would think that it will take you at least a day to get from Omaha to Cheyenne. I'd say another four days to get to Sacramento." Bo and Daniel sat, looking at each other. Daniel was amazed.

"We can travel more than half way across this country in five days?" he asked.

The judge nodded. "I'm not sure about that, but that would be my guess."

Bo stood up. "Let's start getting ready. It's going to take us that long to get to Omaha."

Daniel stood and they rushed out of the judge's office to prepare for their next adventure. They spent the rest of the day packing and drawing supplies for the long ride ahead. Early the next morning, Judge Roads stood outside the bunkhouse as they eased themselves up into their saddles. "You boys be careful and don't either of you get shot this time," he said, as Bo and Daniel prepared to embark for Omaha.

Daniel reached down from Alala and shook the judge's hand. "Thank you for everything, judge. I appreciate everything you've done for me."

Judge Roads smiled. "You can pay me back by bringing those kidnappers to my court for justice." He stood back, allowing the men to go.

Bo and Daniel spun their horses around and headed off north. It was going to be a long hard ride and the weather was getting worse around this time of year. Before long, there would be snow. Not having the pack mule with them on this trip meant cold nights on the ground. First there was snow, then there was a heavy north wind stirring up the dust and dirt and it was always in their faces. There were no breaks and no study time on this trip. Bo couldn't remember a harder five day ride. The thought of Rose was all that kept him going.

Chapter 8
Omaha

It was a cold, gray afternoon with snowflakes drifting down when they finally reached the train station in Omaha. A stove in the middle of the station was keeping the place warm along with a fresh pot of coffee that was available for the patrons who came through. Bo and Daniel took a pair of tin cups and helped themselves to it. The cups warmed their hands as the coffee warmed them inside. The trip from Kansas had been uneventful with nothing but the flat prairie to look at. Bo and Daniel passed the time with Daniel giving Bo math and reading lessons. Bo's thoughts of Rose haunted his dreams. Shortly after they arrived, Bo went into the empty Omaha station and checked on the next departure time for Cheyenne. He walked up to the ticketing booth and introduced himself. From the clerk working in the ticketing booth, he learned there wouldn't be another train until the next day.

Hearing of Bo and Daniel's arrival from the ticket booth clerk, the station master approached the window to speak with Bo. The station master had received a telegram from Judge Roads two days prior to their arrival. "I've got your tickets right here, Marshal Henry. You're traveling with us all the way to Sacramento. The judge has arranged for you to stay at the Omaha Queen Hotel for the night. You can put your animals up at the stable across the street for the night. The hotel has a good dining room. You'll like it there."

Bo reappeared on the platform to give the news to Daniel. "We're going to be spending the night here. The train will be leaving here around ten in the morning. The judge has us booked in the hotel for the night. Let's get the horses taken care of and see if we can't get a hot bath." Daniel followed Bo across the street to the livery stable.

An hour later they were in the Omaha Queen Hotel having their hot baths. They dressed and met in the hall before going down for dinner. Daniel watched Bo moving his left arm and rubbing his shoulder. "Are you all right? It looks like your shoulder is giving you some problems," he asked.

Bo shrugged. "It's nothing that a big plate of warm peach cobbler wouldn't cure." Daniel noted that Bo had said peach and not apple; there was more than his shoulder on his mind.

Bo and Daniel were waiting at the station the next morning to depart from Omaha to go to Cheyenne, then to Sacramento, when the train pulled to a stop for them to board. They waited as the engine took on firewood and water. The conductor stuck his head out of the conductor's car briefly as they boarded to take their seats and informed the two marshals it would be at least another hour before they departed. Buck and Alala were securely stabled in the car just behind what would be theirs, and their saddles were hung next to them. There was another passenger car in front of Bo and Daniel's and a mail car at the end of the train.

There were several other passengers in the car waiting to leave as well. The other passengers didn't pay much attention to them as they boarded and found places to sit. They each had chosen an aisle seat and put their gear on the seat next to them. Soon, the train lurched forward and then took off at full speed, letting off a whistle of hot steam as the wheels turned on their tracks. By the time the train reached Cheyenne, Bo had been silent for the last two hours. He just kept looking out the window to the south. Every once in a while, he'd rub his throbbing shoulder and try to move his arm around.

A few hours later, the conductor made his way through the car with an announcement for the patrons riding the train. "This train will layover in Cheyenne for at least two hours. If any of you with animals want to take them off the train, you can do so now. I will have the engineer blow the whistle three times, fifteen minutes before we leave."

Daniel stood up abruptly. "Let's get off the train. Buck and Alala need some time out of the stable car." He picked up his gear. "Take your gear with you. You don't want to leave it here."

Bo looked up at him. "Do you really want to drag all of this off the train for an hour?"

Daniel just glared at him. "Get your things and let's stretch our legs. The horses need some time off this train."

Bo wasn't in any mood to argue. He gathered his belongings and walked back to the stable car where Buck and Alala were secured. Buck was happy to see him; he'd missed his afternoon scratching. Alala seemed pleased to be getting off the train as well. Daniel and Bo left the car, leading Buck and Alala by the reins and made their way out onto the train station's platform. Bo slid up into his saddle and rode Buck down off to the street below. Daniel followed him, riding Alala up to the station house and then tied her in front. Bo sat on Buck and watched the scenery and the other train riders move about. After a few minutes, Daniel came back out of the station and met with Bo, who was out there waiting for him. "We can get a room for the night down the street. The livery stable is at the other end of town. The train for Denver will be here in the morning."

Bo was confused. They hadn't talked about going to back Denver. "What are you talking about?" he asked Daniel.

Daniel hoisted himself back in his saddle. "We're going to Denver in the morning. You said you wanted some peach cobbler. I sent a message to Mr. O'Reilly to expect us late tomorrow afternoon. We can afford a day or two. The next train for Sacramento will be through here in four days. That will give you two days to get your fill of peach cobbler. Let's go see about the rooms."

Bo dug his heels in. "We're on our way to San Francisco to find your wife."

Daniel leaned over in his saddle. "Bo I would be dead, hanging from a tree if it wasn't for you. I wouldn't be a U.S. marshal if it wasn't for you. You've given me a chance for a way of life that I never knew existed. I've been accepted unconditionally by men who I've always had to look up to. There is no way that I can thank you enough for all that you've given me. I know deep in my heart that Trisha is in a good place and she is well taken care of. A couple of extra days to say thank you to you will not put her in jeopardy. We are going to Denver to see Rose and that's final!" He spun his horse around and headed toward the stables.

Bo was in shock. "I can't let you do that. We have to be on the train to California in a half hour." By this time Daniel was on his way down the street with Bo and Buck trying to keep up. Bo could see there was no use in arguing with Daniel. The big man had made up his mind and nothing would change that.

The men gathered their gear and walked from the stables to a hotel the station clerk at the Cheyenne train station had suggested to Daniel. The hotel was a two-story building with a large porch out front. The lobby was not deep, but it was as wide as the building. To the rear and the left of the desk, Bo and Daniel could see past the front desk to the dining room. The front windows were covered with heavy, red and gold drapes that hung to the floor. Except for Bo, Daniel and the skinny clerk, the lobby was empty. The hotel provided separate accommodations for Daniel, similar to the arrangements he had been given in Omaha. They found the rooms were clean and comfortable. Bo and Daniel got cleaned up and met in the dining room, but there was no peach cobbler on the menu. Daniel smiled. "We'll have a better menu in Denver."

The next morning, they checked on the train leaving for Denver with the station clerk and learned that the train for Denver was scheduled to leave the Cheyenne station at midday. When it finally left Cheyenne, it would take at least four hours to reach Denver. When midday arrived, they stabled the horses in a designated car for them and found a place to sit amongst the other passengers. This train was very similar to the one they were on previously. They found seats in the second passenger car with Bo on the east side and Daniel on the west. Daniel watched the snowcapped mountains stream past his window as the train chugged toward Denver. Bo said very little during the trip. He kept rubbing his aching shoulder and scanning the countryside out the window. After two hours had passed, the train came up on a steep grade and began to slow down. Bo's head popped up when he heard sharp noises from the car in front of them. Daniel heard the same sounds and he looked over at Bo.

"What's going on up there? Was that a gun shot?" Daniel asked, trying to figure out the source of the odd noises.

Bo straightened himself up in his seat. "I don't know, but it doesn't sound good."

At that moment, the door to their car burst open and two men sprang in with their guns drawn. The first man was waving his gun around. He pointed over his shoulder with his free hand. "Stay seated," he said. "Take out all of your cash and valuables and drop them in the bag as my friend passes it to you. When we have what we came for, we will leave you unharmed."

That was when Daniel stood up. The man in front pointed his gun at Daniel. "I told you to stay sitting." His eyes couldn't help but be drawn to Daniel's holsters where he kept his shotguns. "Now, what do we have here?"

That was all the time Bo needed to grab hold of his weapon. His Colt leapt out of his holster and one shot screamed from its barrel. The bullet hit the first man who was distracted by Daniel in his right forearm, the bullet continuing on and through the window with a crash. As he groaned and his gun went flying in the air the second man, holding the bag, spun around to face Bo. When he did, he found himself staring down the bore of Bo's forty-five caliber Colt and, out of his right eye, Daniel's shotgun. Daniel pointed the barrel at his torso, forcing him to freeze.

"Drop your gun and kick it away," Bo had to tell him only once.

The second man's gun pivoted around his finger and slipped to the floor. His boot sent it in Daniel's direction. Daniel picked up the gun and then he held out his hand. "I'll take the bag."

The man stepped forward slowly and gave up the bag he'd been holding. He looked down at his friend lying on the floor of the car holding his shattered arm. "Can I help him?" he asked.

Bo gestured. "See what you can do."

The man dropped to his knees and ripped the sleeve off his friend's shirt. He tied it tightly around the wound. "That's the best I can do here. You need a doctor."

The rest of the passengers in the car, realizing what had happened, started to applaud. One of them stood up. "Who are you?"

Daniel smiled. "I'm U.S. Marshal Daniel Blue and this is my deputy, Marshal Henry.

Bo looked over at Daniel. "What did you say?"

Daniel laughed. "Now you know how it feels!" Daniel ducked down to look at the window with the bullet hole in it. Peering out, he noticed that the train was nearly at the top of the grade. "That must be their ride." Bo dipped down to look through the window next to Daniel. Off in the distance he could see a lone rider with two extra horses. "He is going to be there a long time if he's waiting for these two."

Bo shackled the two men to a seat where he could keep an eye on them. Daniel spent the next hour recording the names of everyone who'd been robbed and listed what had been taken from them. He informed each of them they would be expected to testify in court during the trial to ensure that justice would be served. When Daniel was done investigating and collecting information from the witnesses, he came back to where Bo was guarding the prisoners.

"That takes care of that," Daniel said. "Everyone has had their belongings returned." He looked down at the names of the two men seated in front of him where Bo had written them down on his note pad. "Aren't these the two men we had warrants on when we came out here the first time?"

Bo nodded. "They just don't seem to learn."

Soon, the train squealed to a stop at the Denver station and all of the passengers departed quickly. Bo and Daniel were the last ones off with their prisoners. A young boy at the station was helping the passengers gather and carry their bags. Bo tossed him a quarter. "Go get your sheriff and the doctor. We've got some business for both of them."

The boy took the quarter, looked at it and smiled. "Yes, sir!" he said, then ran off in the direction of the town's jail.

Daniel could see Mr. O'Reilly at the far end of the platform speaking with two men who had been passengers. Beside him, Daniel could make out Rose's outline. The two men shook hands with William and rushed off to their waiting carriages. Scanning the crowd and then noticing Bo and Daniel, William strode up to them with a cheerful demeanor. He shook their hands. "I see the two of you can't leave your work at home. My friends told me these two tried"—he looked at the two men shackled together with scowls across their faces—"to rob the train and that you had to intercede on their behalf."

Daniel looked at Bo to see his reaction. Bo nodded. "We couldn't allow them to rob the train."

By this time, the sheriff had arrived. The sheriff was an older man of average build with a long handle bar mustache. He wore a wide-brimmed hat with a snakeskin band. "Hello, Bo. I see you've brought me some more business," he said. He and his deputy took charge of the two prisoners.

Rose had been standing behind her father. She stepped around him once the prisoners had been taken away. She looked at Daniel. "Hello, Marshal Blue."

Daniel smiled. "Hello, Miss Rose." He tipped his hat.

Rose looked at Bo. He was rubbing his shoulder. "Hello, Marshal Henry." She reached out and touched his shoulder. "Is it hurting you?"

Daniel nodded. "It's been bothering him a lot, but he won't admit it. He tells me that all he needs is a big plate of your peach cobbler."

Rose tucked her arm under Bo's and led him to the train car where the horses were stabled. Rose smiled. "We've got a special cobbler in the oven for supper tonight." She peeked around the edge of the stable car door. "Is Buck with you?"

With his good arm, Bo pulled the stable car door completely open and stepped in to get Buck. Daniel followed to retrieve Alala. As soon as Buck cleared the door, he trotted straight up to Rose and pressed his nose against her chest. She slipped him an apple from her pocket and scratched him under his chin lovingly. Bo shook his head. "I swear you have that horse spoiled rotten."

They bridled the horses and Smitty helped them stow their gear behind the back seat of the wagon. Daniel climbed up next to Smitty. Rose made sure she was seated next to Bo. The cold breath from the team of horses rose up as they marched to a gallop. Blankets were passed out to cover themselves as they made their way up the hills to Yellow Bud.

The first day they were back, Rose made sure Bo got his fill of peach cobbler and Buck had more than his fair share of apples. The second day took on an air of sadness; Bo and Rose's time together hadn't been long enough. That evening, as dinner finished, Bo stood up.

"Mr. O'Reilly," Bo said, facing him, as well as Marie. "You asked me to come to you and tell you when Rose and I had taken time to talk about our future and what it would be like if we were to marry. We've had those discussions, and I would like to ask you for Rose's hand in marriage."

The request took everyone by surprise and they looked up at him shocked. Marie reached over and put her hand on William's arm. She smiled as a tear crept down her cheek. Even Rose was a little surprised. She'd thought that Bo would have this conversation with her father in the study after supper. William cleared his throat before he spoke. He pushed his chair back from the table and sat for a moment looking at Bo and then at Rose. Rose had slipped her arms around Bo's arm.

William stood up at the table. "Yes, you and I had that conversation. From all the time that you and my daughter have spent together, I will assume that at least some important topics were covered. I've always tried to be a father who gave his daughter what she really wanted. All we've heard since you left is how much she misses you." He stopped and looked at Rose. His voice became softer. "Is this the young man you want to spend the rest of your life with?"

Rose still had her arms around Bo. She looked up at her father. "Yes, Daddy."

"I'm sorry Rose, I don't have your ring with me. I've asked my mother to send it to me," Bo replied sheepishly. "I guess I didn't think this out very well. I just knew it was the right time."

William picked up his glass. He looked down at his wife and she nodded and smiled up at him. "Then, I give my permission." He raised his glass and took a sip. Everyone else at the table did the same. Two of the maids who had been serving supper wrapped their arms around each other and began to cry. Then, William set his glass down. He looked down at Marie. "Have Rose and Bo talked about where and when this blessed event will take place?"

Marie nodded. "They wish to be married in the garden next spring when the roses are in full bloom."

William smiled. "I think that was more our daughter's idea than Bo's."

Marie looked up at William and then at the young couple. "If your daughter had her way, they would be married before he leaves tomorrow. You can thank Bo for putting it off until spring. "

The next morning came too quickly. The gray sky and the light snow falling seemed to set the mood. There wasn't any conversation during the ride to the Denver station. Bo eased out of the wagon, helped Rose out and then, took Buck up the ramp to the stable car where he would ride all the way to Cheyenne to get to Sacramento. Daniel was right behind him with Alala. Rose wouldn't let go of Bo's arm. William and Marie stayed back with the wagon to let Rose and Bo say their goodbyes and enjoy the few tender minutes they had left together. When Bo and Rose reached the top of the ramp, Bo handed Rose the small, silver frame she'd given him when they parted the last time.

"Here," he said. "Rose, take this. It's hard for me to carry. I keep your picture right here." He patted his shirt pocket over his heart.

Rose accepted the frame with a look of disappointment and glanced at it. Then, staring at it, stunned, she began to sob and immediately threw her arms around Bo's neck for a hug that took his breath away. "I love it! I love it!" she cried, studying the image of Bo and Buck that Bo had substituted for hers. "I'll keep it with me always."

The engineer blew the whistle to announce that the train would be leaving soon and Bo had to get Buck in his stall. He gave Rose a kiss and gently pushed her away. "You'd better go back with your mom and dad."

Rose stepped back slowly moving back down the ramp toward the platform, pressing the picture to her heart. "I love you, Bo Henry." Her eyes filled with tears and she made no attempt to hide them. Giving Bo one last longing look, she turned and slowly walked back to the wagon.

Bo was choked up as well. "I'll return as soon as I can," he called out to Rose before she disappeared from his sight

The whistle blew again, three times. Bo pulled Buck into the car just before the train lurched forward. Bo and Buck stood in the doorway of the car watching as the station slipped past. Bo turned and tied Buck up for their journey back to Cheyenne. Daniel was standing next to Alala securing her in her stall, as Bo finished with Buck. "We'll travel to San Francisco, pick up Trish and be back here before you know it. You'll be a married man by the time this snow melts." He pulled Bo into the passenger car and they found a seat.

One of the passengers in the car approached them just after they sat down. "Marshal, I'm Calvin Dagget. I was on this train four days ago when you saved us all. I want to thank both of you for your heroism." He handed each of them a business card that proclaimed him to be the president of the local cattleman's association. "William O'Reilly is a good friend of mine. If there is anything either of you need, all you have to do is ask. I own part of this railroad and a hotel in Cheyenne. If you need rooms when you get there, just show them my card and you will be taken care of. Your supper tonight is on me. It's my pleasure." He tipped his hat and went back to his seat.

They accepted the cards and nodded at Mr. Dagget appreciatively. Bo flipped the card over. It read, *All courtesies are to be extended to these gentlemen at my expense.* And it was signed, *Calvin Dagget, President.*

Turning toward the direction Mr. Dagget had gone, Bo called out to him as he sat with his wife. "Thank you very much, sir. I'll be sure to tell Mr. O'Reilly of your generosity." That seemed to please Mr. Dagget who smiled back at him

Bo and Daniel exchanged looks. Bo smiled. "I wonder how big a steak this will get us."

Their train pulled into the station in the early afternoon. When they arrived, the eastbound train was already sitting at the depot waiting for the train from Denver. As they passed Bo and Daniel, Mr. Dagget tipped his hat as he and his wife hurried to meet their next train. The westbound train wouldn't arrive until the next morning. Bo and Daniel gathered their gear and the horses to disembark from the train. After they stopped at the livery stable to secure Buck and Alala, they walked over to Mr. Dagget's hotel. They walked in and approached the desk. The clerk eyed Daniel up and down. "May I help you, gentlemen?"

Bo handed the clerk Mr. Dagget's card. "Mr. Dagget told us to show you this when we got here."

The clerk took the card and read the note that Mr. Dagget had written on it, never taking his eyes off Daniel. "You are the two marshals that were on the Denver train?"

Daniel nodded. "That's us."

The clerk swallowed to clear his throat. "Mr. Dagget sent word that we are to provide you with anything you want. He says you saved his life on the train the other day, and that we owe you our gratitude." He looked up at Daniel. "I have a large room on the third floor with two beds. Will that be adequate?" He held a key out toward them.

Daniel took the key from the clerk. "That will do just fine, sir."

"The train for Sacramento will be in between nine and ten tomorrow morning. The whistle usually wakes most of our guests. Will you need someone to knock on the door?" the clerk asked.

Bo picked up his gear. "No, the train whistle will be sufficient."

They climbed the stairs to the third floor, located their room and washed up for supper. The steak that night was one of the best they had enjoyed. After a decent night's sleep and a quick breakfast, Bo and Daniel were both packing when they heard the train whistle blow the next morning. Bo looked at his watch. "It's fifteen minutes early. We had better get moving."

They grabbed their belongings and quickly went down the stairs. When they had reached the station, they rushed the horses to the stable car just before the whistle blew again. They hopped into the passenger car, and took the first available seats as other patrons rushed by them to get situated before the train took off. They would mark the next couple of days by the sound of that whistle, while spending the days reading the books Daniel had picked up in Kansas City for Bo to learn from. He would have to find additional books in San Francisco as Bo developed further.

The final whistle blew as the train pulled into Sacramento, California and came to a slow stop. Bo and Daniel gathered their belongings then went back to the stable car to get Buck and Alala. The horses were as relieved to be off the train as Daniel and Bo were. When they had reached the platform, they carefully scanned the busy station to see where they could find information about where the livery station was located. Luckily, they happened upon a clerk who was passing by after attending to other train station guests. The clerk politely pointed them in the direction of the livery stable and a hotel where they could get rooms for the night. Seeing an opportunity to gain information from someone who came into contact with people traveling in and out of the area, Bo inquired about the men they were looking for. Unfortunately, the clerk didn't have any memory of seeing the men they were looking for; he advised them to ask the staff at the hotel. Bo and Daniel dropped Buck and Alala off at the livery and then made their way to the hotel to rest and prepare for the long journey ahead.

The next morning, they mounted the horses and started out for San Francisco.

As they left town, Daniel looked over at Bo. "Just think, by this time next year we'll be able to go all the way to San Francisco on the train."

Bo shook his head in disbelief. "I think I would rather ride Buck."

Chapter 9
San Francisco's Gates

The ride to San Francisco from Sacramento took most of the day on a steady gallop. They rode on Buck and Alala through beautiful countryside with golden hills that seemed to stretch out forever. Along their way, they also passed the crews working on the rail line that would one day connect Sacramento to San Francisco, possibly in the next year; both Bo and Daniel had never seen anything like it on their previous travels. Soon, they rode over a hill and saw the unmistakable glowing of what could only be a city—San Francisco—stretched out before them against a dusk sky. They stopped at the top of the hill to take the sight in. The deep pinks and orange tones in the sky hovered over the twinkling city and a cool night-breeze brushed against their faces as they turned the horses and rode in.

When they eventually reached the edge of the city, they found a man who directed them to a livery stable and Bo and Daniel rode down the street to Hanson's Livery Stable. Across the street from the livery was Hanson's Saddle and Tack. Mr. Hanson came out to greet them as they dismounted. "Good evening. Will you be staying the night?" He reached for the reins of the horses.

Bo pulled the reins back. "Buck's a little particular about who takes care of him. I wouldn't want the two of you to get off on the wrong foot." Bo led Buck into the stable and removed his saddle and bridle. Then, the buckskin trotted off to the first empty stall.

Mr. Hanson's son rushed into the stable from the street. He was a bit small for a ten year old and was wearing tattered work pants and a soiled black and white checkered shirt. His boots were untied and they clattered as he ran in. His blond hair was a mess and it stuck out in all directions at the same time. He'd seen the large buckskin come in and ran up to see Buck. Bo reached for the boy, but it was too late. When Bo had gotten to where the child stood, he could see the boy reaching out and stroking Buck's nose. Buck didn't move a muscle. He even let the youth scratch him under his chin. Moving next to the boy and Buck, Bo reached out and scratched Buck behind the ears. He whispered, "Good boy," into the horse's ear, then turned to the youngster. "What's your name?"

The boy backed away from Buck. "My name is James Hanson, sir."

Bo pulled a quarter out of his pocket. "Well, James Hanson, if it's all right with your father, I'd like to hire you to go to the store and buy a bag of apples or some large carrots. Buck gets one every morning." He looked over at James' father who was standing within earshot, by the stable entrance. "Can he do that?"

Mr. Hanson smiled. "He goes down there for his mother all the time."

Bo handed the twenty-five cent piece to James. "I think there's enough extra for a stick of licorice, maybe two."

James held his hand out and took the quarter. "Thank you, sir. I'll be right back." James turned and headed for the stable entrance.

Mr. Hanson patted his son's arm before he left. "Jimmy, you be careful now." He let the boy go and watched him run out of the stable. He turned back to Bo. "From your reaction I'd guess you didn't expect to see your horse react like that."

Bo smiled. "No, I've only seen him let one other person scratch him like that. If Jimmy can do that with him now, I'd say they were pretty good friends. I wouldn't let anyone else handle him. After Jimmy gets back with the apples or carrots, he can give Buck one. That will bond them like brothers."

Daniel bent over to pick up his saddle and heave it over the top rail of Alala's stall. As Daniel did this, Mr. Hanson got a glimpse of Daniel's badge. It was pinned to his shirt under his opened coat. "Are you lawmen?" he asked.

Daniel nodded. "We're U.S. marshals. We're here looking for some men who abducted several of my former neighbors to be sold as indentured servants. They were most likely sold to some of your local, wealthy families. This would have been a year or so ago. There would have been maybe seven white men and eight or so blacks in a couple of wagons. The people they had taken were kidnapped from Chicago. We have arrest warrants for their captors."

Mr. Hanson shook his head. "I don't remember seeing a group like that around here. If they camped outside of town, then I wouldn't have seen them unless they needed some shoeing done on their teams. The best place to start would be the Powers' estate. If the Powers family weren't involved, they surely would know who was. They live in the largest house on the hill overlooking the city. You can't miss it."

Bo picked up his gear. "I wonder if you could give us directions to a place nearby where we each can get a room?"

Mr. Hanson pointed to his right. "There's a place just up the street... that would be Jack's Place. It's a big, green building. You can't miss it. It gets a little rowdy at night but it's clean. Most of the sailors stay there. There aren't many ships in port now, so I'm sure he's got rooms available."

Bo and Daniel gathered up their guns and saddlebags, leaving their sleep rolls behind with their saddles. Then, they walked over to Mr. Hanson to thank him for his hospitality and advice. They shook hands and parted ways, eager to find a place to recover from the day's ride. The sun was slowly sinking into the Pacific Ocean when Bo and Daniel started down the street to Jack's Place. The bright, red sign shaped like a ship hung out over the doors. The bright light coming from inside Jack's, along with the music and smell of steak cooking made them pick up their steps.

The lobby was nearly empty when they walked in. All of Jack's customers were in the bar or the dining room. Jack was a man as large as Daniel with a mostly gray beard that grew in front of his ears and all the way under his chin. He stood in the lobby behind a counter, waiting for patrons to come in, and smiled as he saw them walk in and approach the main desk. "What can I do for you gents tonight?"

Bo smiled back. "We need a couple of rooms for a few days."

Jacked spun the desk register to face them. "Sign in and I'll get you your keys. Do you want to be in the front or back? I've got rooms on all three levels on both sides. The fleet is out so I'm long on rooms and short on guests."

Daniel dropped his gear on the floor. "I guess we'd like the quiet side."

Jack turned to look at Daniel. "That would be the front. Sometimes the boys go out back for a little sport and it gets loud, if you know what I mean. Sheriff Weston won't let them fight in front; the neighbors put up too much of a fuss."

As he walked back to get the keys out of the numbered slots on the wall behind him, Bo and Daniel heard a strange sound—a shuffle and then a thump—near where Jack stood. Curious, Bo bent forward over the desk counter to take a look. Jack turned around to see Bo leaning over the desk.

"What happened to your leg?" Bo asked.

Jack hit the wooden stump with his fist. "I got washed overboard and a shark had my leg for lunch. I was lucky because some of my mates were there with their spears to keep the rest of them off me until I could get back in the boat. It's hard being on a ship with only one leg. That's how I ended up here." He handed keys to each of them. "You're both on the second floor, right over the lobby. You should get a good night's sleep there." He pointed to the stairs off to his left. "Up the stairs and to your right." Then, he pointed to the doorway off to his right. "The kitchen is open all night. We cook up a mighty good steak." Jack laughed at their reaction to the off-key music coming from the bar. "Pay no mind to the piano player. He's used to playing a busted piano and wouldn't know what to do if I had it fixed." They all laughed at the sounds pouring through the doorway.

Bo nodded. "Thank you. I think we'll take you up on that steak as soon as we've had a chance to get some of the dust off."

Bo and Daniel picked up their gear and with their keys in hand, ascended the stairs Jack had pointed them to. They searched for the rooms above the lobby and went into their respective rooms.

Back at Hanson's stable it was feeding time, too; Jimmy and his dad fed the livestock in the livery. Mr. Hanson watched his son feed the buckskin. Buck didn't pay any attention to the boy as he put hay and oats out into the trough for him to eat. At that moment, Mrs. Hanson called from across the street and Mr. Hanson walked over to see what was needed.

"Jimmy, I've got to help your mother," he called back to his son who was still feeding the livestock in the stable. "You finish up and lock the doors then come in for supper!"

"I'll be right there, Pa," Jimmy called back as he saw his father go up the stairs on the side of the building.

Jimmy finished his chores. He closed and began to lock the big swinging doors on the front of the livery and headed for the front door. A dark, skulking figure was hiding between the buildings on the other side of the street. He'd been waiting there for some time, watching the two men come in with the buckskin and bay. He'd watched as the men paid for the care of their horses and left. He knew what would be in the livery that he needed. He rushed at the door before Jimmy could lock it, shoving the boy back into the room. The first thing he did was to slap Jimmy across the face.

"Where do you keep the money, boy?" the stranger demanded.

Jimmy would have fallen from the blow but the man's grip on him was too tight. The boy didn't know what to do. When the man's hand went up in the air again, Jimmy pointed to the desk. "It's in the top middle drawer." Jimmy replied. His voice was shaky and he was scared.

The man pushed Jimmy to the floor and rushed to the desk, jerked the drawer open and found four dollars. "Where's the rest of the money? There's got to be more than this!" He reached down to hit the boy again.

Jimmy threw his arm up across his face. "My pa only leaves that much here. He takes all the rest of the money to the house."

The man didn't like that answer but he had to be satisfied with the response. "I need a horse. Saddle the buckskin," the stranger said, pulling the boy to his feet and pushing him into the stable. "Get going or I'll give you a real beating." The man gave Jimmy another push toward Buck's stall.

As they approached the stall, the stranger reached out to open the stall gate. By this time, Buck had turned around to face the rear of the stall and as the man's hand reached the top of the gate, Buck kicked the top rail of the gate with his hind hooves. The force of Buck's kick splintered the wood and smashed the man squarely in the face, sending him backward. The sharp whistling sounds Buck made were not friendly; Buck swished his tail and his ears pinned back in anger. Jimmy dove into the stall behind Buck. The big buckskin spun around with the boy under him. The man staggered forward and was met by the massive horse's front hooves once again. This time, the blow hit him in the chest knocking him completely across the stable and into the office wall. When the man collided with it, he bounced off and fell into a heap on the straw covered ground.

Just then, Mr. Hanson burst into the livery. He'd started back to see what was keeping Jimmy so long and had heard the commotion. When he saw the man on the floor and the buckskin standing over Jimmy, he wasn't sure what to think. Seeing his father, Jimmy jumped out from the stall relieved. "He saved me, Pa. Buck saved me!" he cried out as he ran to his father.

Instinctively, Mr. Hanson stepped back into the office, a few feet from where the intruder landed, and pulled a small revolver from the bottom drawer of his desk. The man began to roll over and Buck snorted and stomped his front hooves in response. Mr. Hanson looked down at the man as he was attempting to flee. "I'd stay right where you are or that horse will stomp you to death," he said to the intruder as he bounded toward him. The intruder heeded the warning and promptly froze in place, sandwiched between Mr. Hanson and an angry horse. "Put your hands behind your back." Mr. Hanson pushed the gun in the man's face. "Jimmy, fetch me that rope and then ride down the street and bring back the sheriff."

Jimmy quickly brought the rope his dad had asked for, then threw a bridle on his own horse and quickly took off down the street. It was only a few minutes before Sheriff Weston was back with two of his men to take away the thief. Jimmy told them about how Buck had saved him and whose horse the intruder was trying to steal.

"That's quite the story, young man," the sheriff said to Jimmy. "You say these two horses belong to the U.S. marshals? I think I had better drop in at Jake's Place on the way back and introduce myself. We don't get many U.S. marshals visiting us. We should be hospitable." Sheriff Weston's voice was a little less than friendly as he walked out the door with his prisoner. "We'll be in touch, Mr. Hanson. I'm sure the judge will want to talk to you and the boy in a day or so." He turned away and faced his men. "You boys take the prisoner back to the jail. I'm going down to Jake's Place."

Once he was sure that the thief was secure and Mr. Hanson had control of his livery once again, the sheriff made his way to Jake's where he found Bo and Daniel in the dining room. They were sitting at a table having something to drink and waiting for their steak dinners. From the description Mr. Hanson had given the sheriff, he had no trouble picking them out of the dinner crowd. He walked up and pulled out a chair. "Can I assume you are the two U.S. marshals who have their horses stabled down at Hanson's?" He made an obvious gesture to make sure they saw his badge when they acknowledged him by looking up from their drinks.

Bo smiled. "That's right, Sheriff. What can we do for you?"

The waiter approached the table. "What can I get for you, Sheriff Weston?"

The sheriff didn't look up at the man, but kept his eyes pinned on Bo and Daniel. "Whatever they're having." He looked Bo straight in the eyes as the waiter left to place his order to the kitchen. "Can I assume you are here on business and that you were going to stop by my office first thing in the morning to let me know why you are in my city?"

Bo leaned back; he'd seen his share of pumped up egos. "Very first thing, Sheriff. We wouldn't want to step on your toes. Our business here is on a federal warrant for a group of kidnappers who brought their victims here to be sold."

Daniel leaned forward to address Sheriff Weston. "My wife was one of the people taken. We'll stop by right after breakfast and let you look at the warrants. I'm sure you'll find everything in order."

Hearing this troubling news and finding the men courteous, the sheriff's ego had been soothed. "You may want to check your stock in the morning. There was a bit of a scuffle down at Hanson's earlier. That's how I found out you were here."

He recounted the story that Jimmy had told him. By the time he was finished, the steaks had been brought to the table. The sheriff picked up his knife and fork. "Jake's cook sure knows how to prepare a meal. He's better than my wife and I'll lock you up if that gets back to her."

When the steaks and pie were gone and they had finished their last cup of coffee, the sheriff stood up from the table. "I'll expect to see both of you at my office in the morning. Have a good night, Marshals." He turned and walked out, leaving Bo and Daniel staring at him as he left.

Daniel looked over at Bo. "That was one hell of a story he told. Do you think we should go down there and check on the horses?"

Bo smiled. "No. If there was anything wrong, Hanson would have come down here himself. We'll check on them in the morning and get more detailed directions to that mansion on the hill." They got up and went up to their rooms to rest for the night.

Early the next morning Bo and Daniel ate breakfast and then went to Hanson's for their horses. Jimmy was at school but Mr. Hanson was eager to tell them about the attempted robbery. Bo saddled Buck, gave the horse a pat and an apple. "So you were the big hero, yesterday," he said to Buck patting him on the neck. "That boy must be special to you. You never did anything like that for me." Buck just snorted and finished his apple.

On horseback, Bo and Daniel made the four blocks north of the livery stables to Sheriff Weston's office and local jail. When they arrived, Bo and Daniel tied the horses out front and went in. The sheriff stood as they entered. "Good morning, Marshals. I trust you had a good night's sleep. We didn't have any complaints from Jake's neighbors last night." He stopped for a moment when he saw the weapons Daniel had strapped to his hips. "It's true! A cowboy come through here a month ago and told me he saw those. He never said you were—*that* big."

Daniel smiled. He pulled one of the shotguns out of its holsters and slipped out the shells. He handed the weapon to the sheriff. "They get the job done when I need them."

The sheriff took the shotgun from Daniel, carefully, then turned the gun over and over in his hands. As he examined it, he admired the fine craftsmanship and all of the etchings. "It's a shame to have to fire *one* of these and you have two." He handed the gun back to Daniel. "It makes a man glad to be on this side of the law when you pull one of those out. I don't suppose it takes much aiming to hit what you're shooting at."

Daniel reloaded the gun and dropped it back in its holster. "I've never been any good with handguns. These shotguns are my equalizers." He reached into his vest pocket and pulled out the warrants and handed them to the sheriff. "I think these documents are what you wanted to see."

The sheriff took them, held them flat with both hands, and looked them over carefully. "You don't have any names on these warrants. How do you know who to serve them on?"

Daniel took the warrants back. "We do our investigations and find out who we're looking for and then we fill in the names."

The sheriff wasn't so sure about that. "That's a bit strange, isn't it? How do you know you've got the right men? Dragging some innocent souls back here for me to lock up and then have Judge Bates try them on your hearsay isn't going to set well with our citizens when we pick a jury."

Bo shook his head at this. "They will come with us to Judge Roads' court for trial in Kansas City. You may have to keep them for a day or two while we arrange transportation but, they won't be here long."

The sheriff wasn't convinced. "Judge Bates isn't going to like this at all. Before you go out and start arresting people, I want to talk to him about it."

Daniel was more assertive and interjected. "You won't mind if we do some checking around? We don't want any of these men to find out we're looking for them and have them slip away."

The sheriff thought for a moment. "No, I guess not. If they're here, we'll want them behind bars. If you find any of them, you come back here and get me. We've got to keep this by the law. I'll have Judge Bates send a message to your Judge Roads. We'll let them figure this out. Where are you going to start looking?"

Bo pulled up a chair. "We're going up the hill to talk to Mr. Powers. Mr. Hanson told us that if he hadn't bought the people and their debt personally, then he would know who did."

The sheriff dropped into his chair. "Mr. Powers is the richest man in the state. If you're bent on going up there, then I'll have to go with you. He's a close personal friend of Judge Bates. Damn! This is going to get messy. When did you want to go up there?"

Bo thought for a moment. "I guess you're going to have to talk to Judge Bates first? I guess we'll go up to visit Mr. Powers as soon as you've had a chance to see to the judge."

The sheriff stood up again, this time, he inched toward the door as he spoke. "You boys stay right here until I get back. The courthouse is just up the street. You can keep an eye on the fellow who tried to steal your horse last night...the doc's got him all bandaged up. Your horse broke three of his ribs and gave him one hell of a lump on his head. He won't be much trouble. I'll be right back." The sheriff rushed out the door, climbed on his horse, then Bo and Daniel watched as he disappeared from sight.

Bo looked over at Daniel. "He sure was impressed with your shotguns."

Well, he wasn't all that impressed with your warrants," Daniel said with a smirk.

The two men poured themselves cups of coffee and settled in the seats across from the sheriff's desk while they waited for the sheriff to return. It was over an hour before the sheriff finally shuffled back into his office. When he arrived, he passed by Bo and Daniel, and then dropped into his chair.

"I knew this was going to get complicated," Sheriff Weston said, adjusting in his seat. "Judge Bates said we could go up to the Powers' place to talk only. He said under no circumstances are you to even think about pulling out one of those warrants until he's had a chance to communicate with Judge Roads. Apparently they know each other. It seems Judge Roads' wife's family is very wealthy and they know Mr. Powers. We don't do anything but talk until Judge Bates says it's all right."

Bo and Daniel stood up and passed through the main front door of the jail which was an open area with a row of three cells down each wall. The sheriff used the front area as his office. There was a desk to the left of the entrance with two chairs out front and a large swivel chair behind it. A table faced the desk on the other wall and the stove at the rear of the room had a pot of coffee bubbling on it. One of the sheriff's deputies walked in as they left. "Anything special this morning, Sheriff?" they heard the deputy ask as they inched past him and left.

The sheriff didn't hesitate to answer the deputy as he turned toward the jail cell and responded. "No, Sam. We've got one horse thief locked up back there. I'll tell you all about him when I get back. I'll be up at the Powers' place if anyone wants to know."

The deputy nodded that he understood and went into the back cell to check up on the thief they had in custody. Meanwhile, Sheriff Weston gathered himself to leave his deputy to take charge of the jail, then left the building. He got on his horse and headed out of town, following closely behind Bo and Daniel.

Once Bo, Daniel, and Sheriff Weston reached the Powers' estate, they were met by one of the livery staff who took care of the horses. The livery attendant proceeded to take Buck and Alala from them; they dismounted and handed over their reigns. Bo tied Buck up and warned the man not to get too close.

The front door of the estate home opened as they made their way up the nine wide stairs to the landing. Mr. Arron Powers met them at the door.

"Sheriff, what brings you all the way up here on a nice morning like this?" Mr. Powers asked. The sheriff removed his hat as he stepped forward to shake Mr. Powers' hand.

"Mr. Powers, this is U.S. Marshal Bo Henry and his deputy, Daniel Blue. They would like to ask you a few questions regarding several individuals who were kidnapped out east some time ago. They seem to think the victims may have been brought out here and sold."

Mr. Powers reached out and shook Bo's hand. "I'm glad to meet you, Marshal." He looked over at Daniel and nodded his head. "Marshal Blue, it's nice to meet you, as well." He turned and walked into the house. "Kidnapping is a crime and I've not had any dealings with anyone involved in crimes of that nature. I don't know how I could be of any help." He didn't turn back around until he was well into the entry of the home. The large open entry reminded Bo of the O'Reilly home in Denver. It had a large staircase extending up the middle of the entry with a hallway down either side and candles everywhere. There was a door on either side of the entry. The marshals were ushered off to the room on the right. It was the study with books and memorabilia covering the walls. Bo and Daniel followed Mr. Powers into the room while the sheriff lingered in the doorway.

Daniel stepped forward. "These people would have been offered as indentured servants. Have you hired anyone like that in the last two years?"

Mr. Powers didn't like being addressed in such a manner by Daniel. "I should say not!" he said, sounding a bit offended. "All of my employees are free to come and go as they please. I don't believe in such things."

Bo could tell that Mr. Powers wasn't being completely truthful. "We're here at the request of Judge Roads from Kansas City," Bo said. "He thought that you might have heard one of your friends mentioning some deals of that nature."

At that moment one of the house servants entered the study. She looked at Daniel and he recognized her immediately; she had been one of his neighbors in Chicago. Recognizing Daniel, she dropped the tray she was carrying and it clattered across the floor. Everyone jumped at the sound. Daniel rushed to her side to try to steady her. She sobbed as she pressed her cheek to his chest. "Oh Daniel, I'd given up hope of ever seeing anyone from home," she cried.

Bo's teeth clenched. "I'd say we have more to talk about, Mr. Powers."

Arron Powers stood dumbfounded and looked at the woman and Daniel with a blank stare. "I didn't know! They tell so many stories. How do you know what is the truth? I didn't know."

Daniel lifted the woman's face, using his massive palms. "Sissy, is anyone else here with you? Do you know where my wife is?"

She tried to clear her eyes with the backs of her hands and shook her head. "Just my husband, Bartholomew, and our son, Thomas. He's down in the stables. Oh my." She drooped in his arms and began to cry again. "Trisha was sold after we were dropped off here. I don't know where they took her." Her tears were flowing freely.

Daniel was angry. He stared straight into Powers' eyes. "Where are the men who brought these people here? Where are the rest of my people?"

Bo wasn't pleased with the situation either. "If you don't help us, you will be an accessory to kidnapping and subject to one of the warrants in my pocket. They were issued by a friend of yours, Judge Roads in Kansas City."

Arron's face went pale, he knew Judge Roads' reputation and began to feel nervous. "I th-h-ink..." he stammered as he began to talk," they delivered the rest to George Givers' place. You know George, Sheriff."

Sheriff Weston nodded. "I know where his place is. It's not far from here. I think you should come with us, Mr. Powers. He'll handle the news better if it comes from you."

Several of the kitchen staff heard the commotion and came into the entryway to investigate. One of the maids took Sissy's arm to comfort her and as she rose, Daniel's hand glided over her hair. "I want you, your husband and your son to get your things together. When we get back, you're coming with us."

Mr. Powers stepped forward. "They can't just leave! What about my money?"

Daniel leaned over into Powers' face. "Do you want your money and to go to jail, or to just let these people go?"

Mr. Powers stammered again. "You're right...what was I thinking? These mistreated people have to be returned to their homes. I'm sorry. I'll have my horse saddled and I'll be right with you." He signaled to one of the staff members who stood at the entryway and told them to have his horse prepared immediately. The staff member bowed and quickly disappeared out a back door.

In just a few minutes his horse — as well as the other horses—was brought up to the front of the home by Bartholomew. Bartholomew gave the reins to Mr. Powers and then shook Daniel's hand. "God bless you, Daniel. Bless you."

The men mounted their horses and soon, the four horsemen were at the front gate of George Givers' ranch. When they arrived, the staff took care of the horses and one of the maids answered the door when they knocked and immediately went to announce the visitors' arrival to Mr. and Mrs. Givers who were upstairs. Bo, Daniel, Mr. Powers, and the sheriff waited in the foyer.

George came down the stairs. "What is it, Arron? Why is the sheriff here at this time of the morning?"

The maid who had answered the door returned and couldn't take her eyes off Daniel. She knew that she had seen him before, but was afraid to speak. Daniel turned to face her. "Do I know you?" His voice was soft and kind.

She looked up at him without lifting her head. "I think so, sir. I think we lived in Chicago at the same time."

Daniel spun around on his heels to face the others. "Where are the rest of my people?" he demanded. His voice echoed through the house.

One person upstairs, who recognized his voice, came running down the stairs as soon as she heard it. She jumped into his arms as soon as she reached the bottom step. She kissed him and began to cry. She couldn't hold her emotions back; the tears streamed down her face.

George Givers was stunned by what he was seeing. "What the hell is going on here?" He reached out for the woman who had just run down the stairs. "Get back to where you belong!"

Daniel's hand was faster. Before Mr. Givers could touch the woman, he lunged forward, grabbed his arm and pushed him back. "Don't you touch my wife." His free hand quickly made its way to the grip of one of the shotguns on his hip. Then, quickly releasing his hold on Mr. Givers, Daniel grasped Trisha tightly about her waist.

Mr. Powers stepped in quickly. "George, these are U.S. Marshals Bo Henry and Daniel Blue. There's been a terrible mistake. These poor people have been kidnapped from Chicago. All the stories they've been telling us have been true. These marshals have warrants for the arrest of the men who brought them here." He was very careful to choose his words to avoid implicating himself or his friend. "Judge Roads in Kansas City sent these men to find these unfortunate people and bring those evil kidnappers to justice."

Givers took a half-step back while he thought about what Powers had just said to him. "Kidnapped, you say. How terrible. I could never condone anything like that." He took hold of the stair railing to brace himself. He couldn't take his eyes off the massive hand draped over the shotgun grip.

By this time, the rest of the household staff had gathered in the foyer to witness Daniel's arrival. The rest of Daniel's missing neighbors were there and rushed to hug him. He lifted his hand off the gun and returned their hugs. There was even a tear creeping down Daniel's face.

Bo turned to face the sheriff. "Well, Sheriff Weston, what are you going to report to Judge Bates?"

The sheriff smiled. "I'm going to inform him that we have good news. I've located all of the missing abductees."

Bo glared at the sheriff then he turned to Givers. "Do you know where the men are who brought these people to you?"

Givers thought for a moment. "Yes. I've seen two of them down near the pier. We occasionally go to the pier to buy fish. There's this one captain..." Powers cut him off before he could continue.

"These men aren't interested in where you buy your fish, George. They want to capture the men who kidnapped these people." He was nearly shouting at Givers, bringing Givers back to his senses.

"Yes," George continued. "Well, I guess I will have to show you where I think they are staying. I couldn't possibly give you directions. I never know quite where I am when I go down there. The smell is so disgusting."

Daniel pulled back from everyone who was clinging to him. "I want all of you to gather your things together," he told them. "I have to find the men who took you and arrest them. I'll be back tomorrow to take you home."

Givers stepped in. "You can't just take these people away from here, they work for me! I paid off their debts and they owe me money!"

Daniel's hand went back to his gun. Arron Powers stepped in. "George! These people didn't have any debts, they were kidnapped. If you don't let them go, the marshals will arrest you and we will both go to jail. Do you understand?"

It took just a moment for all of what he said to register with Givers. He sighed and reluctantly agreed. "I understand that I'm out a great deal of money and my only other option is to go to prison. Yes, I understand."

Powers turned to the sheriff. "Well, now that this is all straightened out, I'll be going home."

The sheriff stopped him before he could turn and leave. "I'm going to need both of you to make a positive identification of the men who you bought these people from. You're coming with us."

"I strongly object to this," Powers complained. "We didn't buy these individuals. We paid off their debts and they work for us for wages. A portion of their wages are deducted to reimburse us for our investment. That can hardly be considered buying. Besides, you have George to identify the men. Why do you need me?"

Having no patience to continue quarreling with Mr. Powers, the sheriff guided *both* men out the front door. "I'm not going to have time to clear all of this with Judge Bates, so I want to be damn sure that I have the guilty parties. You're both going to make the identifications. Let's go. I want to swing by the jail and pick up two of my men."

The five men made their way down the hill to the jail. Soon, there were seven of them on their way to the pier. Givers and Powers never stopped complaining the entire way, it was obvious they didn't want to be involved.

Dan Bradford

Chapter 10
The Way to Justice

By the time the seven men reached the San Francisco pier, it was late afternoon. The dock workers were done for the day and sailors were starting to come in off the ships. A crowd was beginning to gather on the docks; bars were open and music began to play. The horses were left at the jail and Bo Henry and the men made their way on foot. Givers led them up one street and then down another. Givers couldn't seem to remember where it was that he'd last seen the men they were looking for. After nearly an hour, he suddenly stopped. "That's it! That's the place I saw them coming out of," he stated with relief in his voice. He pointed to a bar that was just beginning to open up for business. "I remember because we had just purchased crabs and there is a crab on the sign."

They all looked up to see where Givers was pointing and saw a wooden adornment cut out and painted to look like a striking, bright blue crab. The adornment hung over another sign that read, "Blue Crab Inn" in matching blue letters and was poised just above the entrance door.

Bo turned to the sheriff. "It's obvious they're not staying here. Let's split up and see if we can't find them. You take your men and Mr. Givers and go north. Daniel and I will go south with Mr. Powers. If you locate them first, send one of your men to find us. We'll meet back here in an hour."

The two groups divided and started off to find the two men who had kidnapped Daniel's wife and friends. It took Daniel and Bo a half-hour to reach the south end of the pier. They moved in on one block and started back to the north. They'd searched for another five minutes when Powers pointed to the other side of the street. "There's one of the men," Powers exclaimed. His voice was nearly loud enough for the man to hear.

Bo pulled Powers' hand down immediately. "Which one is he? And don't point! We don't want him to know we're looking for him."

Powers began to point again, thoughtlessly, and when Daniel intervened, Powers dropped his arm and said in a low voice, "He's the tall, thin man on the opposite corner with the red scarf tied around his neck. He's probably headed back to the Blue Crab Inn...where we were at earlier."

Bo paused for a moment to make sure of the man's direction. "Let's stay over here and keep an eye on him." They moved north on the other side of the street, following far enough behind inconspicuously, until the man made a left turn toward the Blue Crab Inn. They cut across the street and kept behind him.

The inn was exactly where he was headed. The man went to the Blue Crab Inn and just as he entered, Bo, Daniel and Powers noticed the sheriff with his men and Givers coming toward them. When the sheriff and his men spotted Daniel, Bo and Powers, they halted their pursuit toward two other men who entered the Blue Crab Inn just after the tall, thin man wearing a red scarf. As the two men entered the Blue Crab Inn to head to the bar, Powers raised his arm and pointed. "There are two more of them."

This time, Powers was loud enough to be heard and one of the two men spun around to see where that voice had come from. When he turned toward the direction of the voice, he saw Powers on the street, pointing directly at him. By this time, the sheriff and Givers were only a few yards away and Bo was just across the narrow street. The first man who had seen Powers went for his gun, but before his gun could clear its holster, Bo fired. The bullet hit the man in the forearm and spun him around, collapsing him to his knees. The tall, thin man who'd just entered the Blue Crab's entrance having gone before the man who was alerted by Powers, heard the gunfire and came rushing back out with his gun in hand. As he positioned himself in Bo's crosshairs, Bo's second shot hit him in the right shoulder. The man spun around and crashed into the door frame. He bounced off and fell to the ground.

The sheriff and his men closed in and ran on scene to assist Bo and Daniel's takedown. "You're all under arrest! Don't move," the sheriff yelled as loudly as he could.

The third man had no thought of reaching for his gun. In the chaos, he'd gone to the window to investigate the commotion outside during the gunfire and had seen how fast Bo was. Soon, he was looking at the smoking barrel pointed directly at him as Bo and Daniel made it through the doorway and into the inn to get him. The third man raised his hands high over his head. Daniel's shotguns were panning from side to side. There were several frightened people gathering around them, viewing what had just taken place. Seeing that the situation was under control, Daniel eased his guns back into their holsters.

It wasn't long before a doctor arrived at the inn to take care of the wounded men. Once they were patched up, the sheriff had them taken to the jail. By the time the cell doors were locked, it was late in the evening. After Bo and Daniel had taken the horses to Hanson's livery, they made their way back to Jake's Place. It had been a long day.

Daniel hesitated before Bo pulled him into Jake's to call it a day. "I should go back up and get Trisha," Daniel said with an anxious look.

Bo dragged him through the door. "It's too late in the day," Bo said, knowing that going after Trisha after such a long, stressful day could lead to more trouble and a sloppy rescue. He knew what they needed was to reset for their next mission. "Let her get some rest. She'll be just fine knowing you'll be there in the morning. Let's get something to eat and a good night's sleep." Bo stopped for a moment. "I think this is lunch. Maybe I should order two steaks."

Early the next morning, when Bo and Daniel walked into the jail, the sheriff greeted them, but Bo had other things on his mind. He and Sheriff Weston went back to the cells to find the man who they'd brought in yesterday and who wasn't shot during the altercation at the Blue Crab Inn. The guard opened the cell door to let Bo in.

The man backed up as Bo entered the cell. "What do you want, Sheriff?" the man hissed.

Bo grabbed him forcefully and pushed him down on the cot. "I'm a U.S. marshal, not a sheriff. I have a warrant for you and your friends and I'm taking you back to Kansas City to stand trial for the kidnapping of eleven people and trading them as indentured servants. You are going to prison for a very long time. I can talk to Judge Roads if you help me. Maybe I can get some of the time cut off if you cooperate."

The man leaned forward. "I could use a cigarette." He leaned back against the wall.

The sheriff reluctantly gave him the fixings and waited for him to roll a cigarette and light up. After the man took a puff from the cigarette, Bo grew impatient. He had waited long enough. "I want to know who helped you in Chicago and where they are now," he demanded sternly. Then, he stomped his boot on the bunk rail between the man's knees.

The boot had gotten the prisoner's attention causing him to jerk and sit up straight. "I'll tell you what you want to know," he said, more alert.

"My name is Kemp. There were seven of us. Two are dead and the other two are in jail in Arizona. Marks and Craig were the two you shot."

That didn't satisfy Bo. "I want to know who they are. I'll figure out the rest."

The man puffed at the cigarette and them put it out under his boot. "Mainer got himself killed by a sailor a month ago. The sailor was bragging about some gold he found on an island and was flashing it around. Mainer got drunk and tried to take it away from him. The sailor cut him up pretty bad. Mainer died the next day. The other three were Fitgers, Nellis and Bains. They tried to hold up a bank someplace in Arizona. They got shot up. Fitgers got killed. Nellis and Bains are in jail if they aren't already hung. They killed a teller on the way out."

The sheriff was thinking about what Kemp had just told them. "I remember the sailor. His captain stood up for him. It was a clear case of self-defense. We let him go. The ship sailed that morning. They haven't been back, yet. I'll send a wire down to Arizona and check on the other two. It's most likely they got themselves hung if they killed a teller. I'll check."

Bo slowly lifted his boot off the bunk and stood up straight. "You haven't been much help." He gave the bunk a shove as his boot cleared the edge of the rail.

The man's eyes grew wide as he prepared to protest. "You said if I told you about the others that you would help me! It's not my fault they got caught and killed."

Bo turned to leave the cell, then slammed the bars shut. "I guess I'll have to wait and see how much trouble you are on the way to Kansas City."

Daniel, who was out in the hall listening to the entire conversation, met Bo as he left Kemp's cell. "What do we do now?"

Bo reached over to pat him on the shoulder. "It looks like we've got everything we came for. Let's go up and get Trisha and the others. We have to make arrangements for all of them to travel back to Chicago. It looks like I'm going to have to stay here until the two of the prisoners we shot can travel. You can take Trisha and the others back with you."

Blue agreed. "I don't like being on the road like this without you. We haven't worked apart now, for as long as I've been a marshal. This is going to be a strange trip."

Bo smiled. "Not many marshals get to pair up the way we have. It was bound to happen sooner or later. It's going to be strange for me, too. I won't have anyone to pick on." They both laughed as they went out front and got behind the wagon that the sheriff was sending with them.

An hour later they pulled up in front of the Powers' estate, dismounted from the wagon and Mr. Powers met them on the veranda. He smiled as he shook Bo's hand and gave Daniel a polite nod. Sissy's husband, Bartholomew and his son, Thomas, were standing behind him.

"Marshals Henry and Blue, it's so nice to see you this morning. I was up early this morning with Sissy and Bartholomew. They've agreed to stay on with us. Now that I know the truth of how they came to us, I've agreed to keep them on as employees as part of our staff. They will no longer have any deductions from their pay. They will live here with us for as long as they wish. I've agreed to have their son taught by the same teacher that will be tutoring our children," Mr. Powers said, then turned to face Sissy and Bartholomew.

Bartholomew smiled. "That's right, Mr. Henry. Sissy and I want to stay. Mr. Powers has given Sissy and I our own cabin out back with space for a garden. It's nice and I can make it a good place for our son. If it's all right with you, we'd like to stay here. It will be much better here than what we had in Chicago."

Bo shook his head. "Well, Mr. Powers, it seems that you've figured out a way to keep from going to jail. As long as they want to stay, there is nothing I can do to stop them. There is one thing I would like you to know; Daniel and I will be keeping an eye on you and this arrangement. If at any time I find out that you have not lived up to it, I'll be back here with my warrant and you and I will have to take a trip together. Are we clear about that?"

Bo's threat was very clear to Mr. Powers. He'd received a wire from Judge Roads that morning and he showed it to Bo. "My friend, Judge Roads, wrote the same thing this morning. Sissy and Bartholomew will be taken care of as long as they live under my roof. I promise."

Bo reached out and shook Arron Powers' hand. "I'm glad, Mr. Powers. I wasn't looking forward to that train trip with you at all. It would have been a very sad day for the both of us.

Mr. Powers agreed. "There is one more thing, Marshal. George Givers was here early this morning. I'm sure that by now he's come to the same agreement with his employees with the exception of your wife of course, Marshal Blue."

Bo turned to look at Daniel. "You may be traveling back east with just your wife. Let's get up to Givers' and see if all of his workers are going to stay or come with us." Saying their farewells, they mounted the wagon.

The wagon moved slowly up the road leading toward the Givers' estate. Once again, Bo and Daniel were met at the door as soon as they pulled up. George came out to meet them. "Good morning, Marshal. Have you been to the Powers place, yet?"

Bo nodded. "We just came from there. His…"—he paused again to choose the appropriate words—"servants told us they wanted to stay with him and not to return to Chicago. Is that how it is with you?"

Mr. Givers smiled and nodded. "Yes, we've all been up early to discuss it so we would have an answer by the time you got here. They are all inside waiting to speak to you. I was sure you would want to talk to them in person."

He led Bo and Daniel into the entry of the home where Trisha ran to Daniel as soon as he walked in. Daniel gave her a kiss and then pulled back just a little. "Is it true? Does everyone here want to stay?" he asked.

Trisha nodded. "Yes, Mr. Givers has agreed to pay them the same wages as his other workers without any deductions for food, clothes and housing. They have all agreed to Mr. Givers' terms. It was their choice, he didn't pressure any of us for a decision. Our lives here have been so much better than what we had in Chicago—I just missed you so very much." She reached out to him and gave him a tight hug.

Bo approached Mr. Givers and looked him straight in the eyes. "I'm sure you know about the wire that Judge Roads sent Mr. Powers, so I'm going to tell you what I told him. We are going to keep in touch with these people and if for any reason you don't live up to your agreement with them, I will be back."

Mr. Givers took a half-step back. "I fully understand, Marshal Henry. The only problem I have now is how to replace our children's teacher, Trisha. She has been wonderful with them. We are going to miss her very much." He paused for a moment and then he took Trisha's hand. "You will make a wonderful mother, someday." He stepped back and gave her and Daniel a polite nod.

Bo smiled. "Do you have all of your belongings, Trisha?"

She couldn't have been happier to be reunited with Daniel and for the ordeal to finally come to an end. She pointed to her traveling bag, which was next to the door. "Everything I have is right there."

At that moment, the Givers' two children ran down the stairs to see

Trisha. They were crying and begging her not to go. Daniel had a concerned look on his face. He put his hands on her upper arms.

"Sweetheart," he said, looking deep into Trisha's eyes. "I've got to ask you to do something for me"—he looked up at Mr. Givers—"would it be possible for Trisha to stay with you for a few more days? The two prisoners who were shot can't travel now and I have to help Bo move them."

Trisha objected. "No! Now that we're together I don't want you to go, even if it is for only a few more days."

Daniel tried to console her, bringing her close. "Bo and I have a great deal of paperwork to clear up so we can move the prisoners. I'll come up every afternoon to see you." He held her away for a moment. "Can we make some arrangement, Mr. Givers?"

Givers saw the opportunity to get on Bo's good side. "Of course, Marshal. The children would love to have Trisha with them, even if it is for just a few more days. You and Marshal Henry are more than welcome to come every evening for dinner until your prisoners are well enough to travel. We would be delighted to have you."

Daniel looked at Trisha. "It will only be for a few days. The place where Bo and I are staying isn't the type of place that any man would want to take his wife. Please, Trisha, do this for me. I have my duties as a marshal. I have to do this."

Trisha wasn't pleased. She also knew her husband and if nothing else, he had his pride and his honor. He would do his duty no matter what it took. "I'll agree to stay here as long as you are here every afternoon, Daniel Blue." She gave him another kiss. "I'm sure I'll be fine here for a few more days. It will give me a chance to say goodbye to the children the way I want to. They've been a part of my life here for so long and I love them very much.

Givers smiled. "That's wonderful. You'll be able to see each other every evening and we'll have Trisha for a few more days. Children, take Trisha's bag back up to her room." He looked at Bo. "Trisha's room is right next to the children's—they insisted on it. She's been a loved part of our family and she's had such a positive influence on the children. I don't know what we are going to do without her. "

The issue was settled with minimal objections from Trisha. She wasn't happy, but there didn't seem to be much that she could do or say about it as Daniel had made up his mind.

Each afternoon was the same routine: Bo and Daniel would show up at the Givers' estate and have supper with the family. Then Trisha and Daniel would have a short time to spend together. Later, he and Bo would have to leave for the night. The days passed with the doctor visiting the jail every afternoon to examine the prisoners. Bo would pace the floor outside the cells during these visits and then ask the same question: "Are they ready to travel, yet?"

Finally, the day came when the doctor had better news. "I think they can travel the day after tomorrow. You'll have to make sure they don't receive any hard blows to their wounds or too much jostling around."

Sheriff Weston was as relieved to hear the news as was Bo. "I'll have a wagon ready with one of my deputies to drive it," Sheriff Weston remarked after learning the good news. "If you leave in the morning, you'll only have to spend one night in Sacramento and then you can catch the train east that next morning. Judge Bates has signed all the papers transferring them over to you as soon as you leave the city limits. I'll send a message to Judge Roads as soon as you've gone, letting him know he should expect you in a week or so."

Bo was grateful for the sheriff's help but, it did seem as though he was being forced out the door. "I appreciate your help, sheriff. I wish your deputy was going all the way with us."

The sheriff smiled. "I'll bet he would like that, too, but I can't spare him for that long. You can have him until you get to Sacramento. The sheriff in Sacramento is a good friend of mine. I'll make sure he meets you and puts your prisoners up for the night. I'll ask him to find a place for you, as well. You don't want to be going all over town searching for a room."

Daniel had been listening to the conversation from the office out front and poked his face into the hall where the two men had been speaking. "Trisha is going to be glad to hear that. Let's go, I want to tell her."

Daniel shoved Bo out the front door and up into his saddle.

"Take it easy, Daniel. We still have to get through tomorrow. There's a lot we still have to do. We have to make arrangements for all the transportation back. We should contact Judge Roads and have him arrange for us to be on a riverboat from the railhead to Kansas City. We can send him that wire tomorrow. I doubt there will be any problems getting us on the eastbound train. I will arrange for us to be seated in the end car; I don't want to have to parade these three through the train every day."

Daniel settled down after he thought about it for a moment. "You're right, it's not going to be a fun trip no matter how we get it done. Let's go, I can't wait to tell Trisha that it's almost over."

Back at the Givers' estate, Daniel told Trisha about their plans to leave. She squealed with joy. "Oh! I can't believe it's finally coming. I'm going home with you!" She kissed him while Mr. Givers looked on. Givers was pleased.

"That's great news," Givers said to the couple. "I'm so happy for you. We'll help Trisha prepare for her trip tomorrow. I'm assuming you will pick her up on your way to Sacramento in the morning?"

Bo nodded. "We'll be here as soon as we can load the prisoners and get up here. I would appreciate it if everything was ready when we got here—it's going to be a long day as it is."

Before long, the time had come. Sheriff Weston brought the wagon up to the jail for Bo and Daniel's journey onward, just after the sun rose over the hills to the east. A cold, damp fog crept up the hills and swept over the rolling hills.

The prisoners were loaded and the wagon started out with Bo and Daniel right behind on Buck and Alala. It was going to be a tearful departure for Jimmy who had grown attached to Buck. Mr. Hanson and his son arrived at the jail just before they left for the Givers' estate to get Trisha. Jimmy fed Buck two apples and gave the big horse a hug. Buck seemed to sense the sadness in the air and he hung his head as Jimmy pulled away. Bo gave Buck a nudge and they trotted up the street.

The fog was still hugging the hilltops when they reached the Givers' place. The door sprung open as soon as they pulled up out front. Trisha ran out followed by the Givers' family. Mr. Givers put her belongings in the back of the wagon. The children hugged Trisha and they were all crying as she climbed up into the wagon. "I'll write to you when I have an address," she called out to them lovingly, taking a seat next to Sheriff Weston's assigned deputy in the wagon's front seat. "Be nice to your new teacher. I love you."

With that done, the wagon pulled out and before long they had cleared the tops of the hills and the fog. The sun was out and it became quite warm which brought smiles from Bo, Daniel and Trisha. They stopped only once for water and lunch because it would be late by the time they would reach Sacramento. They wanted to avoid traveling unsafely through the night.

Much later, the wagon finally lumbered down the street toward the

Sacramento jail. Everyone was tired and hungry. As they pulled up in front of the jail, a deputy came out to meet them. "You must be Marshal Henry," the deputy said, greeting them. "We've been looking for you all afternoon…must have been a hard trip."

Bo slid down and out of his saddle. "A lot longer than I remembered when we went in the other direction. Help me get these prisoners into cells." He and the deputy walked to the back of the wagon together, then pulled the men out of the wagon, making sure that their handcuffs were secure. "Can you get them something to eat?" Bo asked as he followed the deputy closely into the jail to secure the prisoners.

The deputy nodded in return. "I'll have something brought over."

Stopping in front of a line of bars, the deputy opened the cell doors and the prisoners were locked up.

After the horses were taken care of for the night, Bo, Daniel, Trisha and the deputy ate supper and then went up to their rooms. Early the next morning they were awakened by the whistle of the train as it arrived. They promptly packed, ate a quick breakfast and then hurried down to the stables. The wagon driver who had been loaned by Sheriff Weston, hitched up his team now that his mission to get them to Sacramento was complete. "It's been a pleasure, Marshal Henry," he said, then shook Bo's hand. Next, he turned to Daniel to shake his. "The same to you, Marshal Blue. I hope you and your Mrs. find a nice place to live in Kansas City." He tipped his hat to Trisha and shook Daniel's hand. He climbed up onto the wagon's front seat and pulled out.

A few moments later Trisha, Daniel and Bo met the Sacramento sheriff at the train depot. He had the three prisoners shackled, fed and ready to go. "I think these belong to you, Marshal," the sheriff said, shoving them at Bo. He then extended his hand. "I don't envy you taking this trio all the way to Kansas City; at least you don't have to do it alone.

Have a good trip." He shook Bo's hand and tipped his hat toward Daniel and Trisha. "By the way, I got a wire from Judge Bates in San Francisco. He told me to tell you that they haven't heard back from any of the jails in Arizona about the three men you are looking for. He said he'd let you know as soon as he hears anything." He turned and walked away. Bo wasn't happy to hear the news that he'd just been given.

After mounting the train and securing the horses, Daniel and Bo secured the prisoners on the train by shackling them down to the last row of seats of their train car, on the northernmost side. The prisoners faced west and Bo sat across from them with his back toward the outer wall where he could watch them. Trisha and Daniel selected seats on the south side of the car facing east. Trisha took the window seat. This was their seating arrangement for the remainder of the trip. The only change occurred when the train pulled into Cheyenne where Bo slid into the seat across from Trisha and gazed out at the tracks that led to Denver. It wouldn't have taken much of a push for him to jump off the eastbound train and onto the train for Denver to Rose.

Daniel leaned a little closer to Bo after noticing his despondent demeanor. "You'll see her soon enough. As soon as we get the prisoners to Kansas City, Judge Roads will give you a couple of weeks off. You can come back then."

His optimism didn't help Bo. "I know. It's hard being this close and having to keep going." He watched out the window until he couldn't see any sign of the city or the southbound train any longer. After passing Cheyenne, the view from their car was nothing but flat prairies. The only break in the monotony was an occasional herd of buffalo or antelope. At one point they saw a small group of Indians making their way west on horseback. If it wasn't for the stops for water and wood for the engine's boiler, there would have been nothing to do during the travel at all.

During one of the supply stops, the conductor came through the train. "This is our last stop before we get to Omaha, folks! This would be a good place to get off and stretch your legs. You can get a bite to eat here if you want. We'll be here for about an hour. I'll have the engineer sound the whistle when we're ready to go."

Bo unshackled the prisoners and escorted them off the train. He let them move around and use the outhouse. Daniel guarded them when Bo went into the station to get some food for the remainder of their trip. It didn't seem as though they had been there for an hour when the whistle blew. Bo looked up the track in the direction of the conductor and saw the man waving at them to re-board.

"Let's get back on the train," Bo called out to the others. "I don't want to have to walk from here to Omaha!" He pushed the three prisoners back up the steps and into the last car to be secured again. The prisoners took their seats and Bo locked their shackles, passed out the food he'd purchased in the station and settled back into his seat. They had been on the move for about a half-hour when two men he didn't recognize walked past him and out the rear door of the car. Bo gave them a hard stare as they passed. Daniel glanced over at Bo as they went through the door. He looked back over his shoulder to see them roll a cigarette and light up. "They're just having a smoke," Daniel said looking at Bo. He settled back into his seat.

Bo leaned over and saw one man with a cigarette in his hand just outside the car. Bo relaxed and slid back against the outside of the train, watching the endless waves of brown grass stream by. The monotony was lulling him to sleep. Trisha and Daniel were having the same problem.

Eventually, the back door of the car opened and the two men stepped back inside and walked past Bo who paid them little attention. In an instant, one of the men pulled his gun and pointed it at Trisha and Daniel.

Bo started to move his hand toward his holster when he suddenly felt a gun in the middle of his back.

Kemp jumped up. "It took you long enough! What the hell have you been doing?"

Daniel and Bo realized—all too late—that Kemp had lied about Fitgers, Nellis and Bains.

Daniel started to move for his gun, but one of the men, Fitgers, stepped a little closer toward him. "If you move again, I'm not going to shoot you. I'm going to shoot her," he snapped.

That was all that Daniel needed to hear. He lunged at the gun pointed at him. Fitgers' gun exploded and the bullet gouged out a wound along the outside of Daniel's left leg. He groaned in pain and landed face down between the seats at Trisha's feet. Trisha screamed and quickly reached for Daniel, pulling him up toward her. Bo began to duck around in his seat when the gun behind him came crashing down, sliding alongside his head and onto his left shoulder, striking a pain into his collar bone that felt as if it had been broken. The impact sent him plunging toward the floor, face down, unconscious.

Trisha reached down to see what she could do for Daniel. He was struggling to get up when Fitger's boot came crashing down in the middle of his back. "Stay right there, boy."

The other man, Bains, began going through Bo's pockets to find the keys for the shackles. Recovering the keys, he then reached over and grabbed Trisha roughly. "You're coming with us." He pulled her out of her seat and pushed her down the aisle in front of him.

The prisoner named Marks was getting impatient. "Let's go. Get these damn shackles off me. What are you doing with her? We can't have any extra baggage. Where's Nellis?"

Bains spun his gun around to make sure that none of the other passengers in the car were getting brave. "He's with our horses and the conductor. We need a little extra insurance," Bains explained. "She'll keep these two off our backs if they believe we'll kill her. Now, let's go."

By this time, the three prisoners—Kemp, Marks and Craig—had successfully utilized the keys and were now free of their shackles. Kemp picked up all the guns and grabbed a bag from one of the women in the car as he walked down the aisle. "Put your money and jewelry in this bag when I pass by or I'll shoot you," he yelled loudly.

Each passenger in the car nervously dropped their belongings into the bag. Fitgers looked back as he reached the front door of the car. "What the hell are you doing, Kemp?" Fitgers exclaimed, realizing that Kemp was robbing the people on the train. "We don't have time for this! We've got to get off this train before it gets to another town."

Kemp didn't stop. "I'm just collecting some travel-expense money." He got to the car door and crossed into the next car where he repeated his demands and collected everything he could before going forward into the next car where their horses and the conductor were being held by Nellis. Soon all the horses were saddled and ready to go. Fitgers shoved his gun in the conductor's face. "Stop this train! We want to get off!" He cocked the hammer and pressed the barrel against the man's cheek.

The conductor hurried forward to the mail car and pulled open the door. He yelled at the man inside. "Go up and tell the engineer to stop the train—we're being robbed!"

At this point Kemp angrily grabbed Bains and spun him around. "What the hell took you so long! I've been busting my rump for days on this damn train."

Bains pulled back, avoiding the question. "This is the best place for us to get off. We can go north from here and be in the Indian territories in a couple of days. I hear there are some gold prospecting camps up there.

We can grab a pouch of gold off of a miner or two and get us a stake."

That answer calmed Kemp just a little. "I still don't know why you made us wait so damn long." The train gave a lurch as it began to slow to a stop.

Bains leaned into Kemp's face. "As long as I'm running this outfit, I'll make the decisions on when and where we get off the train and why."

The door of the cars slid open and the other six men, along with Trisha, climbed down on their horses.

Daniel was leaning over Bo when one of the other passengers in the car rushed toward him. "I'm Doctor Allen," the passenger said. "Let me see if I can help." He examined Bo's head, then his shoulder and noticed a cut on his shoulder where the gun butt had hit it. "The cuts on your friend are minor. The blow to his head is more of a problem. I won't be able to tell how bad until he wakes up. Let me take a look at that leg." He began working on Daniel's leg as Daniel pulled himself up and back onto the seat. He looked out of the window at Bains and his men leaving the train with Trisha. His big hand slammed against the glass as he saw them ride off out across the barren prairie.

Bo began to move and groan. The doctor eased him up onto the seat across from the aisle. "Let me take another look at your head," Dr. Allen said, positioning himself to the side of him. Reaching out, he checked Bo out carefully. "There doesn't seem to be a concussion, but you're going to have a headache for some time."

Bo eased forward. "How are you doing, partner?" As he did he heard Daniel moan with pain.

Daniel was hurting, but ready to go. "They took Trisha...we've got to go after them." He attempted to pull himself up out of the seat and fell backward with a groan of pain slipping past his lips.

Meanwhile, the doctor was busy wrapping Bo's arm and shoulder in place. "You can't move this arm for a couple of weeks. I can see from this scar that you were shot not that long ago and that wound hasn't had a chance to mend properly. If you don't let it heal completely, you could lose the use of that arm altogether. As far as your friend here, he's lost a lot of blood and his leg is a mess. It will be weeks before he can ride a horse. I don't know what you can do except wait until you get to Omaha and gather a posse from there to go after those men."

Daniel pulled himself up. "They'll be all the way into the Indian territories by then. We'll never find them. I've got to go after Trisha—now." He took a deep breath and began to limp toward the front of the car.

Bo lifted himself up and looked at the doctor. "You heard the man. We've got to go get his wife. If he can walk, I can follow him." He turned and stood facing the aisle to follow Daniel.

The doctor held his hand up and stopped Bo. "Here, take this. It's not much, but it may help." He handed Bo a two shot Derringer pistol and a handful of cartridges.

Bo stuffed the gun and shells in his vest pocket. "Thank you, Doctor. I'll see that you get this back. I'm a U.S. Marshal stationed in Kansas City. You can reach us through Judge Roads."

Doctor Allen helped Bo up and through the aisle to the front of the train. "I wish both of you good luck. I'll send a wire to Judge Roads as soon as I get to Omaha and let him know what has happened and where you are. I'm sure he'd want to know."

Bo looked at Dr. Allen. "Just get word to Judge Roads and have the sheriff in Omaha send us some help."

Bo shook the doctor's hand and followed Blue out of the car to the next car where the horses were kept. The conductor had to saddle both horses; neither Daniel nor Bo could get it done alone. The conductor even had to help them up into their saddles. "How the hell are the two of you going to ride down those six men like this?" the conductor asked. "You don't even have any guns!"

The employee from the mail car came out to them with a shotgun and two pistols in holsters. "Here, these may help." He also provided a box of shells for each gun. He stuffed them into their saddlebags as he stepped back. "I overheard their plan. They're headed for the Indian territories and the gold fields. They have the woman with them, so they're not going to make very good time. She didn't look like she was comfortable on a horse."

Bo grimaced. "She's from Chicago. She's never been closer to a horse than on the seat of a wagon."

Bo and Daniel thanked everyone who had helped them, then Bo spun Buck around and gave him a nudge. The big horse charged out of the car and off to the north with Alala right on his heels.

The gallop didn't last long because the pain both men felt was only intensified and the jolting they were getting from the horses' movement was becoming more than they could stand. They slowed to a walk. There wasn't much in the way of provisions and when it started to get dark, they saw the lights from a small town off to the north. They agreed between one another that it seemed like a good place to stop so made their way there. They found stalls for the horses and managed to get a room out back of the livery for the night.

The next morning they weren't feeling much better. They rose to start their day and the man at the stable saddled the horses with Bo's help. The stable hands slowly bandaged up Bo and Daniel and then, Bo and Daniel picked up needed supplies at the dry goods store. While there, Bo gave the store owner a description of the men, particularly of what they were wearing. The store owner didn't hesitate to answer. "Two of them came in here yesterday just after lunch," he went on. "They had a third horse with them and they bought enough stores for at least five men. They packed it all on the third horse and headed off to the northwest. There's a grove of trees up there next to the stream. That would make a good place to camp for the night."

Bo and Daniel thanked him and then loaded everything they had onto their horses. It took them a couple of hours to reach the grove of trees and the campsite the store owner had described. Bo eased himself out of the saddle and checked the fire pit. It was cold. All the other signs Bo and Daniel had noticed around the campsite indicated that the fugitives and Trisha had left the location at least six or seven hours before they'd arrived. "They've got a half day on us," Bo commented. "We're going to have to move faster if we want to catch up to them before they reach the Dakotas."

Daniel agreed. "The horses are up to it. I'm not sure how much my leg will take...it started bleeding again." He reached down and helped Bo back into his saddle. Once Bo was seated on Buck's back, he reached over to Daniel's leg and grabbing the knot firmly, helped Daniel tighten the bandage on his leg. Daniel moaned just a little and winced. "A fine looking pair we are."

They left the trees and headed north, nudging the horses just a little faster as they made their way over the next rise. The trail of the seven horses was easy to track. Bains had no fear of being followed—he had Trisha as insurance.

That night Bo and Daniel set up a dry camp, lighting a fire to keep warm. They camped on the south side of a small knoll which kept the north breeze off them and hid their fire. Bo climbed to the crest of the hill and peered out to the north before preparing for sleep. He saw the glimmer of a fire far off to the north. He turned to call back to Daniel. "I think I've spotted their fire," Bo said. "They're about four hours out in front of us!

We can catch them tomorrow if we push it."

Climbing down, Bo made his way back to the fire where Daniel was seated in front of it. Daniel threw a few more buffalo chips on the flames to build up the fire for the night. They pulled their blankets up to their chins and tried to get to sleep; neither one of them had much luck at that.

They were both up at first light. After a small breakfast of coffee and jerky, they quickly prepared to move onward. When their packs were secured, they helped each other into their saddles and headed north. With any luck, they were on the move before Bains and his gang.

About midafternoon Bo pulled up and stopped Blue just short of the top of a hill.

"They're right in front of us," Bo said. "We've got to figure out a way to get in front of them without losing too much distance."

Daniel looked from one side of the trail to the other. "It looks like we can stay hidden if we cut off to the east. If we pick up the pace for an hour or so, we should be far enough north to cut them off."

Bo agreed and they started out at a gallop that soon slowed back to a trot when Blue's leg began to bleed again. After an hour at the faster pace, they cut northwest and crossed the trail the Bains gang had been following. They slid out of their saddles and found a place to hide on one side of the wagon tracks and left the horses down in a gully to conceal them.

"If we can't stop them here, we'll never get to our horses fast enough to stop them. We've got to do this, now."

Daniel nodded. "We have to kill them all before they can ride off." He put two shells in the shotgun's chamber and two more in his breast pocket.

About ten minutes later the seven horses appeared over the ridge. The good news was that Trisha was in the rear of the line with Kemp. As soon as the men were directly across from the marshals, Daniel jumped up and began firing toward them. Blue hit Fitgers, the first man in the line, with a blast from his shotgun. Fitgers flew up in the air and landed ten feet from his horse. The chaos caused all of the horses to jump frantically and begin to spin.

Bo already had one of his pistols out and he began to fire at Marks and Nellis who were his targets. They never stood a chance. The bullets from Bo's gun were deadly accurate and struck both men in the chest. The shot propelled Marks off the rump of his horse to the ground where he landed in a heap on his back. Nellis spun around with his arms flailing in the air. He bounced on his side as he hit the ground.

By this time, Kemp and Bains had drawn their guns defensively and were trying to control their horses to return gunfire. Kemp had his hands full trying to keep control of his own horse and Trisha's as well, and dropped his gun in all the confusion.

Daniel turned to see Bains charging right at him, bringing his gun down to aim. Blue pulled up his shotgun and let the second round go. The full force of the shot hit Bains in the chest. The horse kept running, but Bains halted midair and fell face first into the dirt. From the ground, Craig managed to get two shots off, both of which struck the ground in front of Bo. He hobbled toward his horse to regain control of it. Yanking on the horse's reigns, he staggered, then heaved his injured body into his saddle, attempting to get away. But Bo pulled the second revolver out of his belt and fired three shots, drilling a nice neat row upward and across Craig's chest, barely missing the horse. The third one struck him just under his Adam's apple causing him to flip over the rear of his horse and drop flat on his back. His mouth and eyes were wide open.

Daniel reached into his breast pocket and quickly reloaded the shotgun. He rushed at Kemp as fast as his leg would allow, with the shotgun pointed at him. Kemp threw his hands in the air. "I give up! I give up!" he cried out.

At that same moment, Bo dropped to one knee and grabbed his shoulder. The pain brought tears to his eyes; he didn't realize it until one ran down his cheek. He looked quickly over at Blue and wiped the tear off with the back of his hand. Pulling himself up, he gave a loud whistle. Buck charged up out of the gully with Alala right behind him. Bo made a circular motion with his arm. "Round them up, Buck."

Buck obediently jumped into action, moving around the horses in wide circles. It wasn't long before Buck had rounded up all the stray horses and Bo retrieved their stolen guns. By the time Trisha and Daniel had tied all of the bodies onto the saddles, the sun was starting to set. Luck was on their side that night; they spotted the glimmer of another small town off to the northeast. They tied each horse's reins to the tail of the horse in front and set out toward the lights.

It was after dark when they reached the town. As they entered the town, the sheriff was alerted and promptly met them. After explaining the situation, the local sheriff was eager to help the weary marshals after their incredible adventure. He helped them unload the bodies, and lock Bo and Daniel's prisoner in his jail. Before Trisha, Daniel and Bo had found a place to stay and a meal to eat, the sheriff delivered good news. "You're less than a day's wagon ride to the Missouri river," he said, pointing off to the east. "I can have one of my deputies escort you over so you can catch a boat downriver to Kansas City."

Kemp identified all of the bodies for the sheriff and they were taken away for burial. Afterwards, he was locked in a cell for the night. Trisha, Daniel and Bo found a place to stay and a hot meal to eat after all of the horses were stabled and fed. Much of the following day was spent taking care of business with the livery stable owner who bought all of the criminals' horses and tack. The sheriff managed to come up with a few dollars for the guns they had confiscated. When he was about to pay Bo, he stood back and looked at the pair of guns strapped to Daniel's hips. "You wouldn't be interested in selling them, would you?"

Daniel smiled. "No, these are the only way I can hit anything." He pointed in Bo's direction. "He's the one that does all the fancy shooting. I just get to admire his work."

The next morning, after all of the necessary paperwork was complete, a wagon pulled out with Trisha, Daniel, Bo and Kemp. A deputy took them to the landing to wait for the next boat downriver. They waited for two days before the next ship pulled into port to leave for Kansas City. After talking to the ship's captain and verifying their travel details, Bo sent a message down to Judge Roads to inform him about when they would be in Kansas City.

When the boat docked in Kansas City, there were five marshals on the pier. Even Judge Roads was there to meet them. The marshals were not gentle with Kemp when they took him off the boat; his complaints did him no good.

Bo and Daniel told their entire story to Judge Roads on the hour-long trip back to the Kansas City Federal Court House. As they got back to his office, all the judge could do was shake his head in disbelief. "If I didn't know better, I'd say you were embellishing it all just a little," he said, then turned to Trisha. "I can't imagine what you've been through, young lady. I'm so sorry. I want you to know that you will not have to suffer any more indignation. My wife and I have made arrangements for you and Daniel to stay in our guest cottage until you can find a place of your own here in Kansas City. We have three houses that we own, and two of them are furnished. I'm sure we can figure out a way for the two of you to have one of them. You can look them over as soon as you feel ready. There's no rush." He turned back to Bo. "Right now, we have to get the two of you healed up. First of all, I think you should have some good home cooking and a good night's sleep. Tomorrow we'll take care of all the paper work regarding the prisoner, the five corpses and any back pay that's due to you; I'll expedite any rewards on the six of them."

Daniel shook the judge's hand. "We appreciate all of this, Your Honor. I don't know how to thank you enough." Daniel shook his head. "It's hard for me to comprehend all that's taken place during these last few months. Finding Trisha and then the events on the train all seem to be so far away now. All I can think about is what our lives are going to like from now on."

Judge Roads sat behind his big desk. "There is one thing I would like to discuss with you, Daniel. It's probably better that we talk about it now, so you and Trisha can hash it out over the next few days. I've been speaking to my colleagues here in Kansas City and we all agree that we would like you to stay here and study the law. It wouldn't be long before you could take on a few cases of your own. Until then, we would keep you on as a deputy U.S. marshal. We would pay you the same salary as you would be making running around the countryside with Bo, but you wouldn't be out on the prairie. You'd be home every night. I'm sure Trisha would prefer that. In a few years, you could become a prosecuting attorney and perhaps, if you wished, you could have your own court. We don't expect to have an answer right away. We do want you to think about it and let us know as soon as you can.

Bo smiled. "Just think about that…'Your Honor, Judge Daniel Blue.' It has quite the ring to it. I'm sure you're going to have to get rid of that hat if you become a judge."

Blue turned his head in Bo's direction. "That's not funny, Bo. This is an opportunity I never could have dreamed of." Daniel looked over at

Trisha who was now sitting next to him. "We've got to talk about this. It's a major step for us, Your Honor," he said to Judge Roads.

Trisha didn't say a word. She squeezed Daniel's hand. She knew from the look on his face that this was something he would really like to do. She turned to the judge smiling. "Thank you, Judge. We'll talk about it and he'll let you know soon."

Judge Roads stood up and walked around from behind his desk. "That's wonderful. I've got my carriage out front to take you to my home where my wife, Darlene, is waiting for you. She and our staff will see to whatever it is that you may need." Gesturing toward Bo and Daniel, he continued. "The first stop, however, will be the doctor's office to have the two of you looked at."

Trisha, Daniel and Bo made their way out of Judge Roads' office and the court house to the carriage that waited for them outside. They swung by the doctor's office where Bo's wound was wrapped properly and Daniel received a new set of stitches. Then, it was off to the judge's home for Daniel and Trisha and the barracks for Bo. It would be the first decent night for any of them in a very long time.

The next day, the paperwork started; there seemed to always be paperwork. The days sped by and soon Trisha and Daniel moved into one of the judge's homes. They settled in but Bo was restless; things were unfinished for him. They had been back in Kansas City for two weeks when Bo was invited out to the Blue family's new home. As Bo rode up, Daniel called out to him. "Put Buck out with Alala then come on in," he said.

Bo did as Daniel instructed and took the saddle and bridle off Buck, then put him in the meadow with Alala. A few minutes later, Bo walked up the path from the meadow and met Daniel at the front door. Bo looked at Daniel and was surprised. "Well, look at you without a cane! When did you put that down?" he asked, moving past Daniel into the house as he held the door open for him.

Trisha came in from the kitchen. "He hasn't had the cane for two days now. He's still limping a little, but, his leg is much better. You still have your arm in a sling. When is the doctor going to let you take that off?"

Bo slid into one of the large chairs in the living room. "It's going to be another week before he'll let me start working the arm normally. It would have been sooner except for the bullet I took in the same place. I can't wait to get rid of this thing." Bo took a deep breath. "What smells so good?"

Trisha went through the menu for supper. "I've baked a ham, sweet potatoes and greens… and an apple pie. The two of you sit for a while. It's going to be another twenty minutes before it's all done. By the way, we got your housewarming gift; the lamp is beautiful. Darlene brought over a rocker for us with the lamp. I love both of them." Bo smiled at her warmly and then, she went off to the kitchen to finish supper.

After supper, they cleared the dinner table and then moved back into the living room to talk. Bo looked at Daniel. "Have you made up your mind about studying law with the judge?"

Daniel leaned forward in his seat. "I intend to see him tomorrow. I've decided to take the judge's offer. It's an opportunity that I don't think I can pass up. In five or six years, I would have my own law practice."

Bo smiled. "I'm glad for you. You've worked damn hard and you deserve it. Just think, in a few years you could be my boss." They both laughed over that.

Trisha noticed there was something else on Bo's mind because he was looking out the window while he spoke. "What's wrong, Bo? You've had your mind on something else all night."

Daniel knew what it was. "His mind is in Denver. Rose is on his mind."

Bo turned around and looked at his two friends. "I've decided to go back to Denver in the morning. There's a boat leaving at ten and I intend to be on it. I don't know what's going to happen, but I can't live like this without knowing. We haven't talked in a long time. It's been nearly eight months since I've seen her and I have to know if she still feels the same way."

Trisha reached over and put her hand on Bo's. "If she loves you the way you say, then even a year is nothing. She will be waiting for you without question."

Bo stood up. "If I'm leaving in the morning I've got a lot to do. I have to write a note to Judge Roads and let him know what I'm doing and where I've gone."

Daniel smiled. "I'm going to the office in the morning. Leave the note in my mailbox and I'll give it to him when he comes in. I'm sure he'll understand."

Trisha and Daniel followed Bo outside and watched him saddle Buck. "Thank you for the wonderful dinner, Trisha. Your apple pie was the best I've ever had. You've got a wonderful woman there, Daniel. Don't let her go."

Daniel put his arm around Trisha. "I know what I've got, Bo. Now, go and find yours."

Early the next morning, Bo slipped the note into Daniel's mailbox and rode Buck straight to the boat leaving for Omaha where he would catch the trains to Denver. Daniel, who was going in to work early, picked up the note from his mail slot before going to the courthouse. Then, he sat in the marshals' office finishing up paperwork that Judge Roads had requested before the trials began. He heard the judge come in and unlock his office door so got up and went over to his office. He knocked on the door's frame. "May I came in, Your Honor?"

Judge Roads looked up. "Come in, Daniel. What can I do for you this early in the morning?"

Daniel handed the note to Judge Roads. The judge opened it and read it. "Well, it's about time. I was beginning to think he would never get out of here. Did he say how long he was going to be gone?" He paused. "I guess it doesn't matter. No matter how long it is, he's earned it."

Daniel pulled up a chair in front of the judge's desk. "He visited my place last night for dinner. He didn't say how long he was going to be gone." Daniel shifted uneasily in his chair. "You know..." he hesitated. "Judge, he may not come back at all."

Judge Roads read the note again and then he looked up. As he spoke, his voice was full of emotion. "If he decides to stay out there, he deserves that as well. I've loved that boy like he was my own and if that young lady is that important to him, then I wish them both all the luck in the world."

Daniel saw the judge's eyes were tearing up. He stood up. "I'll have those trial statements written up for you by this afternoon, Your Honor." He turned and walked out the door closing it behind him.

The riverboat slowly traveled up the Missouri to Omaha. When the boat finally met the pier there, Bo and Buck disembarked and made their way to the train depot. He found the ticket booth and went straight to the window, towing Buck closely by his reins in one hand. "I need one ticket to Cheyenne, please. I've got one horse with me that will need feed and water."

The attendant told Bo the ticket price and Bo paid him. "The westbound train will be leaving here at nine tomorrow morning," the attendant said handing Bo the ticket. "Be here at least a half-hour before so we can get your horse bedded down for the trip."

Bo thanked him and left to find a place for Buck and himself for the night. After housing Buck in a livery, finding himself a place to sleep, and eating supper, Bo went down to see Buck. The big horse was always glad to see him. Bo scratched his ears and nose and offered him an apple. "What are we doing? She may not want to see either of us." Buck gave Bo a nudge with his nose and a snort. "You're right, I'm being foolish." Bo went back to the hotel and settled in for the night.

Bo and Buck were at the station at eight-thirty the next morning ready to disembark for Cheyenne. When the train arrived, Bo settled Buck in and gave instructions to the conductor about Buck's feed and water. He found a seat and settled in for the long trip to Cheyenne.

The train seemed to take forever to reach the Cheyenne terminal. After what seemed to be a very long layover, Bo finally saw the southbound train that would take him to Denver standing on the tracks. He rushed through the terminal to get his ticket and within a half-hour he and Buck were on the train headed south. The train couldn't cover the one hundred miles fast enough to suit Bo.

Very late in the afternoon, when the dark blue sky was dotted with pink and orange clouds and the sun crept closer to the mountains, the train arrived at the Denver station. Bo pulled Buck from the train and began to ride toward the O'Reilly's home. Buck felt Bo's nervousness, his body tensing, the closer they got to the house. Buck pranced the last few yards.

William was sitting in his study when he heard one of the dogs begin barking. He stood up and looked out the window to see Bo riding up the pathway. He was surprised to see him and ran to the door. "Well, I'll be damned! Why didn't you send us a wire telling us you were coming?" he called out to Bo as he walked outside toward him.

Bo slid out of his saddle and reached out to shake Mr. O'Reilly's hand. He couldn't look William straight in the face after not seeing him for such a long time. "I wasn't sure Rose would want to see me."

William placed his hands on Bo's shoulders eliciting a moan from him. "Wouldn't want to see you?" William said, looking at Bo head-on. "You're all she's talked about since you left." William pulled back and looked at Bo's arm that was in a sling. "What happened? Is the gunshot wound still giving you trouble? I've got a doctor in Denver who will fix that up for you."

Bo straightened himself up. "No, sir. This is much newer than *that* gun shot."

Soon, the rest of the household had heard the commotion and rushed out to where Bo and William were talking. Suddenly, Rose and Marie appeared at the front door, to see who was speaking with William and then —Rose saw Bo. A wave of excitement washed over her and she nearly tripped as she ran out to him. She launched herself at him, threw her arms around his neck and kissed him. The blow pushed Bo back against Buck.

The kiss seemed to go on for a long time. William smiled. "Let the boy catch his breath, Rose. He's been injured."

Rose pulled back to see Bo's arm in the sling. "What happened? Is that the gunshot wound?' She spun around to look at her father. "Send for the doctor, please, Father."

William was still smiling. "I don't think he came all this way to see a doctor. I think you're more of what he needs than any medicine could fix." He led the couple up the veranda stairs to the front door and inside.

This was only the beginning.

About the Author

A former engineer and military veteran, Nevada resident Daniel Bradford turned to writing first as a hobby, then as a full-time endeavor. After three science fiction novels, three children's books and numerous short stories, he began the Bo Henry saga. He has a fourth science fiction novel and a fifth western in the Bo Henry saga currently in process. He particularly enjoys his time with Charyl Wojtaszek, his Rose O'Reilly, significant partner and enthusiastic supporter of his projects.

Learn more about Mr. Bradford at www.authordanbradford.com.

Dan Bradford

Bo Henry at Three Forks

Chimney Bluffs by David B. Seaburn
The Loons by Sue Dolleris
Light Surfer by David Allan Williams
The Judas List by A. G. Hayes
Path of the Templar—Book 2 of The Jumper Chronicles by W. C. Peever
The Desperate Cycle by Tony Tame
Shutterbug by Buz Sawyer
Blessed are the Peacekeepers by Tom Donnelly and Mike Munger
The Bellwether Messages edited by D. S. Janik
The Turtle Dances by Daniel S. Janik
The Lazarus Conspiracies by Richard Rose
Purple Haze by George B. Hudson
Imminent Danger by A. G. Hayes
Lullaby Moon (CD) by Malia Elliott of Leon & Malia
Volutions edited by Suzanne Langford
In the Eyes of the Son by Hans Brinckmann
The Hanging of Dr. Hanson by Bentley Gates
Flight of Destiny by Francis Powell
Elaine of Corbenic by Tima Z. Newman
Ballerina Birdies by Marina Yamamoto
More More Time by David B. Seabird
Crazy Like Me by Erin Lee
Cleopatra Unconquered by Helen R. Davis
Valedictory by Daniel Scott
The Chemical Factor by A. G. Hayes
Quantum Death by A. G. Hayes and Raymond Gaynor
Big Heaven by Charlotte Hebert
Captain Riddle's Treasure by GV Rama Rao
All Things Await by Seth Clabough
Tsunami Libido by Cate Burns
Finding Kate by A. G. Hayes
The Adventures of Purple Head, Buddha Monkey and Sticky Feet by Erik and Forest Bracht
In the Shadows of My Mind by Andrew Massie
The Gumshoe by Richard Rose
In Search of Somatic Therapy by Setsuko Tsuchiya
Cereus by Z. Roux
The Solar Triangle by A. G. Hayes
Shadow and Light edited by Helen R. Davis
A Real Daughter by Lynne McKelvey
StoryTeller by Nicholas Bylotas

Coming Soon:
Cleopatra Victorious by Helen R. Davis

Savant Books and Publications
http://www.savantbooksandpublications.com

217

Dan Bradford

and from our imprint, Aignos Publishing:

The Dark Side of Sunshine by Paul Guzzo
Happy that it's Not True by Carlos Aleman
Cazadores de Libros Perdidos by German William Cabasssa Barber [Spanish]
The Desert and the City by Derek Bickerton
The Overnight Family Man by Paul Guzzo
There is No Cholera in Zimbabwe by Zachary M. Oliver
John Doe by Buz Sawyers
The Piano Tuner's Wife by Jean Yamasaki Toyama
Nuno by Carlos Aleman
An Aura of Greatness by Brendan P. Burns
Polonio Pass by Doc Krinberg
Iwana by Alvaro Leiva
University and King by Jeffrey Ryan Long
The Surreal Adventures of Dr. Mingus by Jesus Richard Felix Rodriguez
Letters by Buz Sawyers
In the Heart of the Country by Derek Bickerton
El Camino De Regreso by Maricruz Acuna [Spanish]
Diego in Two Places by Carlos Aleman
Prepositions by Jean Yamasaki Toyama
Deep Slumber of Dogs by Doc Krinberg
Saddam's Parrot by Jim Currie
Beneath Them by Natalie Roers
Chang the Magic Cat by A. G. Hayes
Illegal by E. M. Duesel

Coming Soon:
Island Wildlife: Exiles, Expats and Exotic Others by Robert Friedman

Aignos Publishing | an imprint of Savant Books and Publications
http://www.aignospublishing.com